WOLF TAKES THE LEAD

TERRY SPEAR

sourcebooks
casablanca

Published by Sourcebooks Casablanca, an imprint of Sourcebooks
P.O. Box 4410, Naperville, Illinois 60567–4410
(630) 961-3900
sourcebooks.com

Printed and bound in the United States of America.
OPM 10 9 8 7 6 5 4 3 2 1

To Michelle Scaff, who reads everything that has my name on it and tells the world about it. You are a writer's dream come true! Thank you!

CHAPTER 1

DEREK SPENCER WAS RUNNING ALONG THE beach with his Irish setter rescues, Red and Foxy, his bodyguard Will Wolfson following him, when the billionaire gray wolf realized he hadn't heard from his human girlfriend, Brenda Connors, in a few days. Since he was taking her to a charity gala the following night, he figured he'd better touch base with her when he got back in to make sure she was all right. She'd been moody of late, irritable with him, but no matter how much he had pressed her to learn what the matter was, she wouldn't share with him. Maybe she didn't even know herself what was bugging her.

Despite telling himself he should take the chance to date some she-wolves, Derek balked at going out with any of them. He told himself that after opening his heart to two of the she-wolves he'd loved and then lost to other wolves, he couldn't let it happen again. It just wasn't worth it. He couldn't see a way past the anxiety he felt about even trying to date another she-wolf and risking falling in love again if she wanted nothing to do with having a permanent relationship with him. Hell, he was a billionaire and made all kinds of tough financial decisions. He could do just about anything he set his mind to, except when it came to dating she-wolves.

His friends had given up on trying to convince him to date the ones they knew. He did a lot of stuff with his male friends, but when they included their mates, he just felt like an outsider. He felt he was never going to be able to do anything but see human women he wouldn't lose his heart to. He would never consider turning one of them either. Yet he wanted something more.

He wanted the connection he would have with a wolf mate that wasn't anything like being with a human, no hidden secrets about what they were. That would be a relief—to let their wild selves out and enjoy spending the time with each other on wolf outings; to understand what it meant to be wolves; to be free to talk about wolf issues and to have that bond they shared. Sure, he talked to his wolf staff and his friends, but the bond between wolf mates went even deeper. He certainly wasn't a lone wolf at heart.

He ran up the stairs to his ocean-view estate in northern California, removed the dogs' leashes, and headed into the kitchen to pull a bottle of water out of the fridge to drink.

Will joined him. "That was a good run."

"Yeah, the best." Then Derek grabbed his phone to call Brenda.

"If you don't need me for anything, I'm going to do a perimeter search."

"Okay, thanks." Ever since Derek had started dating Brenda six months ago, she'd wanted him to wear something that wouldn't clash with what she was wearing to social engagements. It was a quirk of hers that he didn't mind accommodating. But she hadn't called him about it yet, and he wondered if she was in another one of her moods. He could deal with them better if he just knew what was bothering her. Then he had another notion. He hoped she wasn't sick.

He called her several times before she finally answered her phone. He didn't hear any sounds in the background indicating she was out on the town and too busy to answer the phone.

"Listen, Derek," Brenda said. She didn't sound like she was happy with him, and that made him suspicious. "I'm tired of all my friends asking if we are getting engaged and me hemming and hawing around about it. I like your little social gatherings just fine, but unless you're going to propose to me soon, I'm no longer going out with you."

Derek nearly choked on the water he was drinking out of the bottle. Her declaration surprised him because she hadn't once hinted at wanting to be engaged at all. That was what the mood swings were all about? He sure hadn't expected her to just give him an ultimatum. Why hadn't she talked to him about this earlier instead of putting on the pressure right before the social event? Well, he supposed that was the reason—to convince him to get off the fence and take a stand. He understood that she might eventually want a commitment, but he just wasn't the one to give it to her.

"Okay, well, I'm sorry you feel that way. When we started dating, I told you nothing serious could come of it, but I understand. If you're looking to marry someone, you'll want to be free to do so." He tried to sound amiable about it, though he was annoyed with her that she would wait until this late date to call it quits with him.

"Not with anyone else, Derek! With *you*. I'm not interested in seeing anyone else. I just believe we've been dating each other for long enough that we need to make more of a formal commitment to each other. An engagement, I mean. I'm not seeing anyone else, and I don't want to."

He had always told her this was a way for both of them just to have a nice time. A way for her to social climb and for him to have a date at the charity functions. But marry her? She wasn't a wolf! So there was no chance of that ever happening.

He'd always been completely honest with her about the situation. Except for the part about him being a *lupus garou*. With other human females he'd dated, he would never make an official commitment to them, and they had given up on him. Brenda knew that. He assumed she thought she could change his mind—but only a she-wolf would. If he had decided Brenda was the only one for him, that would have meant biting her, turning her, and being mated to her for life. They lived very long lives. So no way.

"All right. I understand. I'm just not—"

Hell, how did he say this without telling her what the real issue was: he was a wolf; she was not. Besides that, he wasn't in love with her. "I'm not making any commitment to you or anyone else for that matter. It all has to do with me. Not you." Which was partly true. She hadn't even said that she loved him because he knew she didn't. It would have been more of a marriage of convenience, certainly not love. He didn't need that.

"Yeah, I know it does. You have a phobia about commitment. *Fine.* Find someone else to go with you to the gala tomorrow night or go alone. You can deal with it. But if you change your mind about us, you can give me a call," Brenda said.

"All right." That was all he could think of to say. It had been fun while it lasted? It was better to just leave it at that and not say anything further.

Brenda waited a minute more, but he wasn't going to tell her what she wanted to hear. That he'd changed his mind. That he couldn't live without her. That they would become engaged and he wanted her to go with him to the social event. Then she hung up on him.

He called his wolf friend Rafe Denali to see if he knew of anyone he could take to the ball. Since the event was the following night, Derek was afraid it was a little late to call anyone out of the blue. Maybe, if Rafe didn't have someone in mind, his twin brother, Aidan, or their mates might know of a convenient prospect for Derek to take to the gala.

"Hey, Rafe, do you have a moment to talk?" Derek always asked now that Rafe had a mate, Jade, and her four-year-old son he'd adopted as his own.

"Yeah, buddy, I heard Brenda Connors said she was demanding you become engaged with her or she would dump you," Rafe said.

"Yeah, she did it. She waited to the very last minute before the gala to tell me too."

"So you wouldn't have time to get a replacement date. Not as choosy as you are, and for good reason."

"How did you know about Brenda ditching me for the ball?" Derek asked, the notion sinking in that he shouldn't have known. Though bad news did travel fast through their social circles.

"She posted all over the social networking sites that she had broken up with you. Jade happened to see one of her posts. She thought it was rotten of Brenda to wait until the last minute before the gala to tell you to marry her or else."

Great.

"You know Lexi Summerfield's assistant and

bodyguard, Kate Hanover, would be an excellent choice."

That was whom Derek had been afraid Rafe would suggest, since she was the only eligible she-wolf he knew of in the area.

"She might not like that. I didn't hire Kate when she applied for a bodyguard position that I suddenly had to fill," Derek finally said. He'd never told anyone except his staff. He hadn't expected Lexi to hire Kate as *her* bodyguard! By then, he had never mentioned it to his friends because he hadn't seen any reason to do so.

Rafe sighed. "All right, well, I don't know of anyone else offhand who you could take to the ball. I'll ask my brother and our mates if they have any ideas. But if I ask our friend Lexi, she's going to recommend Kate."

"Kate will be there as a bodyguard for Lexi, if Kate's attendance at past charity events is any indication," Derek said.

"Lexi has a mate and Mike Stallings to serve as her bodyguards, and they're always there as well."

Derek didn't want to let on why he had always noticed Kate at the functions. Maybe he had been feeling a little guilty about not hiring her. She had great qualifications when he interviewed her, but he'd already had a built-in bias. He'd dashed her hopes with one little statement that he couldn't hire a woman for the job because of the inherent problem with relationship issues. He had felt strongly about the issue and he still did. She had been nothing but professional and had tried not to let on that she had been offended by his comment. He had smelled her annoyance, courtesy of his heightened ability to smell emotions as a wolf.

He hadn't meant to imply that she wanted to be his bodyguard because she wanted more than that. Though what better way to get to know him than to be with him day and night—while protecting and serving? Even if he had been dating her, he wouldn't have wanted her to serve as his bodyguard—just as his best friend and lover, if they were suited to each other. Even in his youth, he'd had a bit of a phobia when it came to dating she-wolves because back then, the she-wolves had only wanted what he could offer them—his wealth and prestige. They hadn't been interested in really being with him as much as they enjoyed telling their friends they were dating him. Once he had learned the truth— he could be a bit dense at times when it came to women's motives—he hadn't dated any more she-wolves when he was younger. It hadn't been until much later that he had dated the first she-wolf he was head over heels for and she'd dumped him. He suspected the second one he had fallen in love with was a case of rebound, needing something from her that she couldn't give to him.

In reality, Derek had not been so afraid of *Kate's*

intentions but of his own. She was an attractive she-wolf, with poise and good sense. But in the matter of male wolves and she-wolves, all that could be tossed out in a heartbeat. Then what? He would have had to let her go? How would that look when someone else wanted to hire her? He hadn't wanted to do that to her. Sure, she might have worked out fine, but he supposed he would have felt differently if she had been seriously courting a wolf at the time. Or if she'd been mated, then he would have had no difficulty hiring her. It was the fact that they were both single that had given him major heartburn.

As if Rafe knew just what Derek was thinking, he chuckled. "You need to get your own she-wolf. I'll ask Jade if she knows of any single human woman who might fit the bill. One who would be fun to date. I still say your best bet is Kate. She'll be attending the ball already, so she'll have a new gown for it. She'll be there for Lexi, but she can be your date too. On the off chance you need saving, she can pose as your bodyguard. Everyone always has a date at these functions. How will it look if you don't have someone with you at least in the beginning, when you first enter the ballroom? You know how it is. Brenda would drift off and talk to everyone. Kate would do the same thing, keeping an eye on Lexi too. You could even dance with Kate, just to 'prove' to anyone else you're with her."

"Okay, thanks. I'll consider it. Ask Jade first though if she can think of anyone else I might take."

A half hour later, Rafe called Derek back. Once Derek learned Jade said she couldn't think of anyone else but Kate Hanover to go as Derek's date and Aidan's mate, Holly, said the same, Derek knew they were attempting to railroad him into taking Kate to the dance. He sighed. Okay, so what harm would there be in asking? Still, he felt it went against his better judgment. He was almost hoping Lexi would tell him that Kate was needed elsewhere and wasn't attending the ball. Or that Lexi needed her at the ball and so, no, Derek couldn't take Kate as his date.

He couldn't believe how hard this was for him. It shouldn't have been that big a deal. Hoping he wouldn't regret it, Derek called Lexi.

———

Kate Hanover and her boss, Lexi Summerfield, who were best friends, were working on Lexi's website, uploading all the photos of her new fall cosmetic line for her company, Clair de Lune Cosmetics, when Lexi got a call. Kate waited for Lexi to finish her call so they could resume their work when Lexi smiled and glanced at Kate.

Kate wondered if they'd just gotten another big order for the cosmetics from another department store. Kate sure hoped so; business was booming.

In the meantime, Ryder Gallagher, Lexi's mate, brought Spirit, Lexi's rescue wolf dog, inside. Spirit went straight to Kate to greet her as if she hadn't seen her in ages—when she'd seen her earlier this morning. Kate had to pet her and hug her. Animals just seemed to gravitate to Kate. She had wanted to keep one of the wolf dogs Lexi had taken in, but they had so many offers to take them, they ended up just keeping Spirit. All the wolf dogs were well loved. Who better to care for them than *lupus garous* who were part wolves too?

"I'll take Spirit out of here so the two of you can work, but she just had to greet you, knowing you were still here while she was outside," Ryder said.

"Thanks, Ryder," Kate said.

"You're welcome. Sometimes I'm not sure if she realizes we run the pack, not her." Ryder smiled, Kate laughed, and then he took Spirit back outside to play with her.

Ryder was right about that, but Spirit was such a sweet wolf dog, and Kate was glad they had given her a home.

Kate glanced at Lexi to try to glean what the call was about.

Smiling at Kate, Lexi raised her brows. "Thanks, yes, I'm sure she would be delighted, and I know I am… Oh, yes, I have enough bodyguard muscle for the night. I'll let her know… All right, see you at the event tomorrow evening. Good night." Lexi ended the call. "So you know Derek Spencer, right? One of our billionaire wolf friends."

He wasn't *Kate's* billionaire friend. Though Kate knew him, sure. She'd had a huge crush on the wolf from the first time she'd seen him playing fetch with one of his Irish setters on the beach below his estate, though she hadn't known who he was or that he lived in a home on the cliffs at the beach or that he was a billionaire at the time. But she had smelled that he was a wolf, and that had intrigued her. She'd learned Derek had a home for Irish setter rescues, and he didn't keep them in kennels. He believed a dog belonged with his master, and that meant in a loving home environment. They weren't working dogs but companions. She admired him for that and thought he had to be a decent person.

"Of course I know him. He's at all the functions that you attend." Kate hadn't meant to sound so annoyed at the mention of his name.

"Oh, well, I hope it's all right that I made a date for you and him for the ball tomorrow night," Lexi said.

Her jaw slightly dropping, Kate couldn't hide her surprise.

"I mean, as in that his girlfriend, Brenda Connors—"

"Can't go with him for some reason or another." Kate sat back in her chair and folded her arms.

"She dumped him. Now he doesn't have a date

for the gala," Lexi said, back to working on the website, and Kate leaned over to check it out to see what else they could do to make it look even better.

Kate smiled. Not because Brenda's ditching Derek meant that Kate's going with him would mean she had a chance at mating him—and she wasn't going down that road anyway—but she was just amused that a human female had ditched Mr. Hotshot Moneymaker. "Did she give him an ultimatum? Either marry her or else?"

"That was about the gist of it. Of course all of us put our heads together to come up with someone else Derek could take to the ball, and the natural choice was you." Lexi made some minor tweaks on the web page.

"All of us?" Kate raised her brows.

"Jade and Holly and me."

"You left me out of the discussion." Even though Kate wasn't mated to a billionaire wolf or one herself like Lexi was, they usually included her in their social outings. Lexi said they needed her as their bodyguard, but it wasn't just that. She was one of the four she-wolves whom they included in about everything. She was more than just an employee. She was a friend. Why hadn't they asked her first? Actually, why hadn't Derek asked her to accompany him instead of going through Lexi? "You know he isn't interested in dating me for real, don't you? I'm just filling in for the one event, and then he'll start dating some other 'safe' woman."

"Until he finds a she-wolf he can't live without." Lexi began adding descriptive details to her new product pages.

"Okay, just so you ladies know it won't be me." That was all Kate needed was for her friends to all try to convince Derek she was the one for him. She could envision more "dates" set up with him until he finally said enough was enough—or she did. "What about me serving as one of your bodyguards at the event?"

"Mike will be there, and so will my mate. I don't need you to guard me. I need you to have fun. Since I mated Ryder, I haven't wanted you to have to work as a bodyguard at the social functions. You do enough as my personal assistant."

Kate sighed. "All right. I guess I don't have an alternative."

Lexi laughed. "Sure you do. If you really don't want to go with him, you can just call him up and tell him so."

Why should Kate have to cancel on him? Everyone else had set this up behind her back. Still, the curmudgeon part of her wanted to do just that. Tell him she couldn't. Which of course was a big lie.

"We have another problem," Kate said.

Lexi arched a brow.

"My gown."

"It's beautiful on you. You look astonishing in it."

"Right, and that's the problem. I mean, if I'm supposed to be complimenting you and your gown, suddenly I'm not, and instead I'm Derek's date. The gown is way too—"

"Sexy?"

Kate rolled her eyes. "I wouldn't want anyone at the event to get the idea that I'm the new girlfriend. *His* new girlfriend. He was afraid of that happening when I applied for his vacant bodyguard position. At a gala, you know how the paparazzi are."

"Yeah, do I. You don't have anything to worry about. It will be a one-time occurrence. You'll do what you always do, except you'll arrive with him instead of Ryder, Mike, and me. You're great as my one-woman promotional team. You always like talking to prospective and current customers at these events, and everyone's eager to ask you about the products. You do just what you enjoy doing as usual. Derek already said he just expects you to walk with him into the function, and if you don't mind, you could dance once with him. Of course you'll leave with him after the ball is over. Beyond that, it's your night to have fun."

"He has his own bodyguards, right? You wanted me to wear this dress because I wouldn't have to actually protect you, but if I have to protect him, then I'll need to wear something more functional." Actually, she could strap a gun on her thigh and reach for it through the split of her skirt if she had to. She might as well take it, just in case Lexi needed protection and Mike and Ryder weren't there for her. Not that she thought anything bad would happen—but just to be safe.

"He has his own bodyguards," Lexi assured her. "They're always with him. This is strictly a platonic date. Don't worry!"

Kate did worry. She didn't want to be in the tabloids! She figured she *would* be once they realized she was with him and then *not* with him. Envisioning getting hit up for interviews, Kate sure hoped she was wrong about all of it. At least if Brenda was going with him, Kate wouldn't have that issue to deal with.

"What do you think of this layout, Kate?" Lexi asked before they called it a night.

They didn't usually work this late, but they'd paid someone else to do the layout, and it had looked like a disaster, so they were redoing it.

Kate concentrated on the website, thinking the following night could be a disaster too.

CHAPTER 2

THE NIGHT OF THE CHARITY BALL, DEREK couldn't believe how nervous he was. He supposed it was because he hadn't taken a she-wolf on a date since he'd given up on she-wolves. Though this wasn't exactly what he would call a date, since he had arranged it through Lexi and not with Kate and he didn't plan for it to go anywhere beyond this one event.

Lexi had told him to pick Kate up at her home instead of Kate's. When he arrived, he hadn't expected Ryder Gallagher to answer the door and ask him in, as if Ryder was the alpha pack leader and Kate was his ward. "You'll have her back by—"

"Oh, for heaven's sake, 'Dad,'" Kate said to Ryder in a teasing way as she walked into the room. "We'll be fine. This is just a pretend date, no kissing, just a one-time occurrence. Mr. Spencer realizes I know all kinds of martial arts—since he has already seen my résumé—so he will be on his best behavior." Her black hair in a long bob, she glanced her blue eyes at Derek and headed past him for the door. She had no smile for him either, no word of greeting, even for a fellow wolf.

Derek knew this was a bad idea, but he watched the beautiful she-wolf headed for the door anyway, her long, sky-blue satin gown reaching the floor, the off-the-shoulder cut showing off her creamy shoulders and the slit in the gown revealing a shapely leg for brief glimpses. Tonight she was all Derek's—except for the kissing part and all the rest. He looked back at Ryder to see his take on the situation.

Ryder cast him an evil smile. "Have a great time, you two."

Derek would have to make sure Kate didn't call him Mr. Spencer for the rest of the night! He had expected to walk her outside to the car and get the door for her at least. Maybe one of his bodyguards would, since she tore out of Lexi's home so fast and they were following in the Land Rover.

Lexi came out of a back room looking like a million bucks too, dressed in a darker-blue gown that complimented Kate's. She smiled. "Have her back by midnight."

Their wolf dog, Spirit, bounded out to greet Derek. All dogs loved him. Especially when Spirit could smell his Irish setters on him. Once Derek returned home, his dogs would be able to smell Spirit on him too.

"Or she'll turn into Cinderella?" Derek asked Lexi, petting Spirit. He didn't expect Kate to act this way at all. He was hoping she wouldn't have minded being his date for the night. Well, not a date. Instead, she seemed miffed at him. Because he hadn't asked her directly? He guessed he should have. Maybe because it was a secondhand invitation. Probably because he hadn't hired her for the bodyguard position.

"She might turn into a wolf," Lexi said teasingly.

Not that Kate would. She was a royal like him and could shift at will. The moon phases didn't cause any problems for her. That was one thing she made sure he knew when she applied for the bodyguard job.

Derek smiled and saluted them. "See you at the ball."

Then Derek exited Lexi and Ryder's home and found Kate sitting in his Maserati already, his bodyguards watching him from the Land Rover, smiling. He sure hoped one of them had been gallant enough to get the car door for her since he'd missed the opportunity.

When Derek climbed into the car, he said to Kate, "You look lovely."

Good enough to eat, he thought. He had seen her in summer dresses on occasion when the women all got together and he and the guys did something with each other; a bathing suit a time or two, which he had tried not to notice; shorts and a tank top, which had reminded him of how shapely she was; a gown at charity functions a couple of times. He didn't remember her wearing anything this spectacular at a black-tie event before. She was absolutely stunning.

"Thank you. So the men in the Land Rover are your bodyguards?" She ran her hand over her lap. His gaze shifted to the silky creation draping over her legs, but he quickly refocused his attention on the road.

"Uh, yeah, Will is. Allister is on loan from Rafe." Derek didn't mention their last names, figuring she wouldn't care to know them. He suspected that neither of his men had gotten the car door for her then. He would talk to them about it later. "Thanks for agreeing to do this with me on such short notice."

"No problem. I was already going. As long as you escort me in, I go about my business, and you take me home, it won't be a total waste of my time."

He smiled at her choice of words. "But one dance as well. You agreed to that, right?"

She hesitated to answer him. He always danced with his, well, date, and he and Kate were supposed to be keeping up appearances. It would seem odd that he wouldn't dance several times with Kate, as much as he enjoyed dancing at these affairs, so he had to at least take her to the floor one time. Then again, maybe she didn't know how to dance or didn't like the activity.

"Right. After that, you're free to tango or waltz with whomever you please. It's really the perfect situation for you. No attachments. A thoroughly platonic relationship," she said.

Hell, he always ended up with his human partner in bed when the night was through. Not that he would with Kate. But Derek wasn't into platonic relationships. Though Kate was right about the no-attachments business, he wouldn't take out different women for dinners and movies and have sexual encounters with them only once like some wolves did, knowing they couldn't mate the human.

Because he was in the public eye, how would that look? Like a billionaire playboy who had one-night stands with whomever would have them with him? He was too much of a wolf at heart who truly did want a family someday.

Even if that meant opening himself up to a world of hurt all over again.

He wasn't into all the pomp and ceremony that went along with the social functions or business dinners he went to. He just felt it was his duty to give back to the community where he had made so much money. He'd rather spend time in the great outdoors, being one with nature. That had a lot to do with his wolf temperament.

When he thought of platonic relationships between a woman and a man, he thought of a sister and a brother, and he couldn't see Kate in those terms at all. The slit up her long gown had parted, and he glanced down to see her bare leg and her feet in strappy sandals. They were the kind of shoes not meant to be worn in a combative situation, and he was glad Rafe had loaned him one of his extra bodyguards in case he needed one so Kate didn't have to take on the role.

"Are you still miffed at me for not hiring you for the bodyguard opening I had last year?" Derek asked quietly, not wanting to stir up a whole lot of trouble before they arrived at the clubhouse, but maybe if they cleared the air, she would feel better about it. Maybe he would too.

She smiled sweetly at him, but it was more of an attempt at sweet. "I wasn't annoyed with you for not hiring me. You had any number of hotshot *male* bodyguards you were interviewing, and I figured I didn't stand a chance. I was irritated with you because of the *reason* you didn't hire me."

"That I thought things might spiral out of control between us and—"

"You would lose a bodyguard."

"I was afraid I would have to—"

"Fire me?"

"Let you go." He sighed with exasperation. No matter how he tried to make it sound like he'd been reasonable and had both their best interests in mind, he felt he was falling far short of his goal.

"Okay, well, let me ease your mind *if* you feel the least bit guilty over not hiring me, since I am highly trained and could have done the job right for you. I couldn't be happier working for Lexi instead. She's a dream to work for. I will be forever grateful I didn't get the job to work for you."

Was she implying Derek *wouldn't* have been a dream to work for? Then again, had she been his bodyguard, he could see how he'd be ultraprofessional with her—not joking with her like he did his men, afraid it would appear he was interested in having more of a relationship with her. It just seemed like things would have been too strained between them. He just couldn't see her as one of the guys, and that was all on him.

He did wonder about Lexi's other bodyguard, Mike Stallings, and if Kate had any romantic interest in him since he was a bachelor wolf and Kate was in close proximity with him all the time.

"So how are you and Mike getting along?" Derek figured he might as well have some polite conversation with Kate on the way to the clubhouse.

"Famously."

So much for polite conversation. Derek changed the subject. "Uh, there might be a reporter or two outside the clubhouse. They try to capture photos of who is with whom and—"

"Share it with the tabloids. I know. Lexi gets a lot of that." Kate folded her arms.

"But you're not usually the focus of the photo shoots." He wanted to prepare Kate for the onslaught if she hadn't thought of it.

Kate waved her hand, dismissing the notion. "I know. Don't worry. I won't tell anyone our dirty little secret."

"That I didn't hire you? That you're a bodyguard?"

"No, I'm sure everyone knows that I work for Lexi since I'm with her so much of the time at these social gatherings. I meant that I'm a fill-in date because Brenda dumped you."

He chuckled. For some reason, Kate's words just amused him. "It was mutual. She was looking for more than I could give her."

"Marriage."

"Right."

"But you were up-front with her about the fact that you hadn't planned to marry her, right?" Kate asked.

"Absolutely."

Before long, he pulled his Maserati into the circular driveway of the clubhouse, and before he or a valet could get Kate's door, she was getting out of the vehicle. She did a great job of it too; it couldn't have been easy in that slinky dress, and she still managed to look sexy and not clumsy in the least. Once she was standing under the patio cover, he was hoping she wouldn't just go inside without him! That would be difficult to explain, and several people would make it their business to say something about it. People at these functions were used to seeing him with Brenda and might have gotten word that he and she had broken up, so they would most likely be intrigued that he was with Kate now.

Photographers hurried over to get photographs of him and Kate, but she took his hand and pulled him out of the limelight just as he had moved around the car and was in a position for a photograph. He smiled. Her actions would make the reporters even more curious about him and Kate. And truly, he didn't mind that she didn't want to be photographed with him. Especially if this was a one-time deal, but damn if the she-wolf didn't intrigue the hell out of him!

He finally slowed her down, wondering how she could walk that fast in the killer heels she was wearing. Even his bodyguards were having a difficult time keeping up with them. The bodyguards took their places at a couple of strategic locations at the edge of the ballroom where other bodyguards were hanging out.

So many eyes were on Kate and Derek, he realized taking Kate as his date was causing more undue attention than he'd thought possible— even more than going alone. Then he saw Brenda. Ah, hell. He really hadn't expected to see her, and he hoped she didn't cause trouble for him and Kate. Especially for Kate's sake. Brenda was with another guy, a much older billionaire, and she was dressed to the nines. Financially, he was worth even more than Derek was. So much for getting thrown over for a younger model, which Derek thought Brenda would do to spite him.

"I see Brenda's here. Her date must have also had a last-minute cancellation. Maybe he told his girlfriend he wouldn't marry her either," Kate joked.

Derek smiled at her.

Then to Derek's astonishment, Kate slid her arms seductively around his neck, tilted her chin up, and looked like she was ready for a kiss. He lowered his head and kissed her, sweetly, but she didn't release him right away, and what the hell? He might as well play the game too. He wanted to. Desperately. He pressured her lips for more, but she wasn't going for a deep kiss. This was damn nice anyway. Soon, she was pulling away but giving him another brief kiss as if to say they would resume this later—or at least he hoped so.

She smiled at him, pulled completely away, gave him a little wave, and then left him standing there, wondering what had just happened between them while she sauntered off to make her rounds to their cosmetics customers. He just stared after her, lost from the kiss, and wondered if she'd been as affected by it as he had. He figured she was playing her role, and well too, before she did what she'd told him she would do.

So much for her saying there would be no kissing involved between them. Seductive minx. He wondered what else she might do. She definitely had thrown him off balance.

Rafe and Jade soon joined him, and Jade said, "I thought this was supposed to be a pretend date."

Rafe was smiling. "We told you she was the one to take to the ball."

"It *is* a pretend date. Kate is just very good at playing her role." And working Derek up. He couldn't believe how much that brief little kiss had affected him. "She's doing her usual, visiting with clients."

Rafe and Jade were watching Kate move through the crowd, someone getting her a glass of champagne. That should have been Derek, he thought belatedly.

Then two more men were talking to her—about cosmetics, Derek hoped.

"She seems to be very popular tonight," Jade said.

Too popular. Now that Brenda didn't have Derek's undivided attention at one of these affairs—or she would throw a fit about it—he couldn't help but watch Kate and see her growing crowd of enthusiastic potential suitors capturing her attention. She was sipping from her champagne glass and then laughing. He frowned. At least they were humans, not wolves.

He had noticed that everyone had taken notice of her when she had walked into the ballroom. She had been all smiles, independent, seeming to just connect with people, the way he liked his women.

Rafe motioned to her with his head. "If you need me to rescue her, just let me know."

Derek wouldn't need Rafe's help in rescuing Kate. And Derek didn't think she needed his assistance either. He certainly didn't want to interrupt her business talks with the other men, if that was what they were, when he had agreed to the rules of engagement.

Rafe slapped Derek on the back and took Jade's hand to head over to one of the tables. Even though the wolves liked sitting together as a wolf pack at different social gatherings, the couples often sat apart at a charity function like this so they could meet and greet others too.

Then Derek saw Brenda headed his way, and he had the sudden urge to rescue Kate, if by doing so, he got himself out of having to deal with Brenda. He was totally an alpha, so he didn't know why he was feeling that way! Before Brenda reached him, Rafe's brother, Aidan, and his pregnant mate, Holly, came to speak with him, but Derek noticed that didn't stop Brenda from continuing in his direction.

"So why aren't you with Kate?" Holly scolded.

Derek wondered again when Holly's twin babies were due. Holly looked like she was ready to give birth any minute.

Derek shrugged. "She wanted to take care of business. It was the deal we made."

"It looks like Brenda's coming to speak with you," Aidan warned.

"Yeah. I hope she doesn't make a scene." That was all that Derek needed. He really hadn't expected Brenda to show up to the gala, but he knew word would have soon gotten back to her that he had a date. He figured she was dying to see if he had someone to take to the ball on such short notice and who might replace her or maybe that he was alone at the affair and she had a chance to make it up to him.

"Well, don't let the other men monopolize Kate's time," Aidan said.

Derek would, if that was what she wanted and it made her happy. Then Aidan and Holly told him they would talk to him later as soon as Brenda drew close.

"So," Brenda said, joining him. "That was fast."

"I could say the same thing about you," Derek said.

"Isn't the woman you came in with Lexi Summerfield's assistant and bodyguard?" Brenda asked as if she didn't really know whether she was.

"Yeah. We've been friends." Not exactly. Especially not after he had turned her down for a job.

"I could see. So how long has this been going on behind my back?"

"I haven't been out with her before." Though Derek and Brenda had agreed that they weren't dating each other exclusively. He hadn't been seeing anyone, but he didn't know about her. "I'm glad you found someone new to date." He suspected

Brenda had seen Kate kiss him, and he wondered if Brenda was jealous. Here he thought Kate had just kissed him to play her role in front of anyone at the ball who was observing them—not just the ex-girlfriend.

"Oh, that. I'm just with him as a fill-in. His girlfriend wasn't able to attend, and I told him I was available. He was thrilled to bring me here," Brenda said.

Kate suddenly appeared next to Derek like a wolf would on a hunt, silently and self-assuredly. "I'm glad your new relationship is working out so well for the two of you, Brenda." Kate acted as though she hadn't heard what Brenda had said, but with their wolf's hearing, Derek was certain she had. Then Kate smiled brilliantly at Derek. He was getting a big kick out of her. "Do you want to dance?" She slipped her hand around Derek's and pulled him away from Brenda, not giving him a chance to say yes or no.

"I thought you were busy." Derek pulled Kate lightly into his arms on the dance floor, modestly, not like how he wanted to hold her close as they were waltzing. Hell, already his wolf hormones were firing up a storm.

"All work and no play..." Kate danced superbly with him, all her concentration on him as if she truly were his new temporary girlfriend. Because all his girlfriends were temporary.

"I hadn't expected to see Brenda here," Kate began, "but I should have known. She's just an opportunist. Pardon if I'm stepping on your toes, as they say."

Derek shook his head. "Not at all. Everyone knows she'll go with anyone she hopes will marry her and leave her a nice billion-dollar nest egg. I guess she'd been after me for some time to make up my mind about us. I just hadn't seen the signs. But it wasn't in the cards."

Kate slid her arms around his neck and pressed her body closer. He settled his hands around her waist.

Okay, so this wasn't what he thought would happen once he'd picked her up at Lexi and Ryder's home, but he was certain that was exactly where this would have headed had she been his bodyguard. Maybe not as quickly as this, since she was serving in the capacity of his date this time. Kate seemed to want to show Brenda he was with her, so lay off him, which worked well for him as long as Brenda didn't try to take it out on Kate.

"Is Brenda watching us?" He assumed that was why Kate was getting so intimate with him.

"Hmm," Kate said.

He started to glance in the direction he thought Brenda might still be, but Kate warned, "You will blow the whole scene if you scan the ballroom to see if Brenda is observing us. I can tell you right now she is, and I don't even have to look. Why else would she have come over to talk to you when you're with me? She's not ready to give you up, and she wants to know if we're really an item or not. Since I *wasn't* protecting you from her earlier and instead visiting with other men, she figures"—Kate smiled and laughed a little, and he thought that was more of Kate's act—"that we're just putting on a show for her benefit."

"Well, you put on one hell of a show."

"Thank you. But it isn't for real."

He knew it wasn't real for her, but he couldn't hide how real this felt to him, his body ready for a whole lot more.

When the dance was done, he asked, "Did you want to get something to eat?" This time he wasn't looking to see where Brenda had gotten off to. He didn't care one little bit. He knew she was a gold digger and as long as they both had filled a need, he'd been fine with taking her places. But now? He was ready to move on.

Kate sighed. "All right. I guess we can eat together."

Immediately, he wanted to tell Kate she didn't need to put on this faux scene for him or anyone else. He was perfectly fine eating something with the others. He didn't want her to feel that she was doing a job for him. She was just supposed to be his date and enjoy herself like she did when she accompanied Lexi, only this time she was on more of a—dare he say it?—date.

She went with him to eat at one of the grazing tables during the drink reception time. They snacked on lobster and shrimp canapés and champagne before they sat down at a large, round dinner table covered in a white tablecloth. Even though the wolves usually sat at separate tables at a gala like this, tonight they seemed to gravitate to one table, maybe worried for Kate if Brenda tried to cause trouble for her and Derek. The pack was gathering, like wolves who had to protect one of their own.

Charity auctions and raffles were in full swing, and everyone was getting into the business of donating money to the event. Several charity organizers were giving speeches, and in between raffles, live music was playing.

Steaks and lobster were the main courses for dinner. Some of the attendees were offered some kind of vegetarian dinner, but the wolves loved their meat.

"You know," Rafe said, offering a toast to Derek, "this is the first time we've been at a gala where you could comfortably sit with us."

Which had to do with Derek's date being a wolf this time, which meant they could talk freely among themselves.

"I agree," Derek said, raising his glass to Rafe. Visiting with the wolves was really nice.

"Are you having a good time?" Lexi asked Kate.

"Yeah, we made some sales—"

"No business talk," Rafe warned playfully. "Jade's rules at one of these functions."

Jade smiled at her mate and caressed his hand with hers. "You're right. You learned so fast."

But Derek was certain the others were interested in just how Kate was getting along with him and vice versa. He had to admit he was enjoying himself with her, but he still felt she believed she was only on a mission.

CHAPTER 3

KATE DIDN'T KNOW WHAT GOT INTO HER TO rescue Derek from Brenda. For all she knew, he'd wanted to make amends with the woman. Though when Kate led Derek onto the dance floor, he hadn't been reluctant in the least to dance with her. Still, she could have let him fend for himself. He hadn't been in any real danger.

Kate felt the tension between them as she sat next to Derek. And she felt awkward among her friends. None of them had seen her on a real date before, even if this wasn't an honest-to-goodness date. It was as close as they came. Derek was cute and sexy all in one hot package, his light-brown hair streaked with blond. His amber eyes always drew her in, and he had the most kissable mouth. She hadn't expected him to kiss her back like he had. She loved it. She hadn't been kissed like that in a long time. She had the unfathomable urge to take it further—an alpha female wolf wanting to claim the alpha male.

If she'd really been on a date with a wolf, she wouldn't have felt this uncomfortable. She kept feeling she had a role to play, but she wasn't sure how far to go with it. Like rescuing him from Brenda to dance with him. Kate thought she'd gone a little too far with that. Then again, she was a wolf, and he'd brought her to the ball, so he wasn't available to anyone else. Not tonight. She wanted to make that clear to any women who were getting any ideas about him being free.

Women could line up to give him their phone numbers for some other occasion, but tonight, he was hers. Okay, now that she had that worked out, she felt a little better about it.

While eating their delightful dinner, everyone was talking about a camping trip they were all going on next weekend, and she thought it would be fun. Derek hadn't been on one with them since Rafe and Aidan had met their mates. Lexi hadn't been on one with them either, so it would be the first time for all of them to be together.

From what Jade had told Lexi and Kate, their camping trips were wolf affairs, all of them running as wolves in the dark of night. Kate was looking forward to camping with Lexi, Ryder, and Mike, but she and Mike would have their own separate tents. Kate was good friends with Mike, but they didn't have what it took to be wolf mates. Of course she was looking forward to being with the others too.

Derek looked so left out of the conversation, Kate felt bad for him. "You ought to come along." Kate thought afterward that she shouldn't have invited him—it was someone else's call. She'd probably had a little too much bubbly.

Derek actually smiled at her.

"I mean, I'll be in a single tent." That didn't sound right, like Kate wanted to share her tent with Derek. What was the matter with her? "Mike will be there in his own tent too. You could bring your own or maybe even share with Mike if you wanted to keep each other company, though he'll be serving guard duty some of the time. Me too." Why she was suggesting that Derek stay in Mike's tent, she didn't know! Mike would probably be furious with her for offering if Derek wanted to take her up on it!

Everyone else at the table was sharing small, conspiratorial smiles. She should have kept her mouth shut. The others could have invited Derek to go camping with them if they'd wanted to. She knew he hadn't gone on the trips before because he'd been dating a human, and even if a human date had wanted to go on the trip, she couldn't have. Not when one of the purposes of going camping as a pack was to run as wolves.

Derek was still smiling at Kate as he pulled out his phone, and she could see he was checking his calendar. "Well, that's good news. I'm free that weekend. I'll be going to a business conference with Rafe the following week, so that works out perfectly for me. I would love to take you up on it."

Not *her*. The *others*. She felt her face warm in embarrassment. What was she supposed to say now?

She sighed. "Good. I'm sure everyone else will be glad to see you there." Kate purposefully didn't tell him *she* would be glad to see him there. Maybe she should bow out and stay home and do her nails or something. Not that she would really consider skipping out on the adventure when she'd been really looking forward to it.

When they had finished their meals and had flaming chocolate balls for dessert, the others were still talking when Derek leaned over and asked Kate, "Would you like to dance?"

His sexy voice warmed her. "We had our one dance." Though Kate loved to do it and she had enjoyed dancing with Derek the one time already.

"That was a rescue."

She smiled at him. "Okay, so if that didn't count as one, let's go." She had learned to enjoy these functions, though the first time she'd ever gone, she'd felt out of her element. Even though she'd been saving up her money, Kate felt that she was a nobody when all these people were rich somebodies. Now, she was comfortable with the affairs. Oh, sure, some treated her like a nobody still because she wasn't one of the fabulously wealthy. To them, she was just a bodyguard and personal assistant to Lexi, but she'd learned to ignore them.

She had thought she and Derek would dance just one more time, maybe because he wanted to show Brenda he was really with Kate or maybe because he just loved to dance. But once Derek had escorted Kate to the floor, he wasn't letting her go. She was thoroughly enjoying herself though, and she couldn't have been happier. Dance after dance, they swayed and shimmied on the floor to the live band music.

During one of the breaks, they stopped to get drinks of water, and then she excused herself to go to the bathroom.

When she was in the restroom, she heard three women come into the room. She had just finished her business in the stall when one of the women said, "Can you believe that bitch came here with Derek?"

Brenda.

"Yeah, you ought to trip her or spill a drink on her. You and Derek aren't meant to be over yet," another woman said.

Kate left the stall, not about to hide in there, listening to their conversation. She walked over to the sink to wash her hands. "You know, you had a great thing going with him, but you wanted more than he was willing to give."

"You think you have what it takes to make him marry you?" Brenda asked, getting in Kate's space. It really wasn't a good idea to badger a wolf.

"Yeah, I do. But it would have to be mutual." Which Kate was beginning to think it could be.

"You've been seeing him behind my back, haven't you?"

"Nope. Of course I've known him since I interviewed to be his bodyguard. And he's friends with all my friends, but I've never dated him."

"Yeah, right. As if the two of you would be kissing so hot and heavy when you hadn't already dated him."

"There's just something so sexy about him that it's hard not to give in to temptation, don't you think?"

Brenda glowered at her. "He turned you down for the job because you weren't good enough."

"No, he turned me down because he was afraid it would lead to this. And he'd fall in love with me when I was supposed to be working for him. So now we're free and clear of that hurdle." Kate smiled. She needed to dry her hands, and she wanted to return to dance with Derek, but the women were blocking her in. She really didn't want to get physical, but she would if she had to. "Excuse me, I need to dry my hands."

Brenda crowded her more, reaching out to shove at her just as the door opened, and Kate planted her wet hands on Brenda's bodice to gently move her aside. Brenda shrieked when she saw Kate's wet handprints on her dress. She went to swing a fist at Kate, but Brenda must have forgotten the part about Kate being bodyguard trained. She easily blocked the blow.

"Is there a problem?" Jade asked.

Everyone turned to see Jade, Lexi, and Holly standing there frowning at Brenda.

"Did you see what she did?" Brenda said, outraged, showing off her wet gown.

"We saw her ask you nicely about moving out of her way so she could dry her hands and you trying to shove her," Holly said, rubbing her belly full of babies.

"And when she tried to move you out of her path, you tried to hit her. I mean, what else was she supposed to do when you're bullying her and there are three women against one?" Lexi said.

"It seems to me—given that she's a highly trained combatant, knowing several forms of martial arts and combat maneuvers—you would realize it's not a smart idea to mess with her," Jade said.

The wolf in Kate had wanted to fight it out, but she was glad her friends had shown up to save the day so she wouldn't have to resort to anything more violent. She might have felt good about it, but Derek might have thought she should have reined in her wolf tendencies more.

"She started it," Brenda said, finally moving out of Kate's way, Brenda's girlfriends already backing off as if they finally realized Kate could kick their butts too.

"Are we in kindergarten?" Jade asked.

"She has been seeing Derek behind Brenda's back," one of Brenda's friends said.

"No, she hasn't been," Lexi said.

"And I would never give Derek an ultimatum to marry me. If we're well suited, it will happen. Time will tell."

"Bitch," Brenda said, and she brushed past Kate, who fought the urge to trip her and send her sprawling on the restroom floor.

Then Brenda and her friends quickly left the restroom.

Kate finished drying her hands. "Did Derek send you to rescue me?"

Lexi smiled. "He saw Brenda and her friends go into the restroom after you, but we also saw it and were headed here to save you. He was much relieved."

"I was more worried about how you would deal with them, and since Brenda had witnesses on her side, no telling what they would say. I liked the wet handprints on her bodice," Holly said. "New fashion statement, courtesy of a she-wolf."

The ladies laughed and hugged each other.

"Thanks, ladies."

"You're welcome. You would be there for any one of us if the situation required it," Lexi said.

"I certainly would." Then Kate left the restroom, and the other ladies stayed to do their business.

Kate saw Brenda and the other women glowering at her. She smiled sweetly and joined Derek, who was eagle-eyeing the situation.

"Are you okay?"

"Yeah, I'm okay. Brenda's pissed off though."

Derek shook his head. "She has only herself to blame for that."

But Kate didn't tell him about what she had done to Brenda's dress. "Are you up for more dancing?"

"I'm sure am." He took her back to the dance floor. "I've enjoyed our evening together."

"I've had a lot of fun."

"Thanks for inviting me to go camping with the group."

"You looked like an omega wolf on the outskirts of the pack." Which she had hated.

He chuckled. "An omega wolf?"

"Yeah, with some great dance moves. I knew you would have a great time camping with the other guys."

"And with you?" Derek asked.

She shrugged. "I'll be there having a good time whether you're there or not."

He laughed.

"It's true."

"I know. Your comment just struck me as funny."

Kate noticed Brenda glowering at her from the sidelines, the handprints still visible on her dress. It wasn't really the water that had stained the fabric but the minerals in the water. Easy to remedy, but for tonight's event, it was perfect. Brenda's date apparently hadn't wanted to dance. Kate remembered seeing Derek and Brenda dancing a lot when Kate was at affairs like this before, once she had started working for Lexi. "I think Brenda's rethinking her hasty decision to tell you to marry her or else. It doesn't appear that her date wants to join her on the ballroom floor, and I just bet she wishes she was dancing with you instead."

"She can rethink our relationship all she wants. Once a woman starts telling me she wants me to marry her or else, I'm out of there. Because they're human, of course."

"Ha! Even when she's a wolf, you think the same." Whoops, Kate hadn't meant to mention that. She'd definitely had a little over her limit of two glasses of champagne that night. She was a lightweight when it came to drinking alcohol.

"I have my reasons."

Oh, sure, he would probably be besieged by humans and she-wolves alike to date them. Kate hadn't really thought of that since she hadn't been on the market for a billionaire. Not that she didn't still have a super-sized crush on him. She did. But she sure didn't want him thinking she was after him for his money.

Suddenly, a loud pop sounded. Something struck a chandelier overhead, breaking part of it, crystal shards raining down over a table, and some-one shouted, "He has a gun!"

CHAPTER 4

KATE SLAMMED INTO DEREK, TAKING HIM TO the floor. She pinned his body with her own, slid her hand beneath her gown, and grabbed the gun strapped to her left leg. People screamed and started running all over the ballroom, trying to make their escape. After hearing about shootings at other businesses all over the States, it didn't take much for people to panic and for good reason.

Derek started to move, but Kate said, "Stay down—don't move a muscle."

From where they were on the dance floor, they couldn't see who the shooter was, but people running through the building could make for easy targets.

Chaos ensued as people scrambled to leave the ballroom or hide. Some guests were still screaming, some crying. Kate worried about what had happened to Lexi and the others. But for now, she was protecting Derek.

Then she saw Rafe and Jade crouched near one of the tables closest to the dance floor. Rafe motioned to Kate and Derek to go out the side door. The shooter had fired the shot from the direction of the front entryway, which was a long way from the door Rafe indicated, but Kate didn't know where the gunman was now. Some people were running out through the side door.

"Let's make our way to that door." She nodded to Rafe and then finally slid off Derek. But she was also moving them toward Rafe and Jade, since Kate was the only one who was armed and she needed to protect all of them.

She saw Mike running at a crouch to join them. "Go," she told Rafe and Jade. "Derek, go."

"No, I'll stay with you." It appeared Derek wasn't budging.

"You don't have a gun," Kate reminded him.

But to Kate's disquiet—wanting him to get himself to safety—Derek stayed with her, while Mike remained with them and Rafe and Jade headed out through the door. Then Kate saw Holly and Aidan nearby, and she waved to them to go out the same way. Holly's twin sons were due in three weeks, and she needed to be out of there pronto. Then Kate saw Aidan's bodyguards racing to escort them outside. At least some of her friends would be safe.

"Derek, go!" Kate said. "I need to find Lexi and Ryder."

"No way in hell. I'm staying with you."

No more gunfire had sounded, so she hoped the threat had been eliminated. Sirens were wailing off in the distance. She trusted that someone had called in the shooting. Probably several people had once they were outside and felt safe enough to do so.

She and Derek moved closer to the door where attendees were still piling up on each other, frantic to escape. She didn't want to move him into that mass of bodies until they cleared out, or potentially, she could get them both shot.

"I didn't think you were armed." Derek got his phone out and said, "Hey, Will, what's going on? Do you have eyes on the situation?"

"Yeah, the shooter's dressed as waitstaff. Where the hell are you? In the crowd of panicking people, I can't see you."

"We're moving toward the side door. Kate's protecting me."

Will didn't say anything. She assumed he didn't believe Derek was being serious.

"Seriously. She's armed and everything." Derek sounded proud of her.

She was good at her job. She had tried to tell him that during the job interview!

"Okay, good. Stick with her then. I'll move in your direction, but if I can get an eye on the shooter, I'm going to stop him."

"All right. Just don't get yourself shot. I don't want to have to replace you."

"No chance of that," Will said, chuckling.

Then she and Derek saw a waiter running away.

She couldn't see if he was armed. Two security guards waiting in the wings made the move against the waiter, and Will raced out from behind a table and tackled the guy. "Where's your gun?" Will shouted.

With all the conversation going on before the shot went off and the band playing, she wasn't sure now if a gun had been fired. Especially if Will couldn't find a gun on the waiter, unless he had ditched it. She didn't put her gun away in case a threat still existed or someone else was involved.

"I... I don't have a gun. I'm new at the job," the waiter said, frantic to get away. "I... I only opened a bottle of champagne, and the cork flew up to the ceiling and hit the crystal chandelier. Then people were shouting that there was a man with a gun, and all hell broke loose. I didn't even know they were talking about me."

Kate looked at Derek to see his take on it.

Derek shrugged. "It could have been that way. Like you, I responded to the loud pop, the chandelier crystals breaking, and then someone shouting that the waiter had a gun. All of it combined and then everyone panicking added to the confusion."

Police vehicles roared up to the clubhouse and slammed on their brakes, the sirens going off, the flashing lights filling the windows. Kate tucked her gun back in her leg holster. She didn't want the police thinking she was an armed shooter before everyone could vouch for her. Mike likewise tucked his gun back in the holster he was wearing under his suit jacket.

Since she and Derek and Mike had witnessed the men tackling the waiter, they waited in the ballroom to give their testimony to police about what they'd seen. She hoped the waiter had been telling the truth, and she hoped none of the guests or staff had been injured in their rush to leave the clubhouse.

Lexi and Ryder joined them, and then their other friends came back in to stand as a unified pack. Lexi and Kate hugged, and then there were hugs all around.

"Are you okay?" Kate asked Holly. She was thinking Holly should have gone home and the police could have talked to her later. She couldn't imagine carrying twins so close to delivery and having to go through a nightmare like this.

"Yes, I'm okay. Thanks so much for asking," Holly said. "It gave me a scare, and the twins were kicking like crazy, probably recognizing my anxiety."

"What happened?" Lexi asked.

"Kate saved my life," Derek said, winking at her.

"You were in my way, and I was trying to see who the shooter was," Kate corrected him. She told the others what the waiter had said to Will.

"Wait. We ran out of there like a bunch of scared geese because he opened a bottle of champagne?" Lexi asked. "It's a good thing no one was hurt."

"Right." Derek rubbed Kate's shoulder. "I liked your maneuver, Kate, after I got over the initial shock of you throwing me to the dance floor and covering my body with your own."

"Any of the guys would have done it for you if they'd been closer to you than I had been."

"Yeah, but it wouldn't have been the same."

That time, she smiled at him. "The key to taking someone down to protect them is using the other person's body to cushion your fall."

He chuckled.

She brushed off his back where he had gotten a little dusty while he was lying on the floor.

Derek ran his hand over her shoulder in a light caress. "You didn't tell me you were armed."

"Always, when it can come in handy."

Will and the security guards were talking to the police about what had happened.

Once they realized no one was involved in any shooting, they let the management handle dealing with the poor waiter.

Kate wondered if he would be fired and also charged with damaging the chandelier. She felt bad for the guy. She could imagine herself doing something like that!

Afterward, all the attendees and clubhouse staff began to leave. Kate just wanted to ride back with Mike or even Lexi and Ryder; no sense in Derek having to go out of his way to drive her back to the

Gallagher estate. What had started out as a beautiful and elegant night had turned into something wild and unexpected. She wanted to laugh at herself for throwing Derek to the floor on a date. At least she showed him she could do her job as a bodyguard if he'd had any doubts about it.

"I could just ride home with Lexi," Kate told Derek.

"We'll be fine," Lexi said, giving Kate another hug. "Go. Ride with Derek home. You protected him once. He may need your protection again."

"She's right," Derek said, trying to look positively serious, but he was smiling ever so slightly.

Kate shook her head at him.

"Are you ready to leave?" Derek asked Kate.

"Yeah, I am. I had a lovely time. Thanks for inviting me." Even though she would have had a lovely time just going with Lexi and Ryder. She had enjoyed dancing with Derek though. "Are you sure it's really necessary for me to ride back with you? You'll have to go out of your way to go home. Truly, I can hitch a ride with Lexi since I've fulfilled my obligation for the night and your former girlfriend has already left so I don't need to play a role as your date any longer. I'm sure that even all the paparazzi have left, so no one else is here to attempt to get pictures of anyone important."

"I would never take a woman to a social event and not return her home afterward."

Kate raised a brow. She knew Brenda would have gone home with him for the night. Probably the other women Derek had dated too. Kate wasn't that naive.

"Okay, so sometimes it was not until the next day. Though I never brought them to the house." He smiled. "Come on. I'll take you home."

She went with him then, and once the car had been brought around, he got the door for her this time. Then they headed to her home. "I have to thank you for saving me back there."

"You said that already."

"But I don't think you believe I meant it when I did."

"You thought I was just getting friendly."

He chuckled. "Hell, no, but I have to admit I really did like your maneuver."

"I bet. And I figure no one has ever tackled you like that at a ball before."

"No." He smiled. "You might not believe this, but I've never needed saving by a bodyguard before tonight." He turned onto the next road. "Not to change the subject, but thanks again for inviting me to the campout. I haven't been to one with the guys in a couple of years. They have invited me, but I just felt like the odd man out. You made me realize that I didn't have to be with someone to enjoy myself."

"I'm sure you enjoyed doing that with Brenda at some time or another." Kate shouldn't have even mentioned the woman. She wasn't sure why Brenda irked her so much. Maybe because Brenda acted as though she might still be in the running with Derek when he had a new woman he was with at the ball! Not that anything more would come of it, but Brenda wouldn't know that.

"Are you kidding? She was *not* into camping. Five-star hotels were more her style. Being waited on hand and foot. She's worth about a hundred million dollars herself, and she's not about to sleep in a sleeping bag, hassle with the bugs, fish for dinner, and go hiking all over the place. I finally convinced her to stay with me at a cabin one time, and she hated it. They didn't have a heated swimming pool. She didn't like the lake water because she couldn't see what was in it. And it wasn't heated to a perfect temperature. The place had no maid service, and the bathroom was standard, no whirlpool tub. When I caught fish and cleaned it, she was totally grossed out."

Kate laughed. "Can you imagine her seeing you catching fish as a wolf?"

"She saw me as a wolf the one time we stayed at a cabin in the woods," Derek admitted.

"Oh?" Now that totally surprised Kate. "But she didn't see you shift." At least she suspected Brenda hadn't or he would have had to do something about it.

"She didn't. That night she had been sound

asleep, and I wanted to run as a wolf in the worst way. Being a royal with so few human roots, I can change whenever I want to, but when I'm out in nature like that, when I have the chance, I want to run as a wolf. I walked into the woods, removed my clothes, shifted, and then ran for a few miles. When I returned, I heard the door open to the cabin, and I saw her standing there on the deck looking for me. She never wakes when I slip away, so at first when I saw the door open, I was worried that an intruder had broken into our cabin. As a wolf, I would have stood a better chance to scare him off. I was just as surprised as she was when we saw each other. I just stood there for a moment. Even though it was dark out, a full moon helped to light the sky. I'm not sure how well she could see me even then. Though she was looking in my direction."

"Oh, wow, you never told anyone about that, did you?"

"No. There wasn't any need. I turned and loped back to my clothes in the woods and dressed. Then I walked way around the cabin so that I wasn't coming from the same direction the wolf had been in. Though I'm not sure she would have suspected I was the wolf, but she might have been worried about me running into him. I did think about coming from the direction of the wolf and telling her I had run into a big, old, friendly dog. Then she wouldn't be worried about going to a cabin in the woods again."

"It didn't work." At least that was what Kate guessed had happened.

"Nope. She'd seen the wolf, was terrified I had been killed in the woods, and what would she have done? She couldn't even find my keys to the Land Rover so she could go home."

"She was going to abandon you to the wolves?" Kate laughed. "Precious."

He chuckled. "Yeah. I was glad I had left my keys in my jeans' pocket when I went running in the woods. So no more camping trips with Brenda. Most of the women I know are like that. One loved ski resorts, another enjoyed island retreats. But none of them liked camping."

"Well, I'm sure you'll have a great time then."

"I have another social event coming up Monday night if you would like to go with me to that. I know it's short notice, but—"

"You wanted to see how this went between us first. I would have to check my calendar to know for certain, but I'm sure I have something I'm doing with Lexi. I'm a busy working woman, you know."

He smiled. "Okay, well, if you want to go, I'll give you my number."

"Lexi has it." Kate didn't want Derek to think she would be his convenient date for all his social activities now until he found someone who was safer to be with—some woman who was not trying to marry him, at least not right away.

He got a call on his phone and answered it on Bluetooth. "Hey, are you okay?" Brenda asked.

"Yeah, what about you?"

Kate was annoyed that Brenda would be calling Derek after she had broken up with him and he was still on a date with Kate, though she understood to an extent that Brenda would want to make sure he was okay after what they had thought initially was a shootout. But she didn't think that was the only reason Brenda was calling him.

"I'm good, though I broke my high heel in the crush of people trying to get out. I'm sure I got a few bruises too."

"What about your date?"

"Oh, he left me. He was definitely not the hero type. He was out the door before I even realized he was gone. For an older man, he sure could move fast."

"I'm glad you're both okay. I need to go. I'm taking Kate home."

Silence.

Kate smiled. She was glad now that she had allowed Derek to drive her home.

"Okay, well, if you need to talk about what happened, just give me a call when you get home," Brenda said.

"You'll be in bed by then, surely," Kate said.

"Though, come to think of it, he might not even be going home tonight. We haven't worked out the logistics quite yet."

Derek smiled at Kate for saying so, and then Brenda hung up on him.

He pulled into Kate's driveway. She got out before he could barely park the car, the Land Rover parking behind them.

She quickly said good night, waved, and headed inside her house. If he was expecting a good-night kiss, he'd have to take another woman out on a date to get it.

He finally drove off. What a night. She sighed. She was glad the incident at the clubhouse hadn't been anything serious. And she was glad she'd said what she had to Brenda. It would give the other woman something to mull over.

Recalling fondly how great the rest of the evening had gone, Kate twirled around in her foyer, imagining the fun she'd had in dancing with Derek—debonair as usual. She'd even managed to dodge the paparazzi and annoy Brenda in the process. Best of all, she'd had a great time. Another date with Derek? No way. Not when he had such a commitment phobia with she-wolves. What if she fell hard for him and then he broke her heart?

She shouldn't have invited him to the campout. She hoped she wouldn't regret it. She and Mike would have served as bodyguards and just had a great time. She hadn't needed to ask Derek to join them!

He had his own way of life, and that was how he chose to live it—dating human women with no pledge to marry.

Yet she was curious about how he would interact with everybody else on a campout—with her especially.

CHAPTER 5

DEREK KNEW KATE WASN'T A BETA WOLF, BUT the way she had tucked tail and run into the safety of her house made him think of her that way. He sighed. He hadn't meant to imply anything by asking her to accompany him as his date to another social function. He had just enjoyed being with her. And he thought they could have another fun social engagement out together, that was all.

Maybe she worried about what others would think if the paparazzi began taking pictures of them being together too much. He could just imagine what his bodyguards were thinking. That he'd screwed up big time with her at the very end of the date and that was why she'd hurried off and hadn't even let him walk her to the door.

Still, he drove home, feeling like a billion bucks. He hadn't felt that good in a long time. Partly it was because he had a great time being with Kate, dancing with her, visiting with her, eating with her, but he'd also enjoyed dining with his fellow wolf friends for a change, like he was part of the pack again because he hadn't had a human female on his arm this time.

Maybe he could convince Kate to go with him to a different charity event after the campout, as long as they had a great time at it. He was really looking forward to the campout in any case. He wished he'd gotten another sizzling kiss from Kate when he dropped her off at her home to confirm what he'd felt was real between them—that moment of connection between two wolves when sparks fly. He hadn't expected that or for her to disappear so quickly before he had a chance to kiss her again. He suspected that way of thinking was going to get him into trouble again with the she-wolf.

Still, tonight, he couldn't help but think about the camping trip coming up and seeing Kate again.

He entered his home, greeted Foxy and Red, and waved good night to his bodyguards. He wished he could have brought Kate to his home for a nightcap or more. So much for not wanting to get involved with her. But she wasn't working for him, so why not? At least she didn't seem to be upset with him any longer for not hiring her.

———

Kate could barely sleep that night. All she thought about was shimmying to the music with Derek and how much fun she'd had. She was already thinking that maybe there was just an inkling of a possibility between them. She always wondered that when she dated a wolf. This time, she really was having a hard time putting aside the thoughts—of him and her dancing the years away, all the way into their golden years. Silly of her, really. He would go back to dating human women, and she would go back to dating a wolf every once in a while.

When Kate woke the next morning, she was still thinking about Derek. *Give it up for the moment!* She dressed and went over to Lexi's house to work on some more promotional campaign ideas.

Spirit bounded to the door and greeted Kate. Kate gave Spirit hugs and petted her, then Ryder came and got her so Kate could join Lexi in her office.

"Hey, how did it go with Derek last night?" Lexi asked Kate as they sat down to have mimosas.

Okay, so maybe Kate wasn't going to get away from thinking of him like she thought she was.

Kate took a couple of sips of her mimosa, delicious as usual. They always tried to make work fun and usually had fruity teas with their early morning business routine. Usually mimosas were reserved for celebrations. Kate hoped Lexi wasn't celebrating Kate's conquest over Derek.

"It was fine. We had fun dancing." Kate had thought she and Lexi were going to do a few things quickly on the website this morning and then Lexi was taking off the rest of the day to spend with Ryder. Which meant Kate had the rest of the day off too. She wasn't sure what she was going to do with it. Maybe catch up on some movies. Though she really wanted to get some exercise in.

"*Every* dance after dinner." Lexi smiled at her.

"He likes to dance. I like to dance, so sure. You told me to have fun."

Lexi laughed. "You looked like you were having a great time. We didn't expect you to invite him camping."

Kate was afraid that might come back to bite her. "Yeah, I'm sorry about that. I shouldn't have invited him. It was up to one of you to do it." Kate swore the champagne had done the talking for her last night.

"Not at all. You know we told you if you wanted to invite any wolf camping, you were welcome to."

"Yeah, but he hasn't gone camping with his friends in ages, and after I proposed he could join us, I felt I'd overstepped my bounds."

"Nonsense. Ryder said Rafe and Aidan are thrilled Derek would come, just like the good old days. They've been friends with him forever. They've asked him in the past, but Derek didn't want to go by himself and feel like a fifth wheel to them and their mates. And he was always dating a human woman he couldn't bring along."

Besides the fact that the ones he had dated hadn't liked camping. Kate smiled at the thought.

"Ryder got a kick out of how Derek jumped at the chance when you offered for him to come."

"Yeah, I noticed. I was afraid Derek got the wrong impression—that he thought I was offering to share my tent with him. No way."

"Not unless he needs a bodyguard."

Kate scoffed. "He has two very capable body-guards of his own. Besides, Derek would have to pay me double time for the job because the time period would be over the weekend and through the night. But like I told him, I so much prefer working for you."

Lexi laughed.

"Well, I do. I get to do all this fun stuff with you"—Kate motioned to the website—"when I would have been bored to tears working for him. All he would think of was that I would be after his money."

Lexi smiled. "I noticed you kissed him a couple of times."

"Oh, sure. I was playing my role to the hilt. I had thought of letting him just hang out with Brenda a while longer, but some wolfish part of me made me step in and haul him off to dance with me. The woman had the nerve to talk to him when she was with someone else and so was Derek."

"I know, right? Brenda was glowering at you from the edge of the dance floor all night. But it was her choice to tell him to marry her or else. She had a nice thing going for her before that happened. He always took her to the best places, and he didn't expect anything in return," Lexi said.

"He asked me to go with him to a charity dinner on Monday." After Kate mentioned it, she wondered why she had! She knew Lexi would give her the time off to see him and probably even encourage her to go if Kate was hesitant. Which she was at this point. Why should she be the fill-in date until he found a human woman to see who seemed safer than dating a she-wolf?

"Hmm, so are you going?" Lexi asked.

"No. I told him I would probably be busy." Kate was beginning to think Lexi had just asked her over to her house to grill her about Derek, which couldn't help but amuse Kate.

Smiling, Lexi shook her head. "You are never too busy to go out with someone socially. I want you to have fun. Oh, and if you're worried someone might consider you and Derek an item, you don't have to worry about it. It's all over the tabloids, so everyone believes it anyway. I've already been asked to give an interview to tell them all about you. Of course, I wouldn't say anything. I do want to ask you something important though. Would you consider being my partner in the cosmetic business?"

"Are you serious?"

Lexi smiled. "You have increased my sales tenfold. As of this morning, I'm making you a partner. As long as that's okay with you."

"Ohmigod, are you kidding?" Kate couldn't believe it! She was thrilled!

"No, I'm not kidding. With all the promotional ideas you come up with and all the help you are at marketing, you're much more than an assistant. And you're way more than just a friend. You're like a sister to me, part of my family. Not to mention I *need* a business partner. If I were to lose you—"

"I feel the same way about you." Kate wiped away a couple of tears. She couldn't believe how generous Lexi was to her or how much she appreciated that Lexi felt like her sister too. "Don't tell me you think I'm going to get hitched to a hot wolf and leave you alone. Didn't I tell you that's going to be part of my dating regimen? Whoever I find to mate has to agree to my conditions—that I continue to work full-time for you."

"As a business partner. He can come along, whoever he ends up being." Lexi gave Kate a big hug.

Kate hugged her back. "You're not doing this because you think I'm going to mate Derek, are you? And then I would be too busy with him, jet-setting around the world or whatever it is he does, to spend time working with you, right?"

"You might end up with him, but regardless, I want you to have vested interest in the company. You've helped me really make the company take off and be as successful as it has been. I couldn't have done it without you."

"I accept. How much do I need to pay to buy into the business?"

"We're splitting the net profits. I'm giving you half the shares as a bonus. We're going to make this company even better."

Kate smiled. "I never thought a bodyguard position could turn into so much more. Wait until Brenda hears I'm not just your personal assistant any longer."

Lexi laughed. "She'll really be annoyed more than she is already. From what I've learned about her, she does nothing all day. I can't imagine a more boring lifestyle. All her wealth is inherited, and she prefers spending her date's money rather than her own." Lexi drank some of her mimosa. "Oh, and the lawyer will be over in an hour with the documents for us to both sign. I'm making an announcement to the press shortly after that so everyone knows. I'm so glad you're going to be my partner…especially because Ryder and I are having twins next year."

"Ohmigod, I was so hoping you would give me the good news soon. That is wonderful." Kate hugged her again. "Oh, that's why you want me to help run the company."

"Yep. That's my devious ulterior motive. I'll have a nanny to help out with the kids, but I'll need you to run the company—not as my assistant but as part owner. You've managed the business on your own anytime I've needed you to. Heck, when we go on trips together, even when they're supposed to be vacation trips, you're working. So yeah, that's another reason."

"I've got this. Do you know what sex the twins are going to be?"

"Not yet, but soon. Are you happy with the idea of being a partner? I know I should have discussed it with you more, but I just thought you would be thrilled, and I know I am," Lexi said.

"Yes! I couldn't be any happier." Kate was ecstatic.

"Good. Oh, and about the tabloids, they managed to grab some photos of you and Derek dancing and kissing. I love the one where you're dragging him into the clubhouse. That was Ryder's favorite too. He said he'd never seen anyone take charge of Derek—dance with him—like you did. We were all smiling about it."

Kate sighed. "Someone had to do it." Then she thought of the campout and Lexi carrying twins. "So what about camping now that you're pregnant?"

"I've been feeling fine. I haven't had any Braxton-Hicks contractions at all. And it's early enough that I won't have any discomfort with carrying a couple of babies," Lexi said.

"Okay, good." Then Kate frowned. "Your mimosa! You were drinking champagne with your orange juice."

"Mine had carbonated mineral water. Yours had the champagne."

"Oh, okay, great!"

Then Lexi and Kate began to work some more on the website.

"Rafe said he'd never seen anyone move him like you could in all the years he has known him. Aidan agreed. And when you kissed Derek in front of the ex-girlfriend? If Derek is looking to date another woman soon, he might have to explain all about you," Lexi said.

"There's nothing to explain."

Lexi smiled. "Yeah, well, you know what they say. A picture is worth a thousand words. I'm glad you convinced Derek to come to the campout though. I was thinking we could do another woodsy video session for the cosmetics. Holly and Jade said they would be glad to be models for the products. The guys said they would help us set up and then they're going fishing."

"That would be great." Kate loved it when they still had their girl time together.

CHAPTER 6

AFTER SIGNING THE PAPERWORK TO MAKE KATE a partner in the Clair de Lune Cosmetics company, Kate congratulated Lexi on the babies and thanked her again. Then she walked back home to do some gardening. Even though Lexi had gardeners for the property, Kate liked to tend to her own flower beds. Before Ryder became Lexi's mate and Mike moved onto the premises as their bodyguard, Kate had lived at the house with them. But to give them privacy and a place of her own, Lexi had built Kate the guest house. So Kate had a home of her own that was within walking distance of the main house.

That way too, when Lexi's parents visited from Silver Town, they would stay with Lexi and Ryder. Mike continued to stay at the main house to provide around-the-clock protection.

Kate dressed in her old clothes, opened the garage door, and grabbed the gardening tools. She settled down to work in her garden, weeding—a necessary evil—before she could plant her purple coneflowers; black-eyed Susans; red, purple, pink, and yellow zinnias; and blanket flowers—what she truly loved. While Kate was weeding, Spirit bounded up to her and poked Kate with her nose, wanting Kate to pet her. Kate had to oblige and gave her a hug. "Are you supposed to be out here?"

"Nope, she's not." Mike hurried after her so he could take her back to Lexi's fenced-in yard. "But when she saw you out here gardening, she had to check on you. As soon as I opened the gate, she bolted."

"I'm glad you were there to see her."

"Did you need any help with that?"

"Gardening? Nah. You're dressed so nicely, and I'm just in my old clothes. But thanks for taking Spirit back. She won't dig in my garden, thankfully, but she'll want to be petted the whole time she's out here, and you know how hard it is to ignore her."

Mike laughed. "Yes. Come on, Spirit. Let's go play fetch."

Spirit loved playing the game and would play it until everyone was worn out but her.

Mike returned Spirit to Lexi's yard, and Kate really began weeding the garden with gusto. Twenty minutes later, a red Porsche she didn't recognize drove up and parked in front of her flower beds. When she saw the driver, she couldn't have been more surprised. Randall Roberts. She'd dated him on and off for over a year. She hadn't really been interested in mating him. They'd had some good times when she'd wanted to be with a wolf, but that was last year's news.

Wearing slate-gray dress pants and a light-blue

button-down-collar dress shirt, he got out of his car and joined her. She rose to her feet, and he gave her a light hug. For old times' sake, she gave him just a light one back—albeit a little sweaty—not wanting him to think she was really glad to see him. His curly red hair was cropped short, his blue eyes smiling as he observed her. "You're looking great."

She was dressed in old, well-worn sneakers she wore only for gardening, her legs dirt-splattered from pulling up weeds, her hair windblown, and her light-blue tank top sporting a perspiration stain in the front and under the arms; her blue jean shorts featured holes that she put there as she'd worked and played hard—not commercially torn and sold in the stores that way. This was her gardening look. Not a pretty sight. And she knew she wasn't "looking great."

She despised when people gave compliments they didn't really mean.

"I didn't know where you'd ended up after you moved, and then my aunt was reading one of those tabloids, and here you are." He sounded enthusiastic to have finally found Kate.

Had he seen the pictures of her dancing with Derek? Or kissing him? Why would Randall show up here if he thought she was with a guy now? As if Randall had even been looking for her one iota before the big news came out that she appeared to be dating a billionaire. She didn't think he could have heard about her becoming a partner in the cosmetics firm yet. Though she knew Lexi planned to announce it right away.

"I saw you were with Derek Spencer at a charity ball."

She would have thought Randall's being excited to see her was all an act, but she suspected he had an ulterior motive. "And now here you are!" Uninvited and unwelcome. But she was moving up in the world.

"You got a promotion!" he said.

Randall hadn't liked that she was going to be working as a bodyguard. He was a financial advisor, and he thought that was the kind of job that was important. After she quit her lifeguard job, she'd drifted from job to job. She had even worked at a zoo for a while until the zoo no longer had wolves. She had a doctorate of life in understanding wolf biology and behavior.

But she had always liked trying something new until she could find exactly what suited her the best and then stick with it. Once she started working for Lexi as her bodyguard, Randall had been history. Working for Lexi had been a life changer for her. Especially when she began to work for her as her personal assistant too.

"Promotion?" Kate wondered if he *had* heard that she was a full partner in Lexi's business.

"Yeah, as Lexi Summerfield's personal assistant. You did damn good. How did that come about?"

So he didn't know the really good news. "It came about because of my bodyguard position." She cast Randolph a smug smile. "It turned out that I was really good working as a personal assistant to Lexi in conjunction with serving as her bodyguard, and I used my marketing training to help promote Lexi's cosmetics line. So it all worked out really well. Not to mention we have become like sisters. You never know when jumping around from job to job will finally land you in the one you were meant to be in. I'm sure you'll learn of it soon enough, but Lexi made me co-owner of Clair de Lune Cosmetics."

"Hot damn! Things are really looking up for you. I guess that's why Derek Spencer asked you to attend the gala with him."

"Nope. I just signed the paperwork this morning. He doesn't even know anything about it yet."

"Huh."

What did that mean? Randall couldn't see that a billionaire had found her interesting or intriguing enough to take on a date? Despite the fact that she hadn't had the money and power he did?

"So you never used your bodyguard training?" Randall really hadn't believed she could handle it.

"Oh, sure I did. I'm still trained for protecting her if she needs it." Kate *wasn't* going to explain herself to Randall. She figured he wouldn't believe her anyway.

She went back to her gardening. She wanted to pull all the weeds and plant the flowers she had sitting in pots ready for their new beds before it got too hot out. An ex-boyfriend, whom she *wasn't* interested in seeing again just because he thought her elevated job status made her more important in his eyes, wasn't going to stop her from doing what she loved doing.

Randall took a seat on her wood-and-wrought-iron garden bench, his arms draped across the back as if he were staying for a while and wanted to get comfortable—as if she had even invited him to! He could have at least offered to help her. Then again, she would have had to explain how she wanted to plant her flowers or what weeds to pull, and it would be more effort than it was worth. Not to mention he *wasn't* offering.

"Why are you here anyway?" Kate finished pulling weeds and began digging holes for her flowers.

Randall smiled. "I thought we could have lunch and celebrate your new job—though it's even more elevated than I had thought to begin with. I figured you were making good money as a personal assistant to Lexi."

That was the crux of the matter—Kate earning more money.

He'd never wanted to celebrate any of her new jobs with her before. In fact, whenever she had started a new one—that he felt hadn't been financially acceptable—he would stop dating her for a while, a passive-aggressive tactic to show he disapproved of her job choices. But she hadn't cared. He'd only been fun to date when she wanted a wolf to see, but not for anything long-term.

She wasn't naive either. Now she was going to be a full-time partner in Lexi's successful business and Randall probably believed she needed a financial advisor. Lexi had one, and Kate would use him before she ever considered using Randall to take care of her investments.

"You've never wanted to before," Kate said. "Celebrate with me when I've had a new job."

"I was really busy."

"You didn't think the jobs I had were worthwhile before. And now you do? So now what? You want to be my financial advisor?"

His lips parted, and she knew she had surprised him that she realized just why he was here. She would have to have been clueless not to figure that out. "You're transparent if you didn't realize that."

Randall opened his mouth to speak, but then someone else drove up her driveway in a blue Jeep and parked next to Randall's car, and she wondered who that was now! She wanted to garden in peace.

A dark-haired man got out of his vehicle, and he was wearing khaki pants, brown shoes, and a short-sleeved shirt—giving her the impression he was a salesman, except he had a camera in hand. She suspected he had a recorder hidden on his person. He headed her way, smiling as if he were her friend—when he wasn't.

Randall frowned at him, but he didn't leave his relaxed pose where he sat on the bench. Still, if the guy was trouble, she knew Randall would come to her aid. He was a wolf after all.

"I'm Watson Brown, but everyone calls me Watt. I'm a reporter for *the Stargazer*. I would like to do an exclusive story on you about how you're seeing Derek Spencer now."

"Sorry, this is my reporter friend, and he's getting the exclusive interview with me. You're a little too late," Kate said, motioning to Randall.

The reporter frowned at Randall. "Which paper do you work for?"

"*The New York Times*. You can read the story when it comes out."

She was glad at least Randall could play along and didn't tell the guy to get lost.

"That doesn't seem to be something *The New York Times* would be interested in." The reporter sounded like he didn't believe Randall. His relaxed posture and the fact that he had no camera, no recorder, no notepad, or anything else probably didn't help.

"You're right. The story will be about the new partnership Kate's in. Whom she's dating at the moment wouldn't be the focus of the story."

"New partnership?" the reporter asked.

Thank you, she wanted to tell Randall. At least he was good for something. Neither she nor Randall said anything further about what the partnership was all about.

The reporter snapped a shot of them and then got into his car.

Great. Now the reporter would undoubtedly make something up about her and Randall, or maybe he was going to try to learn who Randall really was. Then make something up.

Then the reporter drove off.

Randall smiled. Kate didn't.

"About lunch to celebrate my promotion… Sorry, I'm busy." Kate finished planting the last of the zinnias. Except for just chilling, she didn't have any plans other than getting some exercise in. "I guess I'll see you around sometime." She gathered up her garden tools and carried them into the garage.

Randall rose to his feet and followed her into the garage. A stalker came to mind. She guessed Randall was so eager to get some money out of her that he thought he could continue to pursue the notion and maybe soon convince her of it. Which wasn't happening. She might be easygoing about a lot of things, but she didn't like it when someone was only interested in her because she could do something for him.

When she knew him before, he was only a

convenient wolf date. Now, she realized—just like
Lexi had been concerned about with herself—that
Randall could be after her money. In Kate's case, if
not just as a financial advisor, as a mate.

She suddenly got a text from Mike: Hey, do you
need my protection?

She smiled. Mike to the rescue. "I've got to go,
Randall. I've got to take this. Talk to you later." She
waited for Randall to leave the garage so she could
clean up and answer the text from Mike.

Randall hesitated. Here she was the goose with the
golden egg; he had dated her, and he didn't want to
let her go. He'd never said or done anything that had
made her want to deepen their relationship. She sure
wasn't interested in going out with him any further.
Not when she knew *why* he wanted to see her now.

He finally sighed. "Okay, I'll check with you later
and we can get together. I knew I should have called
first, but since we have a history, I thought I could
just drop by and congratulate you."

She suspected he hadn't wanted to call her, afraid
she would have turned him down over the phone.
Which she would have done.

"Let's be honest with each other, Randall. If I
had been working as a lifeguard still or only a bodyguard, would you have been interested in doing
anything with me? No," she said before he had a
chance to answer her. "Bye. Have a great day."

Randall belatedly responded, "Yeah, I would

have. We have chemistry. We're both wolves. We have fun together. But you think you've got a chance with Derek Spencer now, don't you?"

She laughed. "He's a confirmed bachelor, if you didn't know. Do you know how many countless women he has dated over the years?" She didn't know, but she figured there had been lots. "Before you ask, he has a financial advisor already, and so does Lexi. So if you think knowing me is going to give you an in now with either of them, I don't believe so. As for me, I'll be talking to Lexi's advisor to see about investments." Kate figured she better just be clear about it all in case Randall thought he could continue to pester her for dates or something.

Randall scoffed. "You're after him, aren't you? I should have known you were a gold digger."

"Me? Since when have I ever dated anyone who had a lot of money—besides you—and wanted more than a fun date? Besides, *who* came to see *me* suddenly to ask me out?" Randall was only interested because she made more money now and she could possibly be another of his clients.

She hadn't heard Mike arrive, but suddenly he was standing outside her garage, looking like he was ready to convince Randall he shouldn't be here if he needed to be convinced. And Spirit came charging in to greet Kate, and once she'd petted her, the wolf dog sat next to Kate in protective mode, panting, watching Randall, not greeting him. Spirit was good with people, but Randall hadn't even made the attempt to ask about her or pet her or talk to her, so she wasn't going to be friendly with him either.

"Is everything all right, Kate?" Mike asked, looking and sounding growly.

"Yeah, thanks, Mike." She figured he had come because she hadn't responded to his text and he was worried about her when he saw the vehicle parked out front that he wouldn't have recognized. "Randall is just leaving."

Randall scowled at Mike and then got into his car to leave.

Kate put her garden tools up on the rack in the garage. "Thanks for the save. I dated Randall on and off, but I haven't seen him in over a year. He's a financial advisor and saw my name in the tabloids when I was at the ball with Derek."

"One of those."

"Yep. And he had the nerve to call *me* a gold digger. As if anything else would come of being with Derek at one ball. Anyway, I couldn't get rid of Randall easily, so I appreciate that you came out here to help me send him on his way."

"You're welcome. I worried when you didn't text me back."

"I meant to, but I kept thinking Randall was leaving and I would text you then."

"Well, I'm just glad to be of service."

They watched Randall drive off the property, and then Mike asked, "Did you need me to help you with anything?"

She looked at the freshly planted flower bed. "Now you ask me?"

Mike chuckled. "I guess I got out of that, didn't I? Seriously, if you need help with digging holes for your plants later or moving bags of mulch or anything, just let me know."

"Thanks. Next time."

Then Mike headed back to Lexi's house, and Kate closed her garage door and went inside her house to clean up and get a cup of iced tea. She liked the long summer days and nights because she could get so much done outdoors. She'd been up at six this morning and raring to go despite the late-night gala. That was one thing about her: she was an early riser, no matter what time she went to bed at night, which made her wonder if Derek was too. Or did he like to sleep in late?

And why she was even thinking of that, she hadn't a clue.

CHAPTER 7

AFTER A RESTLESS SLEEP DREAMING OF KATE last night—enjoying the wolf comradery they had shared—Derek really wished Kate had agreed to go with him to the dinner on Monday night. At eight that morning, Derek had barely gotten his first cup of coffee when his bodyguard, Will Wolfson, showed him the tabloid photos featuring Derek and Kate. He smiled. Brenda was old news. The tabloid was having a field day with the news that Derek already had a new girlfriend. He flipped through the pages of the tabloid and didn't see one photo of Brenda with *her* new boyfriend. Even though she said she was just filling in for the guy's date and not really seeing him for anything beyond the gala. Derek suspected she still held out hope that Derek would change his mind about her.

"There were others, some with different shots of the two of you." Will smiled. "When you parked at the clubhouse and she pulled you inside the building so fast, Allister and I hadn't expected that. You looked so surprised, I guess you hadn't either. We had to race after you to keep up with the two of you."

"She was eager to see everyone." Though Derek was certain that wasn't the reason.

"She was trying to avoid the paparazzi photographing the two of you together."

Derek sipped from his coffee and smiled. Will was a great bodyguard. He was observant, and no one got by him if Derek didn't want to deal with someone's unwanted attention. "I tried to warn her. I think she's used to Lexi being in the limelight, but not herself. She might be in photos with Lexi, but the focus isn't on her."

"Well, the limelight's going to be on her now," Will said.

"It was only one time." Derek wouldn't presume he could change Kate's mind about going out with him again.

"No, boss, she's just getting started on her own claim to fame." Will showed him his cell phone. "She has just become Lexi's partner in Clair de Lune Cosmetics."

"What?" Derek couldn't have been more surprised. He read the news on Will's phone. "Well, I'll be damned. I knew they were close to each other, as much as they worked on the business together. I just never suspected Lexi would hand over half the business to Kate."

"That changes things," Will said. "Even if she never goes out with you again, though I thought from the way she kissed you and danced with you the rest of the night, that might be an indication there were more dates coming up. But she's going to be inundated with date offers herself now."

Now why did that notion bug Derek? He refilled his coffee mug. "Did one of you guys get the car door for her when she bolted out of Lexi's house before the dance?"

Will chuckled. "I did. I saw her coming out of the house, heading straight for the car, and you were nowhere in sight. I jumped out of the Land Rover, sprinted to your car, and opened the door. She saw me coming and waited for me at least."

"Good. Lexi and Ryder held me up."

"Have you asked Kate out on a date again?" Will asked.

"We're camping with Rafe, Aidan, Lexi, and their mates next weekend."

"What about your charity dinner on Monday night?"

Derek gave him a look to drop the interrogation.

"Oh, she's busy since it was such short notice. Gotcha. So the follow-on date will be after that." Then Will frowned. "You don't want to ask her out before then? Man, I sure would, especially now that you've broken the ice with her."

Well, Derek *did* want to ask her out again, but she was already balking about doing anything further with him. "I imagine she's going to be busy with her new role in the company."

Will shook his head. "That wouldn't stop me from asking her out. She's still bound to have free time to do something else."

With Foxy and Red on his heels, Cliff Taylor, Derek's longtime bodyguard, came inside to eat breakfast with them. "I did my rounds outside. Nothing suspicious. Sorry about having to take off for family business right before the gala." He'd gotten in early this morning.

"Anytime either of you need to take off for any reason, it's really no problem. If I feel I need another bodyguard to fill in for one of you guys, I'll just ask Rafe to loan me one. Allister did a good job last night. Is everything all right with your mom?" Derek asked, petting both the dogs.

"Yeah, Mom fell and broke her leg—a simple fracture—and I took care of her until my sister was able to finally fly in to stay with her." Cliff sat down at the dining room table with them. "Luckily, Mom was all right otherwise, and with our fast-healing properties, she'll be fine in no time."

"Okay, good."

Cliff said, "Well, I heard there were a lot of new changes since I was gone."

Derek figured Will had told Cliff all about Brenda and Kate already.

"So are there any more dates planned?" Cliff asked.

Smiling, Derek shook his head. "I've got to

get some breakfast, and then I'm off to work." He often worked out of his home, managing his successful investments in real estate and hedge funds and even investing in entrepreneurs' new product lines that had taken off, sitting poolside while he had a view of the Pacific Ocean and beach down below. He hadn't expected his bodyguards to get so interested in his dating habits all of a sudden. Then again, Kate was a wolf, so that made a difference. If he mated a she-wolf, that would change the dynamics in the household.

He heard his housekeeper, Maddie Meyer, in the kitchen making breakfast. She was a gray wolf like the others, midfifties, widowed, and she'd worked for him for about ten years now as his cook and housekeeper, but she also managed the gardeners and cleaning staff. He'd given her more roles, more responsibility because she was always looking at doing more for him and he enjoyed her company.

"I'm making you ham and eggs and toast, all right?" Maddie asked.

"Sounds good to me," Cliff said.

"Yeah, I'm ready," Will said, even though they knew Maddie was talking to Derek.

"Yeah, that sounds good," Derek said. Anything she made was really great.

Maddie soon brought out a bowl of scrambled eggs and another of skillet potatoes for everyone to eat in the formal dining room. She went back for the sliced ham. She always ate at the breakfast nook in the kitchen since it had a view of the pool and the guys could talk guy talk while she read a shifter romance book, just her preference.

Derek picked up the serving spoon to scoop up some scrambled eggs. "Thanks, Maddie."

"You're welcome. I heard you ditched Brenda for a she-wolf Friday night. I told you that you should have hired Kate to be your bodyguard instead of Will." Maddie set the sliced ham on the table and headed back to the kitchen.

Derek smiled at Will.

She brought out the toast, butter, honey, and jam. Then she returned to the kitchen and came back with a fresh pot of steaming-hot coffee to refill everyone's coffee mugs.

"Hey, did you see in the tabloid the way Derek and Kate were kissing and dancing at the gala?" Will asked. "She wouldn't have lasted as Derek's bodyguard for a month."

"Exactly. They would have been mated, and *then* he could have hired *you* to fill her vacated position," Maddie said. "Now she's part owner of Lexi's cosmetic line, and she's going to be too busy to date Derek any further. It's all over Twitter."

"They're going camping together," Will said.

Maddie smiled. "Oh, now that's good news. I will make you the best food ever for the camping trip. Something special for the two of you."

"They're going with Rafe, Aidan, and Lexi and their mates," Will said so Maddie didn't think it was a camping trip just between Derek and Kate.

"Oh, well, we'll have to fix them right up, won't we?" Maddie was talking to Cliff and Will and looking like she had a new mission in mind instead of speaking to Derek about it. She really hadn't liked that he was dating human women, and she had even suggested he ask Kate out on a date when Kate had come to the house to interview for the bodyguard position and Maddie had really liked her.

"I'm not helping with that project," Will declared. "Cliff and I might still have a chance to date Kate ourselves."

Derek smiled.

Cliff shook his head. "She's not interested in me. She's always too busy. I've asked her three times if she would like to go out for pizza, a Chinese dinner, or the movies. She did get a whole lot of interest when the other guys who work for Rafe interviewed for Derek's vacant bodyguard position. I wouldn't be surprised if one of them has started asking her out. And then there's Mike, who works with her all the time."

"We would have heard something about that already." Maddie joined them at the dining table, the first time ever.

Derek guessed she wanted to pursue this

discussion with him dating Kate. Even Will and Cliff looked surprised to see Maddie joining them.

Then Maddie served up eggs and ham for herself. She pointed her fork at Will. "Don't you dare try to mess up anything between Derek and Kate or you could find yourself looking for a new job and you only just got this one."

As if Maddie had anything to do with hiring or firing anyone on Derek's staff.

The guys all laughed. When Maddie had it in mind that Derek should do something—like attend a function he wasn't interested in going to or finding a home for one of the Irish setters because a family wanted one really badly and some of the dogs needed the constant affection—she pursued it until he agreed.

But this time, Maddie would have to try to convince *Kate* of it, not him.

"I agree with Will. You have to ask her out on a date, Derek. Not one that has anything to do with a social function. An honest-to-goodness date. And you have to do it before the camping trip, not afterward! What if things worked out really well between the two of you and by the time the camping trip comes around, she wanted to have even more dates *and* you ended up getting to stay with her in her tent?" Maddie smiled. "Her sleeping bag—or yours even?"

Derek laughed. He'd never seen Maddie so

enthusiastic about anything since she had begun working for him. He swore he had to make it his mission that he found *Maddie* a mate soonest!

His business advisor, Liam McConnell, arrived at the house then, and Derek was glad to get the heat off himself concerning this dating business. "Hey, want some breakfast?"

The dogs hurried to greet Liam, though they were still focused on looking for any table scraps that might fall their way.

"Yeah, you know I always love Maddie's cooking."

Derek noticed that Liam often arrived for meetings around meals; he was a typical bachelor who couldn't figure out what to fix for himself. Since it was Saturday, they weren't meeting at the office. Not that Derek went to his office all the time either. He could do most of his business from home.

"Did you see all the photos taken of Derek with Kate?" Will handed the tabloid to Liam.

Liam smiled. "Yeah. First thing I saw this morning. You know it's my business to keep track of anything that could hurt or help Derek financially."

"So what's the verdict?" Cliff asked.

Maddie got Liam a cup of coffee, a plate, and silverware.

"Well, financially, it couldn't hurt if Derek mated Kate," Liam said.

Hell, Derek's own advisor was now acting like he wasn't even there.

"She's now part owner of Clair de Lune Cosmetics. It's all over the internet. So to get involved with Kate would be an excellent financial decision." Liam smiled at Derek and began to dish up some eggs.

Derek hoped Kate wouldn't believe that about him, should they ever start to really date.

"I told you that you should have dated her already. Now she could think you're interested in adding her half of the business to all your acquisitions," Maddie said.

Smiling, Derek shook his head, though he had to admit he did worry about that a bit.

After finishing breakfast, Derek and Liam sat out on the patio overlooking the beach and the pool from high up above on the cliffs while the dogs lay nearby. A low wall with flowers planted on top of it shielded them from prying eyes.

Liam had a bunch of papers for Derek to sign, moving money around from one stock to another to improve his portfolio. "I'm serious about you dating Kate," Liam said. "Not because of her gaining part ownership of Lexi's company but because she's going to be inundated with offers to date her and more. You know how it is when you're suddenly thrust into the public eye."

"Yeah." Derek did know all about having so much publicity. Kate wasn't exactly used to it. Now he wondered if other people would think he knew about the change in the company's ownership before the gala and *that was* why he had asked her to accompany him. He was certain Brenda would believe that was the case. *Why else would he go out with a woman who was only a personal assistant and bodyguard?* they'd think.

"Even if you and Kate aren't interested in mating, at least for a time, you could take her to some of your social engagements and wolves would leave her alone. Humans are a different story," Liam said. "It might be nice for her too instead of just being there for Lexi. Especially since Lexi now has Ryder."

"I already asked Kate to go with me for a dinner engagement on Monday." Then Derek had to explain about that.

Liam cocked a brow. "Another charity event? And another one that is short notice that you had planned to take Brenda to? Well, hell, don't quit trying. After I leave here, give her a call. Have her come out and walk the dogs on the beach. It doesn't have to be an official date-date. Just something she might like to do. *With you.* You never know, but she might not even like the galas as much as she likes to be one with nature. She's a wolf after all."

Now that was a novel idea. Derek had never invited a woman to just take a walk with him and the dogs. He hadn't thought any woman might be interested in such a mundane thing. They had all been into fancy social affairs.

Brenda didn't even like dogs. He never had her over to his house because of it. He knew Kate loved Spirit, the part German shepherd, part wolf that Lexi had taken in. He'd seen Kate playing with the wolf dog that Rafe had given a home to when she was visiting with the ladies there and Derek had been visiting with the guys. So Derek knew Kate liked dogs. It might work. All of a sudden, he was feeling really good about this. He just hoped she didn't turn him down.

Maybe easing Kate into a date like that would work out much better. "I'll do that."

Liam nodded. "Good. I need to get on with the rest of my day." Then he stood, slapped Derek on the shoulder, and headed back into the house, telling Maddie, "Excellent breakfast, as usual."

Will and Cliff were conducting their morning rounds, walking around the property. Derek had never had any problems that he had needed a bodyguard for, but since Rafe and Aidan had, he figured it would be better to be safe than sorry.

Then Derek got on the phone to call Kate. Not Lexi this time. At least Lexi had given Derek Kate's number. "Hey, it's me, Derek," he said when Kate answered her phone. "I know this is kind of a sudden idea I had, but I was going to take a walk along the beach with the dogs. Did you want to come with me?"

"When?"

He couldn't believe she might be interested. "Whenever it's convenient for you." He was afraid she would turn him down again. "Unless I have pressing business, I usually take a daily run or walk with one of the dogs in the morning and one in the evening too. But if you can come with me, we can take out two of them at the same time."

"Sure, as long as you take care of the poop."

He chuckled. Now *she* was down-to-earth. He couldn't even imagine anyone he'd ever dated saying anything to that effect. He liked that. "Yeah, I've got it. So what time would be good for you?"

"I imagine it's crazy busy out on the beach there on a Saturday with the nice weather we're having."

"It's not too bad. It's early, and clouds are starting to form, so we might have a storm coming in later today."

"I'll be right over."

He was going to offer to pick her up, but if she felt more comfortable driving here on her own so she didn't feel like it was a date per se, he would leave it up her. "Okay, see you in a little while." He wanted to shout out to the world that he'd done it, convinced her to see him further! He hadn't really believed she would. He had been afraid she would keep making excuses why she couldn't see him like she had done with Cliff. Why did he feel some satisfaction in that? He'd even been afraid she'd had a little too much champagne last night and that was why she had asked him to join the group camping. Today she might have regretted extending the invitation.

Will came around to the patio. "Everything's clear. What's your schedule today? Except for Liam coming to have you sign financial paperwork, I didn't see anything else on your calendar."

"I'm taking the dogs for a walk, and Kate's going to join me."

Both dogs perked up at hearing Derek say he was going to take them for a walk.

"Hot damn. You did it."

"He got another date?" Cliff asked, joining them.

"Just a walk with the dogs."

"Take the dogs and Kate for a *long* walk, and you can time it so that she can stay for an early lunch," Cliff said.

Derek couldn't believe his bodyguards were trying to work out his schedule so he could get the most dating time with Kate, but he was all for it.

"Who's staying for lunch?" Maddie asked, calling out the kitchen window as she cleaned up after breakfast, loving to have the windows open to draw in the ocean breeze on such a beautiful day. He swore she had the biggest wolf ears of the bunch.

CHAPTER 8

KATE COULDN'T BELIEVE DEREK WOULD ASK HER out to do something she would really love to do, and she'd already showered after gardening, so she was squeaky clean and ready for a fun walk with him and the dogs. She would run later as a wolf tonight, but she wanted to get out of the house, no fancy ballroom gowns or strappy high heels required. She really was more of a casual kind of girl, and this was just the outing she needed. She grabbed a swimsuit—because she planned to take a dip in the ocean—sunglasses, and a floppy hat, and she was wearing shorts, a T-shirt, and flip-flops. She picked up her sunscreen, applied some of the coconut-scented lotion to her skin, and tossed the container of sunscreen in her beach bag.

She got into her car, pulled out of the garage, and put the top down. She had just closed the garage door and was about to drive off when she saw Spirit running toward her car. Kate had never known a dog that loved to ride with her more than Spirit. She got out of the car and coaxed Spirit back to Lexi's yard. She swore Spirit knew she was taking some other dog for a walk and not her!

Then Kate drove to Derek's place. She'd never been there before, though she knew it was down the road from Rafe's beachfront estate.

She felt on top of the world, first with Lexi making her a partner in the cosmetics business and now with having a whole weekend off and having a wolf friend to walk with. Yes, she was thinking of the billionaire wolf as *her* friend now. She just hoped things wouldn't sour between them, which would make it uncomfortable when everyone got together in the future.

Then she thought of the last time she walked along the beach, when the waves had deposited stinging jellyfish all over the sand. She hoped they wouldn't be an issue today. Otherwise, she'd have to watch where she stepped and she would stay clear of the water when she really wanted to swim for a little bit.

She sighed. She supposed she should let Lexi know where she was going, but she hated to interrupt her and Ryder during their time off together. But Lexi would want to know that Kate was all right and just enjoying herself. Kate decided to call Mike instead, since he would be hanging around the house in case Lexi or Ryder needed him.

"Hey, Mike. It's me, Kate. I was just calling to let you know I'm going over to Derek's place to walk with him and the dogs on the beach."

"And you didn't invite me?"

She knew Mike was teasing her. "You have a job to do. I have the weekend off. When you have *your* days off and I'm serving as Lexi's bodyguard in your place, you can go walking with Derek and his dogs."

Mike laughed. "You know that's going to change."

"What's going to change?" That Derek was going to start dating a human woman again? At least Kate figured he would.

"With you being part owner of Lexi's business now, she's going to want you to concentrate on that. With twins coming, she'll probably hire a second bodyguard and a nanny."

"Oh." Kate hadn't thought of her hiring another bodyguard, but it made sense.

"I mean, hell, if we all run into trouble some-time or another, you'll be worth your weight in gold because you're still a trained bodyguard," Mike said, as if he didn't want her to think all her training was no longer needed and she was being replaced.

Appreciating Mike for saying so, she smiled. "But I just won't be on the books as one of her bodyguards." Kate didn't need the income from that now that she was part owner in the business. She would earn 50 percent of the net profits from the sales. And Kate already had investments to tide her over. She supposed she needed to talk to either Lexi's investment advisor or maybe even Derek's to figure out a new investment strategy.

"Right. You won't be hurting financially without the job," Mike said.

Kate hadn't really thought through all the ramifications of all the changes that could occur. "Okay, yeah, sure, I understand."

"She worries about you now, and I'm supposed to keep an eye on you while Ryder watches out for Lexi."

"No way."

Mike smiled. "Yeah way. Or what if you end up hiring a bodyguard and he intrigues you? Then you could have your very own bodyguard to watch you day and night."

Kate laughed. "That's not going to happen." Yet she could see how she would be put in the same situation as she put Derek when she interviewed for the bodyguard position.

"Well, I know Derek has his bodyguards, so you'll be okay. But if you start running into trouble, don't hesitate to call on me. Ryder will be there for Lexi," Mike said.

"All right, thanks, Mike." Then she ended the call. No way did she want to hire a bodyguard for herself. *She* was a bodyguard! Though she was happy for Lexi, who had hired Ryder and the two of them fell in love and mated each other. Now they had twins on the way...

She thought about Lexi's sporty little car and smiled. Kate suspected Lexi would be getting a van for the family soon. Ohmigod, even though Lexi would be hiring a live-in nanny, Kate would be a nanny wolf too! She couldn't wait.

———————

About a half hour later, sooner than Derek thought Kate would get there, he went outside and greeted her as she parked her vehicle.

She was all smiles, and he thought he'd made her day by inviting her over for a walk along the beach. Even though Lexi's home was sitting on a bluff overlooking the Pacific Ocean and had a beach, it was small, and they couldn't really walk anywhere there. "I brought a change of clothes in case I go into the water."

"Yeah, sure. You can wash up in one of the guest rooms that has its own bathroom. We can even shower off near the pool and then go swimming in the pool if you feel like it and the storm hasn't reached us yet," Derek said.

"Okay, sure. I'm glad you asked me. I've felt I needed to get some exercise, and a beach walk or run is always fun." She carried her bag into the house, and he directed her to the guest room where she could leave it.

Then they went out to see the dogs, the two of them running around, chasing each other in the fenced-in yard he had installed for them. As soon as the dogs saw them, they raced across the yard to greet Derek and Kate.

She petted them and hugged them as they licked her and brushed their noses against her hands to get her to pet them more.

He knew she would like the dogs. "They love to go for a walk, and when I have more of them before I can find them homes, I always feel like I'm singling them out when I only pick one or two."

"Red and Foxy," she said, reading the tags on the dogs' collars.

"All right." Derek attached their leashes to their collars. "Did you want to walk one of them?"

"Sure." She removed her flip-flops and then peeled off her shorts and left them on a chaise longue by the swimming pool. She was wearing her bathing suit and a T-shirt. "Do you ever run as a wolf on the beach?"

"Sure do."

"You don't ever worry about anyone seeing you?"

"No. The beach is closed at ten. We've never had any trouble running along the beach at night. No shops or restaurants are open. The beach is dark. We can see at night without having to use artificial means like humans would, so no one notices us. It's just perfect." Derek left his flip-flops next to the chaise longue and removed his shirt.

Then Kate took Foxy's leash and Derek followed

with Red, and they descended the stairs to the beach where he unlocked the gate using the keypad. That was definitely useful when he went running as a wolf in the dark and didn't want to have to worry about hiding keys anywhere. Will followed closely and the gate locked automatically behind them. Cliff would continue to provide security for the estate.

They walked for some distance, and Derek wasn't sure if Kate wanted to share the news with him just yet, but he wanted to congratulate her. "I heard the good news about you and Lexi and the partnership. Congratulations. It's well deserved. You work at the business as if it were your own, and now it is."

"Thanks, Derek. I love it, and I love working with Lexi. She's like the sister I never had." Kate was just beaming, she appeared so pleased. "It came as a real surprise, and of course, I'm thrilled. Lexi just gave me the exciting news this morning before you called."

"So you were busy working?" He wondered then if Lexi had been with her when he called Kate and Lexi had encouraged her to go walk with him instead of it being Kate's idea.

"When you called? No. I had already gone home. Ryder and Lexi were having some alone time. Mike's there, overseeing the house, but unobtrusively. I had just planned on watching a silly movie or starting a new series or something on TV, no real plans. So when you called, it was perfect timing because I really wanted to walk, but I needed the motivation."

Relieved Lexi hadn't needed to convince Kate to walk with him, Derek smiled. He was so glad he had listened to everyone on his staff who told him to call Kate and not to wait.

"Your dogs are dreams to walk. I had a silky terrier once, and she pulled at me to walk faster all the time, practically choking herself. I envisioned the Irish setters doing that with us too."

"I've worked with them. I've even had Cliff and Will training them so they know how to handle them. How's the German shepherd wolf dog working out for Lexi? She seemed really good-natured."

"She's the sweetest dog ever, but she's a wolf too, so she has a mind of her own. The German shepherd part of her makes her a little easier to train. But she's really friendly, and that's the main thing."

"That's good."

"So sometimes you have a lot more Irish setters?"

"Yeah. Foxy and Red are mine, but I've had as many as ten rescue dogs at the house at one time. When I can find good families for them, I'll let them go—because their welfare is most important to me. I haven't had one rehomed who hasn't loved his or her new family. In fact, the families who took them in send me pictures every Christmas and at other times during the year to show me how well loved the dogs are."

"Oh, that's wonderful. Hey, do you mind?" She handed Foxy's leash to him. "I'm going to dash into the water for a second to cool off."

Kate pulled off her T-shirt, handed it to him, and then ran into the water, waded out farther, and dove into the deeper water. He smiled at her. She was so cute. He hadn't really believed she would swim in the ocean. The swimming pool, yes, maybe—but his other dates wouldn't swim in the ocean because they would get salty and sandy and it wasn't their thing. He'd asked a couple of them about going to the beach, but it was a no-go.

Then Will came up and took the dogs' leashes and Kate's T-shirt from Derek so he could join her in the water. Derek hurried off to enter the water. Then he was moving deeper into the waves with her but glanced at the clouds building as the storm was slowly moving in from farther out over the ocean. Here near shore where they were, it was still sunny.

She laughed when he joined her. "It's hot, and I just had to cool down."

"You sure are. I'm so glad you came."

"Oh, me too. This is fun." Then she swam out farther, and he swam out to join her.

When Derek joined Kate in the ocean, she was thrilled. He was so hot, muscled, and bronzed. She'd hoped he would be all wolfish and enjoy the surf with her. Small fish bumped into their legs, and she laughed. They tickled her, and she hadn't expected it. She hadn't been in the ocean in ages. She loved how uplifting it was to be in the briny sea, the buoyancy of the water making her float. She felt some tidal pull, and as soon as she did, he grabbed her arm and pulled her close to him, being an anchor for her. She loved this. Then he wrapped his arms around her and kissed her.

The kiss he shared with her was sweet, and then he deepened it. Hmm, now this was nice. Really nice. She wrapped her arms around his neck and got into the kiss, tonguing him, enjoying this. He smiled. Okay, she wasn't supposed to be doing this with him... She was trying not to make this too personal, but she was failing miserably. Maybe he knew her better than she knew herself.

"I wanted to kiss you good night when I dropped you off at your place last night, but I couldn't. You ran away too fast. But when you kissed me yesterday at the gala, I didn't want that to be the last one."

She smiled and kissed him again. "I have to admit this is super nice."

"I have to agree. I go for a swim in the ocean every once in a while, but this is the first time I've ever swam with a woman, other than with some teenage girls when I was younger."

"Hmm, well, I've swam with guys before, but never a wolf. Did you tackle the teenage girls?" Kate asked with a smile. She could see him doing that.

"No. You might be surprised to hear this, but I was shy with the girls."

She laughed, never expecting him to say that. He always seemed so self-assured around women. Not with Kate as much, but she suspected that had to do with her being a wolf and his being afraid of a permanent entanglement with her.

She had the greatest urge to play with him. She dove under the shallower water and tackled his legs, expecting to sweep him off his feet. He was solid, his muscular legs just perfect as a runner—sturdy and immovable. Her plan foiled, she wanted to laugh. His legs moved, and suddenly he was diving under the water. She nearly gasped for air, she was so rattled as he went under the water searching for her.

Then he grabbed her around the waist and pulled her up for air and kissed her. She kissed him back. So much for her being in charge. They broke off the kiss, and she hoped Will wasn't watching them. She glanced at the beach where Will was standing with the dogs, her T-shirt draped over his shoulder, his back to them to give them privacy. He was the ideal bodyguard.

"I didn't expect you to tackle me." Derek smiled at her.

"I didn't expect you to be so immovable."

He laughed. "I was trying to keep my feet planted in the sand and make sure we weren't swept away."

"Then you disappeared under the water."

"So I could sweep you up in my arms and kiss you."

"Well, that was nice. Do you want to, um, play in the sand with me?"

He raised his brows. "What exactly do you have in mind?"

"Do you want to build a sandcastle?"

He gave her a broad smile.

"You don't have to do it if you think it's too silly. It could be messy. You can walk the dogs while I build the sandcastle and you can return with the dogs, and we can resume our walk."

"Are you kidding? I've been wanting to do this forever, but I didn't think anyone else would be interested. So yeah, we're doing this."

Thinking he was funny, she was glad he was game. Then she and he released each other and headed into shore.

Suddenly, a rogue wave hit them hard and knocked them off their feet. Kate went under, and when she came up, she saw Derek's bare ass for a minute and was so startled, she couldn't believe her eyes. And then he swam into the surf away from the shore.

She called out, "What's wrong, Derek?" She considered the notion that he might have lost his board shorts when they'd been pummeled by the wave. She had thought they had only been pulled down so that she was mooned. She hoped he hadn't lost his swim trunks completely, but she wanted to laugh if that was the case.

"In all the time I've been swimming in the ocean, I've never once lost my swimming suit." He gave her a cocky smile.

She laughed then. "Better you than me." She called out to Will. "We have an emergency. I can be Derek's bodyguard and you can get Derek some other swim trunks, or I'll go get them and you can stay here and watch over him."

"I'll call Cliff and he'll come with a pair of trunks." Will was trying to hide a smile, but he wasn't very convincing.

"I could just shift," Derek said, smiling.

"Oh, yeah, that would really work. *Not.* There are way too many people out here." She could just imagine Derek diving into the water and then shifting into a wolf and coming out of the water as a wet gray wolf this time. People would worry that the man had drowned if they had been watching him go under. They wouldn't know what to think of the wolf that suddenly took his place.

"Aren't you going to join me out here?" Derek had a wicked gleam in his eyes.

She laughed. "What? To protect you from inquisitive onlookers?"

"Yeah."

She smiled and shook her head. "It's a good thing you didn't take some other woman with you today."

"I have never been with any woman in the ocean and lost my swim trunks. I'm glad I did this with you and not someone else."

Kate laughed again. She couldn't help it. This had turned out to be a beautiful day already. Then she saw Cliff racing down the beach with a pair of blue board shorts. She smiled. This was just too hilarious.

Cliff reached Kate and handed the board shorts to her. It was just a good thing that she hadn't lost *her* swimsuit in the rogue wave. She carried the board shorts out to Derek and handed them to him. The waves kept hitting him, and he was going to have some time trying to pull them on.

"Do you need my help?" She would certainly have wanted his assistance if she'd lost her bathing suit. She was glad she was wearing a one-piece.

"Yeah, try and keep the waves from rolling this way, would you?" Derek had such a boyish look about him, like he'd been caught skinny-dipping when he shouldn't have been. "I would have opted for shifting."

Every time he tried to lift a foot to step into one leg of his board shorts, a wave rolled into him, knocking him over.

She wrapped her arms around his body from

behind him to serve as his legs so that he could climb into his board shorts. She rooted herself to the ocean floor as well as she could as the current tugged at them both but enough that he could finally get his feet into his board shorts, and then he was pulling them up and he was perfectly clothed again.

He turned around and hugged her. "Hey, thanks so much for saving my dignity out here."

"Yeah, it was my pleasure."

He kissed her then, and she kissed him back. Yeah, this was really pleasurable too.

"Hmm." He didn't seem to want to let her go, and she had to admit she loved this. "I think it's time to go in and build sandcastles, don't you?" he asked.

"Yeah, I thought we had already decided on that. Until you lost your shorts."

He smiled at her as they swam to shore. Cliff and Will were smiling at Derek.

"Did you want me to go back up to the house now?" Cliff asked.

"Sure. I think it's safe for you to do so. I'm going to work on building a sandcastle with Kate, and I don't think I'll need your services down here again," Derek said.

"You're building sandcastles? You should have told me, and I would have brought some gardening tools," Cliff said.

"We're going to just wing it," Derek said.

Smiling, Cliff shook his head and walked back to Derek's estate. Foxy and Red were lying on the sand. Kate wondered if the dogs would have played in the surf if Derek had let them. But then they would be more of a mess than they were now.

Then Derek and Kate sat on the beach and began building their sandcastle using a seashell Will had found for them. "I'll go look for another."

Will took the dogs with him while he searched for another seashell.

In the meantime, Derek was mounding the sand up for a base to the castle.

Kate began building a wall. "This is great. I haven't done this in so long."

"Yeah, I agree. I haven't either."

She glanced back at the ocean. "I wonder if anyone will run into your board shorts at some time or another."

He laughed. "Yeah, maybe they'll wash up on the shore and I'll get lucky and find them."

"Hopefully they won't be torn to shreds by sharks and give anyone the notion that there had been a shark attack or that searchers should look for a body."

Will came jogging back with the dogs, and she figured he must have finally found a seashell.

"Okay, boss, here's your sandcastle maker." Will gave Derek the shell.

It was much smaller than Kate's seashell, and she chuckled.

After a while, they had finished their four towers and walls, and then Will had to take a photo of the sandcastle.

"Are you ready to finish our walk?" Derek asked Kate.

"Yeah, I sure am. But I'm all sandy. Do you mind if we take a dip in the water before we walk? Just don't lose your board shorts again."

"I sure don't intend to. But I'll feel better knowing you're there to rescue me again if I need you to."

They went for a quick swim and washed off, and then they hurried back to the shore. As soon as they left the water, Derek said, "I wish I had brought towels for us. I didn't even think of it."

"It's sunny and warm, and we will drip-dry on our way."

Will handed Kate her T-shirt and she pulled it on, and then they walked the dogs again. Both Foxy and Red were excited to walk some more. They would be worn out afterward.

"This has been great. Lexi doesn't have a long beach to walk on like this, so this is nice," Kate said.

The nicest walk she'd ever taken on the beach with a male wolf.

CHAPTER 9

"About the paparazzi," Kate said as Derek and she continued to walk along the beach with the dogs, not ready to have her life under the microscope when it came to dating men. "I tried not to get you into too much hot water with the human women you're bound to hook up with now that Brenda is history."

"I'm not 'hooking up' with any of them right now."

"What about your dinner coming up?" She suspected he'd have to ask someone else to go to it if she didn't change her mind and go with him.

"I'm not deciding about that for a while. I might even just go alone."

"But you've bought two tickets for the event, right?" She figured he would have, just an automatic thing for him because he had been going with Brenda.

"Yeah. But it's another charity event, so the money goes to a good cause no matter what."

"Oh, true. That's good." Kate was watching two teens on the beach, both walking behind people sitting on chairs or chaise longues reading books or tanning. The teens were looking down at the bags by people's chairs, and she knew just what they intended to do—grab a bag and run. "Did you know I was a former lifeguard?"

Derek glanced down at her. "No, it wasn't on your résumé."

"Would you have hired me if it had been?"

"Maybe. I like to swim. You could have guarded me in the water then."

"And your board shorts." She handed him Foxy's leash. "Hold on to her for me, will you? I need to run." Then she dashed off, and she could hear Derek, Will, and the dogs running to keep up with her.

She wasn't very far from the one teen as the other asked the man sitting under a blue-and-white-striped beach umbrella what the time was while pointing at his own wrist, but Kate was watching the teen behind the beachgoer, and when he grabbed the man's beach bag, she tackled the teen to the sand.

Will and Derek reached her right after that, and Will took the other teen into custody when he tried to flee.

"This is your bag, isn't it, sir?" Kate asked the man who was now standing up and looking shocked that they'd caught the would-be thief stealing his bag.

"Yeah, it sure is."

"Do you want to press charges against these teens?" she asked.

"Hell, yeah. It's the only way to deter thieves."

Derek had Will call the police to come and arrest the teens.

"Thanks," the man said to them.

"You're welcome. I hate to see thieves ruining a good day for beachgoers." Kate brushed the sand off her knees.

Once the police were there and taking the teens into custody, Kate took Foxy's leash and continued to walk with her as if nothing had even happened. She was just driven to right a wrong, even though she supposed she shouldn't have done it while she was walking with Derek and his bodyguard on a pseudo date. What would they think? That she was trying to show off?

She supposed she was a little.

"She has eagle eyes," Will said. "Here I was watching for threats to the two of you. And she nabs would-be thieves."

"You got the one or he would have hightailed it out of there." Kate always gave credit where credit was due.

Finally, Derek said to her, "You did that as a lifeguard?"

She smiled up at him. "When days were slow. I had the martial arts training already. I could see them stealing from people, and then I would have to deal with the fallout. One time, five college girls from Australia on a school break were at the beach, four of them swimming, while the fifth girlfriend was supposed to watch their bags. She fell asleep, so naturally, you can imagine what happened. It was awful. Traveler's checks, credit cards, IDs, passports—all gone. It was probably the trip of a lifetime for them, and they were so far from home. No family or friends to call. They had to go to the embassy to get help. I felt so sorry for them.

"I had wished I had seen the thieves who had stolen all their things, but I hadn't. The four women were furious with the one who fell asleep. But the thieves were the ones at fault. It's a shame when you can't go to the beach without worrying about thieves stealing your stuff. But that's when I started monitoring what was going on at the beach too. I learned from one guy I caught that he made any- where from three to six thousand dollars a day!"

Derek shook his head. "I'm in the wrong business."

"Yeah. The police got used to me calling them, once I had ensured that the victim was going to press charges."

Frowning at her, Derek asked, "Did you ever get hurt?"

"Bruises, sometimes. But you know with our faster-healing genetics, any small injuries would be gone in a day or so. The police wanted to hire me to work a beach patrol."

Derek smiled at her. "When thieves saw you on

the beach, you would think they would learn to clear out."

"Yeah, they started to look for me, and when I wasn't there, they would have a field day." Kate was still looking for more would-be thieves on the beach, but she didn't see anyone who looked suspicious now.

"I hadn't known that about you."

"Yeah, there's a lot you don't know about me."

"Why did you become a bodyguard?" Derek asked.

"I saw a man threatening another man with a gun, and I stopped the gunman with a martial arts maneuver, kicked his gun from his hand, and took him down. I wasn't trained as a bodyguard back then. But I got so much good publicity that I had several job offers, so I got the training. My interview with you was my first time applying for a bodyguard position."

"Right, and working for Lexi was your first job serving as a bodyguard, and you did a great job."

"Thanks. At least she hasn't had any trouble recently."

"I agree. What do you think about having an early lunch at my place after we get back to the house?" Derek asked Kate.

"Oh, sure. I was going to just eat some leftovers at home, but that would be great. Thanks." She always had an open invitation to eat at Lexi's home, but she tried not to eat over there most of the time when she was free on the weekends, now that she had a place of her own and could make her own meals. Lexi and Ryder needed their special time. She still couldn't believe Lexi was pregnant with twins.

"Are you watching for more thieves on the beach?" Derek asked.

She smiled. "Are you?"

"Hell, yeah, I don't want you to get the drop on them before I do. You're just supposed to be here enjoying your time with me, not taking risks on beach patrol."

"I don't see anyone. We're good." She smiled at him. "I've had a great time with you today."

"Especially when I lost my board shorts, I bet."

She laughed. "Yeah, that was definitely the highlight of my day."

Then they turned around and headed to the house, jogging the rest of the way back. They finally reached the stairs to Derek's home, unlocked the gate, and went up to the pool patio. Will hosed off the dogs and took them to their yard, and Kate pulled off her T-shirt. She showered outdoors first, and then she jumped into the pool. Derek showered after that while Kate swam a lap. Cliff and Will went inside the house to give them some privacy.

Derek brought the basketball hoop out, put it in the water, and then joined Kate in the pool. He tossed the ball to her, and she caught it and laughed. Then they played hoops.

"This is fun," Kate said, throwing the ball again.

"Yeah, it always livens things up in the pool."

"Thanks for inviting me over today."

"I've had a great time too."

Kate had enjoyed the day so much with Derek that she was thinking that if she could do more things like this with him—and with no paparazzi reporting their every move—she could continue to have fun with him. But she didn't want to be in the limelight. She hadn't realized how much that bothered her. When Lexi was, Kate was just her sidekick, and it had all been about Lexi. Kate liked her privacy when she was not at social functions, but beyond that, she really didn't want her love life on view for everyone. She'd never thought that would ever happen if she started seeing someone. Of course, that would have been par for the course if she'd continued to go to social functions with Derek since he was the one in the spotlight, which put her smack-dab in the middle of it too. But now she would be the center of attention just for being a partner in Lexi's business.

Derek saw the crease between Kate's brows and wondered if she was worried about something.

"As long as the paparazzi don't become an issue, I'm fine with doing things like this," Kate said.

He took that to mean she didn't want to go with him to his charity events or other activities where a lot of reporters were hanging around.

"I mean, you have such a reputation…" she began.

He smiled.

They got out of the water, rinsed off under the outdoor shower, and then dried off.

"Well, since you go out with different women and never commit to any of them, I just don't want to be put in the same category with the rest of them."

So she was worried about her reputation. He could understand that.

"You know it wouldn't be like that with us. You're a wolf. They were human."

"Okay, you have never settled down with anyone." Kate raised a brow.

"Neither have you."

She smiled. "I've never met anyone I've wanted to settle down with."

Well, he couldn't say he hadn't wanted to. He had. Twice. And neither of the situations had worked out. So yeah, he was a little gun-shy when it came to having another go at dating a wolf regularly. Even with Kate, he certainly wasn't sure. He was having a great time with her. But if she was looking for a commitment this early in the game, he couldn't give her one.

But if her issue was being seen with him, they could try to work around that. He never thought any woman he dated would not want to be seen with him. That was a novel situation. Most wanted others to know that he was theirs—for a while anyway.

"Well, the good news is the paparazzi know I don't go anywhere with a date unless it's a special function that's getting lots of publicity. They don't follow me around like they do Rafe. I'm boring. I run with the dogs on the beach, take a dip in the ocean every once in a while, get together with Aidan and Rafe and Ryder every so often. Nothing newsworthy in that. So if we do things like this, we should be good, if you're afraid to be seen with me."

She smiled. "Perfect."

It bothered him a bit that she felt that way, but he understood her reasoning to a degree. He also wondered if it meant she might be interested in dating other wolves because of her newfound status as a partner in Lexi's successful business. That bothered him even more. He did have the concern that unsavory wolves—or humans— might try to get to know her, those who were solely interested in her money. But of course the humans wouldn't stand a chance, no matter if they were the most successful con artists in the world because she wouldn't be taken in by them—not when she was a wolf.

"Okay, good. We'll have to come up with some more paparazzi-free activities we would both like to explore then," he said.

"That sounds like a great idea."

He still couldn't believe that she didn't want to be seen with him. So what would he do about his other social engagements? He suspected Kate wouldn't like it if he was seeing another woman just for his social functions though. He would just have to see how it went. He liked taking a woman to the events. Going alone didn't appeal at all. Maybe he could go by himself a couple of times and then still convince her at some point to start going with him to them. Nothing was static in life. That was what he would do.

She got a text on her phone where she'd left it next to her shorts on the chaise longue. She checked it out. "Well, another guy I went out with a long time ago asked me on a date."

"A wolf?" That was all that concerned Derek. Not that he wanted her to date humans on a regular basis either.

"Yeah."

She got another text and smiled. "Well, and this one is a human. I guess the word is just getting out that I'm a partner in a billion-dollar business." She got one more text and chuckled. Then she turned off her phone.

He was glad she hadn't just started texting them back. He hoped she wouldn't take any of them up on dates, but especially the wolf. Here he thought he would begin to get a bunch of calls from human women interested in getting to know him better now that he was no longer seeing Brenda. But maybe they thought he was now seeing Kate and they didn't stand a chance.

"Who's the wolf? Anyone I know?" he asked.

"The last one was a wolf you know. I have never dated him, just for your information. I don't know if you know the other guy."

"Who is the guy I know?"

"Will? Your new bodyguard. I haven't ever dated him before," Kate said again, sounding highly amused.

"Hell, does he want to get fired?" Derek hadn't meant to say that aloud.

She laughed. "I don't know if I could keep up with all the dates I might now get. I could imagine having to get my own personal assistant to keep me straight on it."

He wanted to groan out loud. He noticed the clouds had swiftly moved in and were now filling the sky.

"Are you about ready to eat?" Derek asked.

"I sure am."

Then it poured rain! First, it was a light shower, and then the raindrops grew bigger and slammed into them, the pool, and the patio. They hurriedly grabbed shorts and phones and shoes and headed inside.

"That was perfect timing," she said.

"I'll say."

They went inside to change out of their bathing suits and into street clothes.

She joined Derek in the living room, and he escorted her to the dining room to have lunch. He'd had such a great time with her, he really didn't want it to end. It just felt right. It was so nice to be with a she-wolf again who liked to do the same things he did.

Will smiled broadly at Derek, just trying to get his goat by texting Kate for a date while Derek was on one with her! Then Will joined Cliff at the breakfast table that had seating for six.

Usually, Derek ate lunch with his bodyguards and Maddie ate by herself in the kitchen. But today, the guys were eating with Maddie in the breakfast nook so that Derek and Kate could have a meal alone. He hadn't even suggested it. He sure appreciated them for thinking of it.

Maddie had made lobster salads for everyone, though Derek had heard her say sometime before Kate had arrived that she was making everyone hamburgers. Maddie must have changed her mind and wanted to impress Kate instead. Which was fine with Derek. He loved lobster any way that Maddie made it.

As to Cliff and Will? Derek suspected they would have preferred hamburgers. But they could grill some for tonight. On summer nights, Derek normally grilled dinner poolside and gave Maddie the night off. Though she was always welcome to eat with them. Sometimes she would.

"This is really great," Kate said. "I would love to have the recipe."

"You should have Maddie's lobster mac and cheese. It's out of this world. Three kinds of cheese and lots of lobster."

"Hmm, that sounds delicious. I'll need that recipe too." Kate took another bite of her salad and then sipped from her red nonalcoholic cocktail, an orange slice garnishing the chilled glass. She buttered another fresh-baked roll. "These are so good too."

"Maddie makes the best baked goods. Now that's something I never got into. I love to grill though. I was going to make hamburgers on the grill tonight, if you want to have dinner with us. That is, if you don't have anything planned."

"Thanks, but I'm going to chill at home."

"We could go for a run on the beach as wolves after we watch the sun set."

She smiled.

He thought he might have won her over on that note.

"Um, okay, because I love to run as a wolf, but

it's a lot more fun to do it with someone. On the beach? I never get to do that. Is it safe?"

"Yeah, sure. No one's on the beach after dark. We'll just run along after that and have a great time."

"Okay, I would love that. I'll go home for a while to get some chores done and come back at…?"

"Seven. We can swim in the pool after dinner, have some champagne, and watch the sun set. Then we can go for a wolf run on the beach."

"That sounds like fun." Kate finished her drink. "This drink is so refreshing. What's in it? I can taste the cranberry juice, but also…grapefruit?"

"Maddie calls it her Ocean Breeze Summer Cocktail. It's made with unsweetened cranberry juice, maple syrup, and grapefruit juice. She can give you her recipe if you would like."

"I would. It would be nice to have some when Lexi and I are working and need something refreshing to drink on a hot summer day."

"Maddie is always trying new recipes out on us. The Ocean Breeze is one of my favorites."

"I can see why."

"I figured we would have champagne to celebrate your partnership with Lexi."

He was getting pretty good with winging date plans with Kate, he thought. If he'd proposed something like that to Brenda—well, minus the wolf run on the beach—without giving her at least a week's notice, she wouldn't have taken him up on it. He realized Kate was really flexible about making plans, and he liked that. Now, when she got really into the partnership business, she might not be as free, but he was glad to have her company again for tonight.

Once they finished lunch, Kate thanked Maddie for a great meal.

Derek thought he was making a little progress with her, even if she was balking about going to another official social function with him where the paparazzi would be sure to hang out and take more pictures of them. So far, they hadn't had any issues today, and he was sure the reporters were following some other celebrity around to get a "breaking" story.

Maybe Derek needed to show Kate that he could just have fun with her like this. Truly, he had thoroughly enjoyed the day so far—though he could have done without losing his board shorts. Still, he'd been a good sport about it, and she'd been amused, so it had turned out fine.

"Well, okay, Derek. I'm ready to go home, and I'll return at seven then," Kate said.

―――――

After such a lovely morning and afternoon, Kate finally returned home. She had plans to do the laundry, dust, vacuum, all the usual stuff. But she needed to let Lexi know she was home and going back out tonight.

Kate texted Lexi: Hey, I'm home, but I'm returning to Derek's place for grilled hamburgers and a swim in the pool tonight at seven.

Lexi texted back: You know you're welcome to use our pool. Ryder and I are going out to dinner tonight at that new Italian restaurant.

Kate texted: No, that's okay. Derek's grilling hamburgers, so I'm sure he's all set up to do it there.

Lexi texted: Okay, well, you have fun.

Kate texted: We will. You too.

That night, Kate arrived at Derek's place to have dinner with him, and she was glad she'd agreed to it. It would have been an otherwise boring night if she'd stayed at home and just watched TV. Derek gave her a glass of champagne, and she sat at the poolside bar, little fire torches blowing in the breeze. So romantic. She felt like she was in Hawaii. He began grilling the hamburgers.

"What can I help you with?" she asked.

"I've got it all taken care of."

"Well, thanks." She wasn't ever pampered by anyone, so this was really nice. If he'd been a real boyfriend, she would stay with him overnight in a heartbeat.

"Well, you deserve it. You saved me from the waiter who popped the cork of the champagne bottle last night, and then you saved my dignity today."

She laughed at him. "You mean about losing your board shorts in the ocean?"

"Yeah. That's what I mean."

She laughed again. She would never forget that. "It made my day."

"I bet."

Then they were sitting poolside enjoying the hamburgers and corn on the cob and watching the sun set.

Derek asked, "Hey, if you happen to be free tomorrow and you want to get together again with me—"

She smiled, amused he was trying to set up another date with her. Whatever happened to him being worried that if she worked for him, she might want a romantic relationship?

"Too much, too soon?" he asked.

She chuckled. "I've had fun."

"Don't tell me you and Lexi work all weekend."

"No, you're right. She's taking off the weekend to spend it with Ryder. I was thinking of having my nails done, having my hair dyed, going to a sauna, working out—"

Derek smiled.

"Okay, maybe none of the above." Having their nails done and their hair dyed didn't really last long for them. One shift into their wolf and both were gone. As for saunas? No way. She would rather swim in a pool. "What did you have in mind?"

"What would you like to do?" Derek asked.

"Hmm, I want to go to the zoo. We can eat lunch there, ride the train and the sky rail. I love seeing all the animals."

He was smiling at her.

"I'm absolutely serious. Here's the deal. You take me to the zoo, and we even can ride on the carousel—"

He raised his brows.

"Okay, maybe not that, but we can do everything else that I mentioned, and"—she took a deep, exaggerated breath and exhaled it—"I'll go with you to the function you have on Monday night." She figured since he was willing to humor her—even building a sandcastle on the beach today—she would help him out on Monday night.

"Deal!"

She laughed. "If you really don't want to go to the zoo…"

"No, it's perfect. There's really nothing better I would like to do."

She didn't think he was being sincere, but maybe he was. She liked a well-rounded guy who could do any number of things and enjoy them with her. Not just do stuff like that when they had kids.

"What time?" he asked.

"When it opens first thing. That way we can enjoy it before all the families with kids arrive," she said.

"All right. Your place is closer to the zoo, so I'll pick you up. The guys are going to love this."

"We don't have to take them. You've got me for protection."

"Yeah, we can do that. They don't go with me all the time."

"Okay, so pick me up at half past eight and we'll be there when the zoo opens."

"Maybe you should just stay the night… We'll have breakfast and then head over to the zoo," he said.

"I'll sleep better in my bed. Alone," she added, just in case he needed her to tell him that.

He only smiled.

If they were really seriously dating, she would have stayed at his estate in a heartbeat. But they weren't. At least not yet…but, man, was she rethinking her position.

Especially after they had a lovely run in their wolf coats on the beach, nipping at each other, racing into the water, running on the sand, having the time of their lives. Yeah, she was definitely thinking of possibilities here and hoping it wasn't premature.

CHAPTER 10

THAT NIGHT WHEN KATE WENT HOME, THE storms had returned and Derek wanted her to stay at his place in the worst way, but she was determined to go home. She was to call him once she made it home though. He was glad he'd left it up to her to decide on what she wanted to do the next day. He would never have suggested going to the zoo, and she seemed exuberant about it. And he really did want to do something with her that she had suggested. To top that off? She had agreed to go with him to the charity dinner, and that made his night.

"Are you sure you don't need at least one of us to go with you to the zoo tomorrow?" Cliff asked, sounding concerned.

"I volunteer Cliff," Will said.

Derek chuckled. "We should be good. If you're worried at all about our safety, you could come in a separate car, but I really don't see that we should have any trouble."

"I guess we can decide for certain in the morning," Cliff said.

"Yeah, sure." But Derek felt he didn't need the

guys to serve as bodyguards while he was taking Kate on a zoo date. He never thought he would love the idea of going to the zoo on a date either. But only with Kate. A she-wolf at heart.

———

On the drive home in the pouring rain, Kate hoped the squall would blow over quickly. She appreciated that Derek had wanted her to stay safely at his place, but she'd driven in bad weather before, so she was up for this. Besides, she didn't have anything she needed for that night or the next morning. Then a pickup truck drove right up to her bumper and just sat there, high beams on, irritating her to no end. He wouldn't pass her, and he wouldn't back off, even though the traffic was sparse that night. She figured the driver had had too much to drink or maybe had road rage. But it sure made her want to turn wolf and take a bite out of him. He finally passed her on the road after following her for quite a ways when he'd had ample opportunity to do so long before that. She relaxed, realizing just how tense she'd been. She watched the taillights of the vehicle disappear in the distance, but she thought he couldn't have vanished that fast unless he was going about a hundred miles per hour. Maybe he had turned off on another road and she had just missed it. Then she saw a black pickup sitting on the shoulder of the road, and a chill went up her spine.

She was certain it was the same one that had been riding her bumper, the lights off now. As soon as she passed the vehicle, the lights turned on, and then they switched to high beam. The truck pulled off the shoulder of the road and tore off after her again. She was only about ten miles from home, and she considered calling Mike to come out and meet her if the situation worsened between her and her stalker, but she figured the driver was just being an ass and there wasn't anything Mike could do but escalate the situation further. She just hoped this guy didn't follow her onto Lexi's property. Though if he did, Kate would alert Mike for sure, and he and Ryder would help her deal with the driver. The pickup continued to ride her tail, and she kept up her speed, not slowing down to antagonize him or letting him pass if he was going to pull the same thing. She would not speed way up to play his game.

When she arrived at the drive into the property, she signaled she was turning left and slowed down to make the turn safely. The guy nearly hit her, speeding past her as she started to make the turn. She slammed on her brakes and swore at the bastard. Then once he was out of her path, she drove onto the property.

The truck continued on past the property, and she took a relieved breath, though she was shaken by the accident he had nearly caused. She drove to the garage, pulled inside, and shut the door.

She called Mike to let him know she had gotten in because she was certain he and Lexi would be worried about her otherwise. Then she wouldn't have to also disturb Lexi and Ryder. "I just got in, and I'm going to the zoo tomorrow first thing in the morning, just to let you know ahead of time."

She figured there was no sense in mentioning the out-of-control driver to Mike. The guy was just being an ass, and hopefully, he wouldn't bother anyone else.

"The zoo?" Mike asked, sounding surprised.

"Yeah, with Derek. We'll have lunch there. We might have dinner together after. I just wanted you to know I'll be gone for part of the day at least."

"Sure, okay, I'll tell Lexi. She and Ryder are swimming, so I'll just send her a text."

"Okay, I guess I could have, but if they'd been busy, I was afraid she might feel she had to check it."

"You're covered."

"Thanks."

"You never told me you liked to go to the zoo. *I* could have gone with you."

She chuckled. "You didn't tell me you liked going." She suspected Mike wasn't all that interested in a trip to the zoo.

"To smell stinky animals, no. But I still would have taken you if it's something you're interested in doing."

"Well, if I'm free and you're free and I feel an urge to make another trip there, I'll keep that in mind. Night, Mike." She hoped Derek wouldn't feel the same way about stinky animals. She would prefer going by herself if he didn't enjoy the zoo like she did.

"Night, Kate."

She quickly texted Derek: Home safe and sound. See you tomorrow.

Derek texted right back: Look forward to it. Night, Kate.

Kate: Night, Derek.

Then she headed into her bedroom, stripped off her clothes, took a shower, and tugged on a peach nightie. This had been one of the best dates ever. So much more relaxed than being on show at the gala, where everyone was dressed to the hilt and checking each other out to see if anyone was wearing last year's fashions or someone else's same gown or wearing the same gown as she'd worn at an earlier event this year—heaven forbid!

But with Derek, Kate hoped she wouldn't end up like Brenda, one of the many women he had dated and discarded over the years. Kate tried not to think about it and see him as just a fun date for a couple of outings, but it made her wonder why he was so guarded with having a permanent relationship with a woman, especially a wolf.

She wondered if some she-wolf had broken his heart. Kate had gone out with broken men before.

She tended to want to fix them when she couldn't really do anything for them. And that had gotten her into trouble before. She didn't want to go there with anyone else like that.

Still, she was excited about going to the zoo with Derek tomorrow because she loved visiting the animals, even if nothing ever came of any of this with Derek. She slipped under the covers and smiled and couldn't wait for tomorrow.

When Kate woke the next morning, she practically bounced out of bed and hurried to get ready for her adventure with Derek today. Brenda, eat your heart out! Not that Brenda would have loved visiting a zoo with the hunky wolf—her loss.

Mike called her while she was in the middle of dressing. She was used to going to the zoo alone, but this would be much more fun, she hoped.

"Hello, Mike?" She hoped he wouldn't tell her he needed her to watch over Lexi today.

"Hey, did you see *The Stargazer* this morning? That reporter pictured you and Randall in it, though luckily he didn't catch you kissing him."

"I hadn't intended to." But she wished the reporter hadn't done that.

"Right."

"Okay, so what did it say?" The picture was one thing since it didn't show her in a lover's embrace with Randall. The made-up story could be an entirely different matter.

"It reads: *Has Derek Spencer got competition? Or is Kate Hanover just playing the field still?*"

She laughed. "Since when do I date? Well, hopefully, Derek didn't see it. But if he does, I hope he doesn't put any stock in it. The reporters for those rags are always sensationalizing some nonsense."

"Exactly. I just wanted to warn you because Cliff warned me."

"Cliff, one of Derek's bodyguards?" Now *that* surprised her.

"Yeah."

"Did he say that Derek had read the article?"

"No, but he said Maddie always reads the rag, and she could have alerted Derek about the story. I just wanted to give you a heads-up if he mentions it to you while you're on your date."

"Thanks. I've got to get ready to go. I'll let you know when I'm home for good."

"All right. Have fun!"

Great! Kate should have figured the reporter would have gotten the story in the press as soon as he could. She swore they were like piranhas, not caring who they hurt with their sensationalist stories, as long as they sold lots more papers.

CHAPTER 11

WHEN THE TABLOID CAME OUT THAT SHOWED Kate with some guy at her house, Derek wondered what that was all about. Maybe she was seeing someone else. Hell, he never even read the tabloids normally. It perturbed him that the reporter had even gone to her house! But the tabloid was sitting on the table at Derek's place setting, opened to the page of the offending photo and topic: *Has Derek Spencer got competition? Or is Kate Hanover just playing the field still?*

Still? Derek hadn't thought she was seeing anyone else. Not that he should expect that of her, since they weren't a couple. But it did mean he might need to really step up his game.

Will came into the dining room and glanced at the tabloid Derek was reading. "I didn't think you read that stuff."

"Someone artfully set it at my place setting."

"I did." Maddie carried in a platter of waffles and set them on the table. Then she returned with butter and maple syrup. To Derek's amusement, she sat down with them at the table as Cliff joined them too. Maddie served up some waffles for herself and poured syrup on them. "That's just a warning that there's some other guy who's interested in Kate, so you need to work faster. No telling how many other wolves there will be trying to date her before she finds one she wants to mate."

Cliff and Will were smiling. Derek served himself some waffles. "You know they sensationalize stories in the tabloids so much that you have no idea what is truth and what is fiction."

"Besides, the reporter who took the pictures at the gala captured Derek and Kate in a lip-lock, and this reporter didn't with this guy and Kate. Do you want me to get a private investigator to check him out?" Cliff asked.

"No." Derek was adamant about that. Unless the guy was trouble for her, it wasn't Derek's place to get involved. "He probably isn't even a wolf." Still, it did make Derek wonder if the guy was or not.

"He has a classic Porsche, and he's well dressed, so he probably has money," Will said. "What if he is someone who is bugging her because of her new status as part owner of the cosmetic firm?"

"I agree. Hire a private investigator," Maddie said. "That way we know if the guy is a good guy or bad. And if he's a wolf."

"I'm *not* hiring a private investigator. It's not my business," Derek said. "Besides, I'm going to the zoo with Kate today." Which meant she *wasn't* going out with the other guy!

"Oh, that's right," Maddie said. "You'll have to ask her all about the guy."

"Take the tabloid with you and just happen to have it lying on the passenger seat with the page open to the incriminating photo," Cliff said, but he was joking. He had to know it would be a real turn-off if Kate saw that.

Derek just shook his head, finished his waffles, and had another cup of coffee.

"Are you sure you don't need us to go with you?" Cliff asked, the worrier of Derek's two bodyguards.

"We'll be fine. Kate will take care of any bad guys." Derek really didn't feel any need to take either of the guys with him. He wanted to enjoy the time with Kate without them having to keep up with Kate and him. "Okay, I'll see you all later."

Then Derek drove his Maserati to pick Kate up at her house. When he arrived at her place, Kate came out wearing a halter top, shorts, and sandals with a bag slung over her shoulder. Anything she wore, she looked great in. She was smiling too, and he knew they would have fun.

As soon as she settled in the passenger's seat, she pulled out a map of the zoo, and he drove to the place.

"I figure we'll visit the big cats first, the bears after that. Oh, and we've got to go to the butterfly sanctuary! The bird sanctuary too."

"Is there anything that you *don't* want to see?"

"Nope."

He chuckled.

"When was the last time you went to a zoo?" she asked.

"When I was a kid. I went with Rafe and Aidan and their parents. We had to see the snakes and the alligators, ride the train and the sky rail. The big cats entertained us too. They were chomping on watermelons."

He hadn't expected Kate to be so organized. He suspected that was why she helped Lexi so much with her business. He liked it, though he enjoyed doing things on the spur of the moment too. But he knew if they had their activities planned out more, they would get more done. And that was great too.

"Oh, and by the way, your bodyguard called Mike and told him about the tabloid picture taken yesterday of Randall Roberts and me while I was gardening. I just wanted to say that I used to date Randall on and off. There wasn't really anything special going on between us, and yes, he's a wolf. I haven't even seen him in over a year."

"Which of my bodyguards talked to Mike about it?"

"I'm *not* getting him in trouble if you're going to chew him out."

Derek sighed. "No. I was just wondering who did it."

"I'm not saying. Anyway, in case it troubled you

or you were worried I was unsettled by the news story, I wasn't, and I wanted to let you know who he was. There shouldn't be any further stories about Randall and me. Oh, and he's a financial advisor, so I assumed that's why he finally 'found' me and was interested in getting back with me. Or at least to offer his financial services. Paid for, of course."

"Oh."

"Just in case you read the tabloids."

"I don't normally. But Maddie put the rag on the dining room table for me to read first thing this morning."

Kate laughed, and he enjoyed her laughter. He was glad she was making light of the whole thing.

"My staff wanted me to hire a private investigator to check him out and make sure he wasn't going to cause trouble for you." He figured he might as well share the whole story with her since she seemed to be getting a kick out of it.

She smiled. "And learn if he was a wolf?"

"Naturally."

"Well, they don't have to worry about it. Mike is watching out for me."

Derek was glad, but it bothered him that she had to have Mike watch out for her. "The guy was giving you trouble?"

"I was having a tough time getting rid of him. I'm sure he thought if he hung around long enough, he would have convinced me to talk to him about financial matters. I told him, though I shouldn't have probably spoken for you and Lexi, that you both have your own financial advisors, so if he thought he might make some headway with either of you because he knew me, forget it."

Derek smiled. "I'm glad you did because you're right. I wouldn't switch to some other wolf I don't even know when Liam does a great job with my finances."

"I was going to either contact Liam or Lexi's financial advisor to set things up for me."

"Let me know what you decide, and if you want to talk to Liam, I'll call him. Or you can, of course." Derek didn't know why he was taking over her business! "But if you have any further trouble with the guy, just tell me. I can help out there too."

She chuckled. "He already might think we're dating anyway because we went to the gala together."

"So he saw the tabloid featuring us."

"Uh, yes, that's how he tracked me down. If I had known I was walking with you yesterday when Randall came by while I was gardening, I would have told him I had to run, and that would have made him leave. But you hadn't called me to come with you to walk the dogs yet, and I didn't want to make up any stories."

"I should have called you earlier."

She laughed. "Mike convinced him to leave."

"We could be dating, you know. I mean, beyond this."

She sighed. "You don't date she-wolves."

"I would be willing to make an exception in your case."

"We'll see." Kate still sounded like she didn't think Derek would ever settle down, and maybe he wouldn't. But she probably thought that he would stop dating her, afraid of a commitment, and start dating human women again.

They left it at that for now, but in his own mind, he was damn well dating her. He would do his best to be a wolf she could trust. He felt good about that.

They finally arrived at the zoo, and he was all set to pay for their tickets, but Kate had a season pass. He would buy their lunch then.

They started to follow the map of the zoo to reach the big cat exhibits. In the first one, a tiger watched them, and then he wandered down to the waterway flowing through the exhibit and took a sip of water. In the next enclosure, a large lion gnawed on a massive bone, looking perfectly content. A black jaguar slept on top of a giant tree branch in another pen. A cougar was nearly indistinguishable from the rocks it lay on way up above on the cliffs, another pacing near the smudged window below in the next enclosure. It made Derek realize just how easily the cougars could leap onto the cliffs where his wolf kind couldn't go unless he climbed them as a human. And just how well they blended in with their surroundings. After that, they checked out a group of enclosures where ocelots and clouded leopards slept on top of tree branches.

Derek got a text message and pulled his phone out of his pocket. It was from Brenda. Couldn't she get a clue that it was over between them? Forever?

Brenda texted: I know you're more into doing things on a whim than I am.

That was for damn sure.

Brenda continued: But I thought we could drive down to the pier and have lunch.

He turned off the text notifications and pocketed his phone. He suspected now that Brenda had the notion that if she kept texting him, she would wear him down until he began dating her again. Maybe if he just ignored Brenda, she would finally get the message.

He walked with Kate to the next exhibit, but he felt a bit of tension between them. He hadn't planned to mention Brenda texting him because he didn't want to upset Kate. But he figured it would be better to tell her what was going on. "That was Brenda. I've told her we're not going out together further, but she's not getting the message."

"What did she want to do with you?"

"Have lunch down at the pier."

"We could do that sometime."

Loving the idea, he smiled at Kate. She had a bit

of the devil in her. He guessed it was her wolfish nature that said she was seeing him and hands off to any other woman. "That sounds great. Just let me know when."

"Okay, maybe the weekend after next since we're camping next weekend."

"That sounds good."

The bear exhibits were next. A big old grizzly lay half-asleep on his bed of straw, his tongue hanging out, one eye watching them. In the next enclosure, a Southeast Asian sun bear stood up, watching all the people observing him; another slept behind him on the rocks.

Then Kate took Derek to see the giraffes and purchased tickets to feed them. "I'm going to take pictures of you feeding the giraffe to show how it's done."

He laughed. He was having a ball with Kate. He held out the lettuce and smiled while Kate took pictures of him hand-feeding the giraffe, its long black tongue snaking out to grab the food. Then it was her turn, and Derek took a picture of her feeding the giraffe next. But she needed one of them together too, and when she moved in close to take the picture, he wrapped his arms around her in a way that said they were truly with one another. He didn't know where she was going to post the pictures, if at all, but he was enjoying this too much not to take advantage of the gesture.

She smiled up at him, and this time, he took the shot.

"I'm going to share them on all the social network sites," she said, "after we leave. And Brenda, if she's watching, can enjoy."

He laughed. "I'll be sure to post them on my sites as well in case she misses your postings."

"You have a deal." After that, Kate appeared to be having a blast taking pictures of them everywhere—at the train station, on the sky rail, even petting the goats in the petting zoo. They got up close and personal to the ostrich who was standing right next to the fence and the baby African elephant that was trying to reach imitation plants in a hanging basket next to his enclosure as he had climbed halfway through the fence.

Derek was taking just as many pictures of them together too. He would be posting his on Facebook, Twitter, and Instagram later.

"It's lunchtime, don't you think?" Kate asked.

"Yeah, we've worked up an appetite."

"I like to go right at eleven when it's not as crowded. A lot of people wait until noon."

"That's a good idea."

They headed to the glassed-in facility that housed monkeys and parrots, quickly finding a seat right by the windows before anybody else took it. "Pepperoni pizza for me. What about you?" she asked.

"Hamburger and fries for me. I'll go get them."

"I was going to pay for lunch," she said, "since going to the zoo was my idea."

"No way. I never thought I would enjoy visiting the zoo like this until I had kids, of course. Besides, you paid for our entrance. You can get dessert later if you would like."

"Okay."

When he returned with the food, she was taking pictures of a spider monkey nursing her infant.

"So what else would you like to do?" he asked.

"You mean today? I think our schedule is pretty full. But next chance we have, we could go to the botanical gardens."

"I thought you would never ask."

She laughed and pulled off a slice of her pizza.

He'd never been to the botanical gardens before, but with Kate? He was certain she would make the trip entertaining.

He ate his hamburger and watched the baby monkey curled up in its mother's lap. "This is a really good hamburger. I hadn't expected it to taste as good as what I would make on the grill, but it does."

"I'm glad you're enjoying it. I love their pizza here. I had thought the same, that the zoo food wouldn't be that good. I was pleasantly surprised the first time, so now I always grab a bite to eat before I leave. I come here about three times a year at least. I enjoy walking around the exhibits; it's good exercise, yet I don't really notice it because I'm having so much fun seeing the animals."

"Do you always come by yourself?"

"Most of the time, sure. I came with a guy on a date one time. Lexi and I went together last year, and we had a really nice time. I can't wait until she has her twins and we can take them to the zoo."

"Twins?" Derek asked, surprised.

"Oh, sorry. Maybe she hasn't told everyone else yet."

"She might have told the others. I just hadn't gotten the word. I won't mention I know until someone else shares the news with me in case she hadn't planned to share yet."

"It could be because you're a bachelor male and she didn't think it would interest you. Thanks for not letting on about it though, in case she hasn't told anyone else about it." Kate pulled off another slice of pizza.

Derek took a drink of his lemonade. "Is that why she made you a partner in her firm?"

"Yeah, that's part of it. She knows I'll be driven to continue to make it succeed when she's busy with the babies."

"You're so good at it." He finished his hamburger and ate one of his french fries. "Fries are good too."

"Great."

"So about the guy you took on the date to the zoo…" Derek wanted to know if the guy was human.

Appearing amused Derek would ask, she smiled at him. Which meant? Was he human or a wolf?

"Oh, well, this wolf kept wanting to take me out to nightclubs. I like them, but I love doing out-doorsy stuff too. A variety of things. I would love to go to a theme park or a water park—or even white-water rafting."

"Hmm, theme parks."

"Yeah, so if you're ever up for it, we can do that."

He realized the more he got to know Kate, the more he was up for it. "Yeah, sure. I would love to."

"Anyway, the wolf was not interested in anything at the zoo. He liked the food, but that was about it. He didn't like how costly everything was. He was a dentist, so he made enough money, but he was a cheapskate. I ended up paying for a lot of the stuff because he balked at the price of things the whole time. Even back then, I had a season pass and could take a friend. So he didn't even have to pay for that. When we saw the crocodiles' yellow teeth, that reminded the dentist of dental cleanings. Then he shared all kinds of stories with me about people's dental issues. Believe me, it wasn't the greatest date material to talk about. At the time, I was working as a lifeguard, so if he was going to share his work expe-riences with me, I figured I would share some excit-ing stories with him about saving people or catching thieves on the beach, and I swear he yawned twice while I was telling him about them."

"Clown."

"Yeah. He didn't know why I kept turning him down for dates after that. His idea of a date was doing a pub crawl. Which can be okay for a special party, but to do it all the time? Nope."

"Yeah, I agree. What about us going for a pedal boat ride sometime? A lake is located near us where we can take out a pedal boat, see the swans and geese and ducks, get some exercise, and we could have lunch at the marina."

Kate gave him another one of her sunshiny smiles. "I would love to."

CHAPTER 12

LATER THAT AFTERNOON AFTER VISITING ALL the primates and the reptile house at the zoo, Derek and Kate had soft chocolate-and-vanilla-swirl ice cream in sugar cones. She normally never had ice cream at the zoo, but this was fun on a date. In fact, she was having such a wonderful time, she decided she was dating Derek, and no other wolf—or human—need apply for the position!

He might not always be this accommodating, but for now, he was a dream date.

She couldn't believe it when he took her hand and led her to the booth to pay for rides on the carousel. "You really want to do this?" She loved that he would be that adventurous.

"Yeah. You wanted to. You pick the animal you want to ride, and I'll stand next to you and take photos."

She laughed. "Okay."

When they finally got onto the carousel, she saw just the animal she wanted to ride and dashed for it before someone else got it. Once she was seated on the gray wolf, he took pictures of her and the wolf and then them together as the carousel began to move. She was having a blast.

After that, they visited the bird house filled with parrots and another filled with hummingbirds. They went through the butterfly exhibit next. One of the brilliant blue morpho butterflies took a ride on Derek's shirt the whole way through, and she was amused, taking pictures of the two of them to show off to the world. Though at one point, Derek pulled her in next to him so he could get a shot of Kate, the traveling butterfly, and him. When they finished seeing all the beautiful butterflies, one of the zoo staff moved the morpho to a piece of fruit, and then Derek and Kate left the butterfly house.

"I thought you were going to take your new little friend home with you," Kate said, grasping Derek's hand.

"I would much rather take you."

"Hmm, speaking of going home, we were at the zoo for so much longer than we planned, I was thinking of us having dinner at my place if that works for you," Kate said.

"That would be great," Derek said.

"If you still want to swim, Lexi said we could anytime."

Derek shrugged. "Maybe we could watch a movie at your place instead."

"Sure, we can do that. We did get tons of exercise with all the walking we did. Relaxing tonight sounds good." She suspected he just wanted to be with her tonight.

Then he drove her home, and she really was glad she had asked him to go to the zoo with her today.

When they arrived home, she wasn't expecting him to come into the kitchen and help her make dinner, but she appreciated that he would. "How about chicken cacciatore? We can have it served over rice. It will take about thirty minutes."

"Yeah, that sounds great. I've never made it, so I'll have to ask Maddie to serve it sometime. But this will give me an idea of how it's made."

"Sure, if you like it well enough. We just need to cook some onions, bell peppers, and mushrooms first." Kate began cutting up the peppers, and Derek cut up the mushrooms and onions.

Once the vegetables were softened, she added tomato paste, garlic, Italian seasoning, and red pepper flakes and let them cook another couple of minutes.

"Then we add wine, heavy cream, crushed tomatoes, and tomato sauce."

"My stomach is already grumbling," Derek said.

She smiled. "It's delicious." She added chicken to the skillet and cooked it for another fifteen minutes.

Soon, she was serving up the dinner, and she added chopped parsley and parmesan cheese on top.

"Would you like a glass of wine?" She brought out a bottle of cabernet sauvignon.

"Sure." Derek poured glasses for them, and then

they took their seats at the oak dining table for six. "This has been a great day."

"It has been. I really enjoyed going to the zoo with you."

"I would never have thought of taking a date to the zoo, but you made it fun." Then they began eating, and he smiled. "Wow, this is so good. I definitely want the recipe for Maddie, but since I helped you make it, I suspect she might want me to make it for everyone first."

Kate laughed. "I'm so glad you're enjoying it. My mother used to make this, and I would help her. I haven't had it in ages."

After dinner, they settled down to watch a fantasy film, and they both kicked off their shoes, but to her surprise, he said, "Why don't you lie down that way, and I'll massage your feet."

"Seriously?" she asked.

"Yeah, no strings attached."

She was getting ready to attach strings to him all over the place! "Let me get some lotion." With wearing sandals, her feet would get rough during the summer, and lotion helped them stay soft. She retrieved the lotion from her bedroom drawer and then returned to the living room. She handed him the lotion, set one of the couch cushions behind her head, and rested her feet on his lap. He began to massage her feet with finesse, making her feel divine, cherished, and sexy. She loved the intimacy.

"Hmm, that feels wonderful." She sighed, his hands working on her feet making her feel pleasantly aroused. "You know what this means, don't you? With us spending the whole weekend together? And that on Monday we're going to another charity dinner together?"

"You want me to stay the night?"

She laughed.

"Too much, right?"

Smiling, she said, "It means we're officially dating."

"Hot damn, yes!"

Once he was done massaging her feet, she worked on his, and they were definitely rough. He needed some lotion to soften up his skin too. She had some samples from their cosmetic line, and she would send them with him so he could use them on his feet every night, but this was too much fun, massaging his feet while he watched her, not the movie. He looked part dreamy eyed, part lustful, and she had to make a decision, right or wrong. Should she let him stay the night or not?

They would make unconsummated love, and she hadn't done that with a wolf ever. Making love to humans, sure, once in a blue moon, but she'd never found a wolf she wanted to be that intimate with. Kisses were all she'd allowed, and though most of the wolves were interested in going further, not a mating, she hadn't been. Which had been a little off-putting for the wolves she had dated, but she did have her reasons.

So tonight she wondered if she would be making a mistake by making love to him. She sighed, glanced at him, and smiled. He looked like he could fall asleep on the couch, she was making his feet feel so good. She couldn't imagine only sleeping with him though. She wanted more. To know if he was as good with her in that department as he was about everything else so far.

"Yeah," she finally said.

He raised a brow.

"In answer to your question. I want you to spend the night. I'll protect you in case you have any trouble."

He smiled. "I would love that."

"We both have work tomorrow, and we can't make this a habit, but for tonight, let's do it." There, she'd said it. She normally made up her mind quickly, but in this case, she'd had to do it before she chickened out and changed her mind. She loved how he didn't pressure her about it in any way, shape, or form.

They finally finished their movie. Now it was a matter of logistics. Couch or bed? She was moving this to the bedroom. She got up from the couch and turned off the TV, and he joined her.

"Guest room?" he asked, as if he suddenly was afraid she hadn't meant she wanted to sleep with him.

"My room, unless you would rather just sleep alone in the guest room."

He gave her a hot, sexy smile.

"I didn't think so." Then she and he retired to her bedroom.

He slipped his phone out of his pocket, set it on the bedside table, and then pulled her close and began kissing her, and she opened up to him right away, her hands resting on his lean hips. Tongues caressed and lips melded in a never-ending kiss. He was hotness personified, the way he cupped her face and got into the kiss as if nothing else mattered but making her feel the passion ignite between them. She was immersed in the sensual sensation of her tongue on his, using long, luxurious passes. His hands shifted to her shoulders. As he caressed her, she thought having a whole body massage under his capable hands would be so nice!

She moved her hands to his buttocks and pulled him closer, wanting him pressed tight to her, to feel his growing erection. He was already fully aroused, probably from her massaging his feet! He swept his hands down her back, settled them on her buttocks, and gently squeezed.

This was such a wonderful way to end a beautiful two and a half days of fun with him.

She kissed his strong jaw, moved her mouth to his throat, and licked and kissed him there. She swore she heard him growl a little. A totally under-her-wolf-spell kind of growl. Then he nuzzled her temple and her hair with his face, like a wolf would.

This was pure ecstasy and made her anticipate the rest of their lovemaking with restless desire. She wanted to go further, to strip him of all his clothes and yank her own off and rub their bodies together, to share their scents with each other, to enjoy the intimacy between two unmated wolves. Their pheromones were coming into play like they did whenever they kissed, pushing for more, for consummated sex, but they weren't ready for that. At least not for now.

She slid her hands up his T-shirt over his muscled abs. He was such a hunky specimen of a wolf. But it wasn't enough to feel him and smell his wolfish desire. She wanted to see him in the flesh. All of him. That was definitely a turn-on for her. She pulled her hands out from under his shirt and began to slide it up his torso to get this show on the road.

He smiled and kissed her mouth again, only stopping when she had to pull his T-shirt over his head and toss it to the floor. She thought about him not having a change of clothes for tomorrow. And about him going home with scraggly chin whiskers that were really sexy, she thought—totally a wolf thing. About how he was going to have to tell his staff he wasn't coming home tonight.

Then she was lost again in the feel of him as he

kissed her and she felt his hands on the button of her shorts while her hands were skimming over all his beautiful smooth skin. He unzipped her shorts and pulled them down over her hips, and she quickly stepped out of them and pushed them aside with her foot. She worked on his shorts next, unfastening the belt. Before she could unbutton and unzip his shorts, he was sliding her shirt over her head. Then she finished removing his shorts. The kissing resumed, their hands on each other, feeling each other up with slow, gentle caresses.

He unfastened her lavender lace bra and pulled it off. He kissed her mouth and then pressed kisses over her jaw and down her neck and breastbone until he reached one of her breasts. He kissed and licked the nipple and then the other, making her feel all tingly and needy, her nipples peaked to the max. His were too, and she took her turn kissing his and licking them.

She swore she heard him moan slightly as he kissed the top of her head.

He slid his hands down her waist, tucked his thumbs under her lavender lace panties, and pulled them down her legs. She only had three sets of matching bras and panties, just for a night like this, and she was so glad she had worn one of them instead of one of her old bras and panties that probably needed to be replaced. Did guys even think about things like that? Probably not! But his black boxer briefs cupped his hardness just perfectly, so he didn't need to worry about it as far as she was concerned.

She slowly slid his boxer briefs down his hips, eagerly watched his arousal spring free, and smiled a little, and then he shook his boxer briefs free of his feet. The next phase would be in bed with the wolf.

She was about to turn and climb into bed, but he scooped her up against his body, set her on the bed, and then pressed his aroused body against hers. His body covering hers felt protective, hot, and comforting. She hadn't ever felt that way about anyone before.

He ground his body against hers in an erotic way, kissing her mouth as she deepened the kiss. Man, oh, man, she could get used to this every night. She ran her hand over his scrumptious back and buttocks. Skin to skin, he felt even better than her just seeing him naked.

He moved off her slightly to caress her breast and then slid his hand down her tummy to her short curly hairs and what she'd been expecting since they started kissing, her nether region already aching for his touch. Then he found her nubbin and began stroking her, and she sank deeper into the mattress, her whole body thrumming with pent-up need. But he wasn't done kissing her, and she wasn't done either, so their tongues collided and stroked too.

Except for her shallow breathing and their pounding hearts, no other sound intruded. He was coaxing her toward climax, and she was getting closer to the end, only seconds away. He didn't let up on his strokes, which was good because she would have had a meltdown. And she wasn't that kind of woman! But this was just too good to be true.

He started to stroke her faster, more determinedly, smelling her need, and that was all she needed to push her over the edge. She felt she was free-falling, her whole world tilting on edge. "Aww," she moaned, the orgasm still rippling through her body, making her feel like a billion bucks. If she hadn't craved finishing him off next, she would have just curled up against him and slept. Instead of dreaming of him dancing with her, she might dream of this.

She lay there for a moment, just in wonderment, thinking how much she had missed by not being with a wolf like Derek. Not any wolf really though, just him. She sighed and pushed him onto his back. His dark eyes were lust filled, and he smiled at her. She smiled back. Then she straddled his legs, took hold of his impressive erection, and began to stroke. She thought this might take a while, but before she knew it, he was coming, she'd primed him so already. He groaned aloud as she finished him off and she lay next to him for a moment, just half cuddling with him, her arm over his chest.

"Do you want to take a shower? With me?" she asked.

"Yeah. I sure do." But he didn't seem to want to move any more than she did.

She finally chuckled. "I'll meet you in there."

Her climbing over him and heading for the bathroom was enough to make him leave the bed and sprint after her.

After washing each other, they toweled each other dry. "I'm going to dry my hair really quick." Having a long bob helped instead of long hair like she used to have. She thought he would just return to the bedroom and call Cliff or Will to tell him he wouldn't be home tonight.

But when she pulled out her hair dryer, Derek said, "Here, let me do that."

"Oh, you are a dream come true!"

He chuckled and combed his fingers through her hair as he dried it.

She'd never expected that. Though she did wonder if he did that with all the women he'd been with.

"No," he said.

She glanced back at him. "No, what?"

"I've never dried a woman's hair."

She sighed. "But you can read minds?"

He laughed. "No, but I could just imagine what you were thinking."

"Well, I've never showered with a guy either."

He smiled. "Ditto for me—with a woman, I mean."

She was ready to melt into the floor as the tips of his fingers lightly massaged her scalp. Then he was done. She gave him a new toothbrush, they both brushed their teeth, and then returned to bed, this time to cuddle and sleep.

———

Derek couldn't believe how lucky he could get. He had hoped he could stay over at Kate's home, but he didn't expect the invite. God, this was great. He really couldn't believe she was dating him. He would make it worth her while. Though just doing things like walking the dogs on the beach or watching a movie with her in her home was just as enjoyable for him as going to the zoo. She really added a lot of spice to his life.

As blissfully satiated as he was, he still didn't want to sleep. He wanted to feel Kate pressed lightly against his chest. Her shallow breathing indicated she had fallen fast asleep. Hell, he hadn't let Cliff know he was staying the night.

He reached over to the bedside table for his phone and texted Cliff: Hey, I'm staying over at Kate's house. Sorry for the late notice.

Cliff texted back: Good show. I already checked with Mike about twenty minutes ago and he said your car was still at Kate's place.

Derek was glad that Cliff was always on top of things. He texted: I'll see you in the morning, but I'll probably have breakfast with Kate.

Cliff: I'll tell Maddie to hold breakfast for you, just in case.

Derek: I'll let you know in the morning.

Then Derek set his phone back on the bedside table and snuggled with Kate. He was sure damn glad he hadn't turned down a zoo date with her!

Early the next morning, Kate lifted her head off his chest, waking him. Her eyes were round. "Did you let Cliff or Will know you were staying the night?"

Derek smiled.

CHAPTER 13

"OH, I'VE GOT TO GET WITH LEXI," KATE SAID, IN a hurry to get out of bed, glad Derek had told her he had let Cliff know he had stayed the night. She was getting dressed, and Derek got out of bed to dress too. "Sorry for the early-morning wake-up, but I've got a meeting with Lexi first thing this morning."

"No problem at all."

Kate threw on a blue-and-white-floral summer dress over her undergarments and slipped on some sandals.

"Do you have time for breakfast?" he asked, figuring he could even make it if she had to do anything else to get ready for work.

"Yeah. Eggs? Bacon?" She brushed out her hair and rushed out of the bedroom.

He chuckled. He hadn't expected her to be a jackrabbit this morning. He finished dressing and headed into the kitchen.

She was already cracking the eggs into a pan, and he made the coffee. "Tea for you?" he asked.

"Yeah, thanks! Sorry for the rush, but I don't usually have a hot wolf in bed with me, and I'm running later than I normally am. I don't want to worry Lexi."

"I'm sure she'll be fine with it." That was the nice thing about Lexi working mostly out of her home. Besides, Kate wasn't an employee anymore but a partner in the business. He didn't mention that Mike had seen Derek's car still sitting at Kate's place.

"Um, okay, so five tonight for the dinner, right?" She served up the eggs while the bacon was still sizzling away.

He made her tea and took the mugs of tea and coffee to the table. "Yeah." He was hoping he could stay the night with her again tonight and take her out every night until the camping trip. He was thinking of Maddie's comment that he could stay in Kate's tent at the campout if he dated her and things were working out well for them. But he would talk to Kate about it tonight at the dinner. She was in too much of a rush to get out of here.

He served up the bacon, and then they sat down to eat.

"Is there anything in particular I should wear tonight?" she asked.

"It's another black-tie event. Wear whatever you would like."

"Okay." She drank some of her lavender tea and smiled. "All right, five then." She hurried to eat, which made him rush to finish his own breakfast.

He hoped it wouldn't always be this way between them. "I guess we can tell everyone we're dating now." He was sure eager to.

"No, let's wait until the campout."

He frowned. "Did you want separate tents?" He didn't want that.

"Uh, yes." She finished her tea and kissed him on the cheek. "I've got to run. You can let yourself out whenever you're ready to leave. The keypad locks automatically. Grab yourself another cup of coffee and anything else you would like."

"Okay." Though all he really wanted was more time with Kate. He rose from his chair and gave her a hug and kiss. "See you tonight then."

"Yeah, can't wait." She hurried out through the front door, and he looked at their plates.

He sure hoped she hadn't changed her mind about dating him.

He finished breakfast, texting Cliff at the same time to let him know he was eating at Kate's this morning, though mostly without Kate. He didn't mention that part. He sighed and was taking the dishes to the kitchen when he heard someone open the front door.

"Just me," she said, sounding breathless. "Sorry, I don't have time for the dishes. I'll take care of them at lunchtime. Bye!"

Then she was out the door again and gone. But he wasn't leaving the dishes for her to do later. He might have a housekeeper, but he knew how to put dishes in the dishwasher and how to clean pots and pans.

After he cleaned up, he got into his car and drove off, not sure what was going on with Kate this morning. He really thought she was rethinking dating him for real or she would have just told the world they were.

He tried to tell himself it was okay, but he really wanted to date her.

━━━━━━

Lexi hurried to get together with Kate and was a bundle of mixed emotions. At Lexi's house, they were working on new product ideas for next spring and more promotional ideas for the fall, but the way Lexi was frowning, she seemed perturbed about something. And Kate forgot all about giving Derek some lotion for his feet. She was never late, and she didn't want to start arriving late now. How would that look? Like she was a new partner and didn't have to arrive on time?

Kate hoped she hadn't been the one to upset her. She could just imagine Lexi wishing she hadn't made Kate a full partner in the business!

Lexi opened up her Facebook page and did a search. "Normally, I wouldn't pay any attention to an ex-girlfriend's rantings, but I don't want this to get out of hand."

"Ryder had an ex-girlfriend who's giving you trouble?" That really surprised Kate.

"No, Derek—Brenda. Even if you're not concerned about it, I just wanted to make you aware of it."

"Sure, thanks." Kate read through the comments and smiled.

Brenda said: *That little nobody, Kate Hanover, has been trying to steal my boyfriend away from me for months behind my back. She has the nerve. Well, I'm not done with her.*

Wouldn't Brenda be surprised when she learned Kate was dating Derek! Though after throwing caution to the wind last night, Kate felt that she would go with him to the dinner tonight and have a cooling-off period so she could be more levelheaded about this whole situation.

One of Brenda's friends responded: *She needs to be dealt with.*

Kate raised a brow to hear the way Brenda was stirring up her friends with the lies she was telling.

Brenda said: *Can you believe she tried to get Derek to hire her as a bodyguard?*

Okay, well, that part was true.

Another friend of Brenda's said: *No way.*

And the list of comments went on. Kate had read enough. Though just in case Brenda decided to really do something nefarious where Kate was concerned, she took some screenshots and sent them to her email. Brenda was a bitter woman, and she needed to move on with her life.

"I'm glad you told me about Brenda. I figured she was just bugging Derek to try to get back in his good graces. I had a human stalker boyfriend once and a human ex-girlfriend of another former boyfriend—a wolf—who gave me grief. I had only dated the male wolf twice and the human guy three times. The ex-girlfriend of the wolf guy gave up on me when he started seeing a human woman, so I figured the stalker ex-girlfriend turned her wrath on his new girlfriend instead. The human guy who had stalked me started seeing someone else, and I have no idea how that all turned out. I really didn't want to know either, as long as they left me alone. So I think it's always important to be aware of a situation where a perfectly normal person otherwise can create real issues in your life."

"I don't blame you. How *are* things going between you and Derek?" Lexi asked.

Kate was sure Lexi was dying to know. She felt Lexi was a like a sister to her, so she didn't mind telling her. "We've had a great time so far. He spent the night last evening. I need to leave later this afternoon to get ready for a charity dinner tonight. You weren't going to that, were you?" Kate hadn't remembered Lexi mentioning it to her before. She didn't tell Lexi that she was dating Derek yet. She really thought if she took a break from him the rest of the week and then went camping with him, she'd know if dating him officially was really the right move for them.

"No. Ryder and I had other plans. I'm glad you're going with Derek. Rafe said he hasn't seen Derek this excited about anything in a long time. He was surprised Derek went to the zoo with you."

"Oh, we're going to the botanical gardens one of these weekends."

Lexi laughed.

"And pedal boating."

"I'm seriously going to have to talk Ryder into doing some of those things."

"Where is Ryder?" For that matter, where was Spirit? She usually greeted Kate as soon as she arrived at Lexi's home.

"We found a veterinarian, Rebecca Ann Young, who is a wolf, and she's going to be giving all the wolf dogs their vaccinations. Regular vets won't do it. But she totally understands where we're coming from. Ryder took Spirit to get her shots."

"Oh, fantastic. Is the veterinarian new to the area?"

"Yeah, she was with a pack up in Seattle, and she got fed up with the leadership there, so she figured she would settle down here."

"Does Derek take his Irish setters to her?"

"I don't know for sure. We shared the word about her with him though."

"She's single?" If she was, would Derek be interested in the vet? Kate hated how her mind would sometimes go on wild tangents.

Lexi added some prices to the web page. "Uh, yes. But she has been really busy, and she's trying to just get her practice set up first before she starts to date, she said."

"Oh, okay." But it made Kate realize she might not be the only she-wolf in the area who was available to see Derek and she might need to make her mind up sooner rather than later.

CHAPTER 14

HOPING DEREK WOULDN'T BE UPSET WITH HER now that she wanted to hold off on telling anyone she was dating him, Kate was ready for him when he came to pick her up at her home for the charity dinner. He hurried to the door to get it for her, but she left the house before he reached her. He smiled and gave her a kiss and a hug. "You look ravishing as usual."

"Thanks. You look like a handsome devil of a wolf." She kissed and hugged him back, wanting to show she really did care about him.

He held the car door for her, and when they were on the way, she casually said, "Lexi was telling me that we have a wolf veterinarian to take care of the wolf dogs now. Have you touched base with her about your Irish setters?" She'd been thinking about it ever since Lexi told her this morning.

"I have. They have their annuals coming up in about a month."

"Oh, that's great. I haven't met her yet. Is she nice?" Kate asked.

"She seems to be. I'm sure she will fit right in with the pack."

"I didn't know anything about her. You could have asked her to the gala instead of me." Yeah, Kate figured he would know she was fishing to learn if he was at all interested in the vet.

"Your name was the one that kept coming up and—"

"You already had me checked out—I mean as far as the job interview went—so I was a little more of a known quantity."

"Truthfully, since the time of the interview, I've watched you interacting with my friends, and you always appeared to be enjoying yourself. I wanted that with you."

Kate smiled. "Really?"

"Yeah."

"But you didn't ask me to go with you to the gala. You went through Lexi instead."

Derek nodded. "That had all to do with me turning you down for the bodyguard job. I was hoping Lexi could convince you to go with me if you were a bit reluctant."

"Well, it worked."

"It sure did."

"So is Brenda going to be at this function?"

"I wish I could say that she won't be, but I suspect she will be since she knows where I'm going to be and I suspect she's going to keep trying to meet up with me," Derek said, turning onto another road.

"Has she texted you anymore?"

"She has. But I'm not bothering to answer her texts."

"Good. Maybe she'll finally find someone else to hassle. By the way, I don't get any tabloids. Since Maddie reads them, are there any news stories about us lately?"

"Uh, yeah, about you."

"Me? Just me?" Kate asked, wondering if that one reporter had made more stories up about her and Randall.

"Yeah, apparently you're a heartbreaker."

"I am. But I think you are too."

He chuckled.

"So what did they really say? The tabloids?"

"That you broke up several relationships."

"Ha! You know who started that rumor?"

"I suspect Brenda did. Even though I hadn't been dating anyone else while I was seeing Brenda, I'm sure she thinks I was with you on the sly. Why else would you be available to date me on the spur of the moment?"

"I was already going to the gala."

"Exactly. But she's not going to see it that way, nor is she going to let on that that's the case."

She frowned. "I never had anything to do with you at the previous events."

"I know, but I always watched you and was interested in you."

Kate scoffed.

He pulled up to the restaurant. "It's true. I wanted to see you, but I just couldn't bring myself to—"

"Date me?" she asked.

"Right. I was afraid to fall for another she-wolf and get my hopes up that she was the one for me." He got out of the car and then went to her side. This time, she waited for him, and he helped her out.

Then he saw the paparazzi, and he pulled Kate into a hug and kissed her. If they were going to write stories about him and Kate, he wanted them to get the stories right.

This time Kate didn't race off either, pulling Derek out of the limelight. She kissed him back. "I'm not after your money," she whispered in his ear. "But all that wolfish hotness? Now that's another story."

"And I'm not after your half of the cosmetics business. But one fun she-wolf—that's a whole other story." He suspected she was beginning to feel more comfortable with the paparazzi taking photos of them together now that she was nearly dating him.

She smiled, took his hand, and led him into the restaurant. "I hope Brenda's here tonight."

He chuckled. "You like to live dangerously."

"I do."

Inside, a hostess was busily escorting all the new arrivals to the banquet room.

Kate smiled and glanced around the room, her

arm around Derek's waist. He had his arm slung over her shoulder.

"I was afraid you wouldn't be coming with me to any of these events. That you didn't want to be to be seen with me," Derek said.

"Well, I changed my mind after we had so much fun this weekend. Brenda also needs to see that this is real between us and to get over it. Besides, I've had the biggest crush on you ever since I saw you."

He smiled.

"I'm serious."

"I knew it! That's why you wanted to work for me, and you knew I felt the same way about you."

She laughed. "Yeah, and you were afraid to lose your heart again."

"I was. You saw me watching you at the social events that Lexi and you attended, didn't you?"

"A time or two." She gave him a cute little shrug.

"You knew."

"Why do you think I applied to be your bodyguard? I saw you running on the beach with one of your dogs, and I smelled your scent, knew you were a wolf, and had to know who you were. It had nothing to do with you having a lot of money. I didn't know you from Adam. Believe it or not, I don't read the tabloids. But I loved how you stopped to play with your dog, tossing a Frisbee into the air."

Kate figured Brenda still wanted to be with a much hotter, virile wolf, though she wouldn't know he was a wolf. They soon saw Brenda with the same guy as before, standing near the entrance to the banquet room. Kate was glad Brenda witnessed that she was still with Derek.

"At least she won't be seated by us tonight," Derek said, smiling at Kate.

"It won't matter." Kate pulled Derek into her arms and kissed him. "Because I'm showing her and you just what I feel for you. Believe me, there are no other wolves waiting in the wings."

"That's just what I wanted to hear. But only from you."

Kate had thought of telling Derek all the bad things Brenda was saying about her on social media, but she figured she would just handle the situation herself. She didn't need anyone else fighting her battles. She could be just as snarky as the woman, but she was trying to hold back her wolf nature and just ignore Brenda, who was acting like a sore loser. Like Derek was handling Brenda, Kate thought that might be the best way to deal with someone like her.

When they finally took their seats, they realized that Brenda and her date were sitting opposite them. Was it a coincidence, or had Brenda bribed someone to rearrange the seating? Kate was kind of surprised that Brenda had come with the same date because he'd abandoned her at the gala. If Brenda was seeing the man now—despite saying she was just a fill-in unless the other woman was still sick or something—why continue to harass Derek for a date? Maybe because she truly was the fill-in. Or the hot wolf was a lot more appealing than the older man with more money.

So money, in that case, didn't buy everything.

The small tables—covered in white tablecloths with red roses in glass vases sitting in the center—made the gathering more intimate. They could eat all the sushi they wanted, artistically prepared by a chef from Hawaii. Along with that and a variety of sautéed vegetables, they enjoyed cocktails while live music played on the other side of the restaurant.

It was really beautiful as they enjoyed the dinner. Derek donated money to funding a cure for cancer. He'd already bid on several items during the silent auction: an all-inclusive trip for two to Hawaii, dinner theater tickets, an all-inclusive ski trip to Vail, Colorado, and dinner for two at one of the exclusive restaurants in their area.

Kate didn't have the kind of money Derek had, so it was hard to imagine bidding so much for a vacation he could pay half the cost for. She had to remind herself it was all for charity and she was glad he was so generous and that he could afford to be so. She noticed Brenda's date wasn't bidding on anything in the silent auction, while Derek was using mobile bidding on his smartphone.

This was really exciting and less stressful, Kate

thought. At the end of the silent auction, the winners were announced, and Brenda looked smugly at Derek when it appeared he hadn't won anything. Everyone else was already paying for their wins, and then Derek leaned over and kissed Kate on the cheek. "Are you ready for an all-inclusive trip to Hawaii?"

"Seriously?" She had never won anything in her life, and she was so surprised. He probably had paid a fortune to win the trip. "Your name wasn't called."

"I used DS Enterprises, a subsidiary that handles my real estate ventures."

She smiled and kissed his mouth. "How wonderful that you won! I can't wait to go. I'll have to get some new clothes for the trip. This is going to be so much fun." She didn't know if it would really happen. By the time he was ready to take the trip, Kate could have been easily replaced. But for Brenda's benefit, Kate was playing it up big time.

Derek kissed Kate back and smiled at her. He seemed pleased at her reaction.

Brenda's glower couldn't have been any harsher. Then she scoffed. "I imagine so since you're wearing the same gown that you've worn before. Is that a wine stain on the bodice?"

"No, and you're just plain rude," Kate said.

Brenda's date smiled at Kate as if he was glad she had said so. Then Kate noticed Derek was smiling too. Good. Kate didn't want him to feel he'd made a mistake in taking her to the dinner because she couldn't ignore Brenda's uncalled-for comment.

When they finally finished dinner and enjoying the night's events, Derek and Kate headed to her place.

"I can't believe you won the trip to Hawaii. I mean, I'm sure you paid a fortune for it, but...were you serious about going with me?"

"Yeah, I am. As long as you want to go, we'll have a great time."

"Oh, sure. When we both have time." She still felt by the time it was scheduled, she and he could have moved on. "Sorry about bothering to set Brenda straight at the dinner table."

"I would have done it if you hadn't. She *was* being rude. If she thinks that putting you down in front of me and others will convince me to date her again, she's gravely mistaken. So would you like to go out tomorrow night or just come over and have dinner with me? Walk the dogs on the beach? Swim in the pool?" Derek asked, sounding like he wanted to ensure he had dates with Kate every night now.

She was afraid of that. She didn't want to make him feel bad, but she thought she needed to have some time away from him so her judgment wasn't clouded about what was going on between them. She would be with him from Friday through Sunday. "Uh, no, really, I need to get my stuff sorted and packed up for the campout, and I'll be busy doing other things after work. Laundry, cleaning the house, you name it. So thanks, but I'll see you on Friday!" She really had to make sure she was doing the right thing with him. She thought taking a breather was the best thing for her—and probably for him. Though he seemed kind of down about it. "We'll have a blast this Friday."

He smiled. "Yeah, sure, we will."

But he sounded like he'd done something wrong, and he hadn't. It was all her. She was worried that the fun would run out and then she would be down about the whole thing.

"You're not changing your mind about us, are you?" he asked.

She smiled at him. "No. I just need to get some things done, or Friday will be here before we know it and I won't be ready to go."

"Okay."

When he parked at her house, she leaned over the console and kissed him, telling him she wanted more, but she didn't want a repeat of last night again so soon after. He kissed her back, but with a little reservation, as if he was afraid she would break his heart.

She sighed, smiled, and got out of the car. "See you on Friday!" Then she waved at him, shut the car door, and headed into the house, hoping she wasn't making a mistake in not going out with him the rest of the week. When it came to dating, she definitely didn't have much of a success rate.

CHAPTER 15

THAT NIGHT ON THE WAY HOME, DEREK THOUGHT
about Kate, afraid she was changing her mind about
dating him and wondering what was wrong. He
wanted to see her at night, just like dating wolves
would. Every evening, he wished she could be sitting on his back patio enjoying cocktails with him,
running along the beach with the dogs or running
as wolves, swimming with her in his pool, but she
had put on the brakes big time. A cooling down?
He was afraid he'd done or said something wrong.
He didn't think Lexi kept her busy working on the
business at night. And he couldn't imagine she had
that much work to get ready to go camping.

Hell, he'd come over and help her sort everything
out. He guessed she wasn't ready to stay with him
in his tent. She could just pack what she needed for
herself, and he'd manage all the camping gear. He'd
fought with himself not to call Lexi to see if maybe
Kate had said something to her about being upset
with him.

He managed to get through Tuesday night without Kate—was that lame or what?

It was Wednesday night now, and he let out his

breath, went down to his exercise room, and began bicycling—again. Will joined him and began lifting weights while Cliff served on guard duty.

"We thought you might be going out with Kate tonight," Will said.

"We went out Monday night." Derek kept telling himself he would see her Friday night, but he was afraid she wouldn't want to tell any of their friends they were dating at the campout either.

"Yeah, but you were with her Friday, all weekend, and then Monday, and now?" Will raised a brow.

"You know you *can* be replaced."

Will laughed. "Yeah, I know, but if there's any chance things aren't working out between the two of you—"

"We're camping on Friday," Derek reminded him. "She has work to do before she can take off to camp all weekend, and she has to get ready for the trip."

"So it's not you who is balking at taking her out."

"I asked, okay? But she was busy. I'm not going to keep bugging her if she needs some time to herself to do other things. I'll see her on *Friday* when we go camping."

"We are trying to limit the number of vehicles we take to the park, but if you think it would work better if Cliff and I are in our own vehicle and you can ask Kate to ride with you, we could do that."

"No. We all agreed that we would keep the number of cars down to a minimum. There's a limit on the number of vehicles allowed to park at each campsite." Derek couldn't believe how much his bodyguards and Maddie were invested in his dating Kate. With Maddie, she would love to have another woman around—a she-wolf, not a human. And she was hopeful Derek and Kate would mate and have kids. But with Cliff and Will? They both were interested in dating Kate. Maybe if Derek couldn't settle down with her, they felt they had a chance to date her.

Derek felt glum about it. What was he doing wrong?

———

While washing her car, Kate had told herself she'd made a mistake in going out with Derek all weekend, making love to him, and then attending the charity dinner with him on Monday night. Not that she hadn't had a great time. She had! But she'd felt like she was just falling into the same pattern he'd had with other women he'd dated. Lexi had told her Derek had dated she-wolves in the past and two had left him for other wolves, so he'd made a commitment to both and then neither of them stayed with him. She could understand the hurt. And truly, she didn't want him to have all these expectations about her either if things shouldn't work out.

She wondered if he was the kind of wolf who had to have a mate and he wanted to see her every day, day in and day out, and even that wouldn't be enough. She didn't want to feel like her life was being overshadowed by a male wolf. She had her own life, and she enjoyed it very much. She could imagine needing to work on things for the company and Derek needing her to attend functions to fulfill his own agenda. She wasn't going to give up on her own dreams to fulfill someone else's.

So she'd made the tough decision to stay away from him until the camping trip. Sure, they would run as wolves together during the campout. And they would eat together with the rest of the pack for meals. Otherwise, she was going to be there to enjoy just doing things she liked with a group of wolves. She didn't want anyone to think of her and Derek as a couple. And yet?

Damn if she couldn't quit thinking of him. If she was being honest with herself, he was the kind of wolf she had always wanted in her life.

Last night, she'd had dinner on her own, but tonight, Lexi had invited her over for a working dinner and a swim in the pool. That was what she loved about working with Lexi. They had a great time doing it. But she hoped the topic of Derek wouldn't come up.

She finished washing her car and drying it off

and then parked it in the garage. She cleaned up and headed over to Lexi's house on the brick path that connected the two homes.

When she arrived at Lexi and Ryder's home, Ryder and Mike were in the basement practicing martial arts moves.

"Ryder and Mike made us veal scallopini and ate already so we would have our dinner/work time in private," Lexi said. "Let's eat and then we can work on some new concepts." Once they sat down at the dining room table, she asked, "So how are things going between you and Derek?"

Kate sighed. "He wanted to get together on Tuesday night. I was certain if I said yes, he would have wanted to date the rest of the nights this week, but I wanted to take time off to get ready to camp and just do some other things."

"So you're not upset with him for some reason."

Kate smiled. "No. We've had a great time when we've been together, and you know we'll all see him when we go camping. It's not like you and Ryder and how the two of you had to stay together. He was helping protect you and then you *both* wanted more than that."

"You don't feel really connected to Derek?"

Kate sighed again. "Yeah, I mean, we're both wolves. So sure, there's that connection." She felt a real draw to him. She couldn't deny she wanted more with him, but she didn't want him to do the pushing away at the end. "We made unconsummated love with each other on Sunday night."

Lexi nodded. "I mean, it's inevitable if you really like each other. But I understand if you are feeling a little like pulling back. Derek will understand, and if it's meant to be, it will be." Lexi smiled at her, as if she knew things would work out between Kate and Derek. If they did, it would make for one neat little wolf pack since she and Derek were already both wolf friends with everyone else.

Kate thought Lexi was right and hoped everything would work out the way they hoped it would.

Then they ate their meal. While drinking sarsaparillas poolside, they talked over some business, comparing sales data for various product lines, phasing out a line of cosmetics and a few products in another line that weren't selling well. Afterward, they swam in the pool. Kate heard the guys watching football on TV in the house and smiled. "Thanks for having me over. We got a lot done but we had a great time as usual."

"You bet." Lexi gave her a hug. "Everything will work out between the two of you."

"I hope so." And really, Kate did. Then she walked on the path to her home.

She'd had a delightful time with Lexi, just liked they'd always had, and she was thinking about the issue with Derek. What if she did mate him? Then she wouldn't live right here, having fun with Lexi on the spur of the moment. Though she would have a romping good time with Derek instead in a totally different way. She could see herself running along the beach as wolves at night, taking the dogs for walks as humans when the sun was setting, and even swimming in the ocean with each other again. Playing tag in his swimming pool? Yeah, she could envision how hot that would get.

Before she reached the house, she saw Foxy, Derek's Irish setter that she had walked on the beach, sitting on her front doorstep. "Ohmigod, what are you doing here?"

Foxy's long red fur was tangled, and she had twigs, pine needles, and bits of leaves that had caught in the strands. She was panting heavily and needed water. Foxy greeted her right away.

Kate quickly took the dog inside the house and got her a bowl of water. Then she pulled out her phone and called Derek, but he wasn't answering his phone. She called Will and Cliff, but neither of them was either. Then she figured they were out running as wolves, trying to find Foxy. Which meant they might very well end up here! She didn't have Maddie's number. She probably had gone home for the night anyway.

Kate left a message on Derek's phone then. "Hey, it's me, Kate. Foxy is at my home, and she's safe. I'm going to give her a bath after I pull all the twigs out of her fur."

Then she ended the call and began pulling out the debris tangled in Foxy's fur. "How in the world did you find my place?"

Sure, Kate had run as a wolf in the direction of Derek's home before. But there was a big gap between his home and hers! Though they all had homes on the beach, Lexi's beach was blocked by rocks, and the only way to get there was to run through the underbrush up above and through people's yards or along the winding road—which was where Kate ran. She and Lexi had walked along that stretch of road too. Then again, Kate had her car's top down when she went to see Derek at his place, since the weather had been so nice. Maybe that was the way Foxy had found Kate—smelling her scent all along the way.

Kate couldn't believe Foxy would have sought her out like this—as if she didn't get enough loving at home! Kate finished pulling the stuff from Foxy's fur and then called Lexi. "Hey, sorry to interrupt you, but can I use your dog grooming room to wash a dog?"

"This sounds like a story and a half."

"Yeah, one of Derek's Irish setters came to my house. She's a mess. I tried getting a hold of Derek and his bodyguards, but I suspect they're running as wolves, trying to track her down."

"Oh, so you're going to have a bunch of naked men at your house too." Lexi laughed.

Kate chuckled. "Most likely. Can I use the bath-house for Foxy?"

"Yes. And Ryder said he would loan the guys some clothes."

"I'm sure they'll need a ride home. They can just remain as wolves. I'm headed over to your house. I'll leave a note on my door saying I've gone to your place to give Foxy a bath," Kate said.

Then she ended the call, scribbled a note to Derek, should he come to her house, taped it to her front door, and tied a short electric cord to Foxy's collar. Kate figured when she returned Foxy to her home, she would borrow one of the leashes Lexi had for Spirit.

Kate had barely reached the dog's bathhouse when Spirit ran out of Lexi's house to join her and Foxy and greeted both of them. They were making best friends when Kate saw Derek running as a wolf to greet her. She laughed.

His wolf bodyguards weren't far behind. Derek woofed at Foxy. She didn't seem to think she'd done anything wrong and licked his face. Then Spirit greeted all of them, glad to have all the company, as if everyone was there just for her.

"Hi, Derek. I'm giving her a bath and then Ryder or Mike can take you guys home. You can chill out by the pool."

But Derek went into the bathhouse with her, and she wondered what he thought he was going to do. Then he shifted—man, he was so hot, muscles and all! He grabbed one of the clean towels stacked on a table, wrapped it around his waist, and came over to give Kate a hug. "Thanks so much, Kate. I thought I'd lost her for good."

She hugged him back, knowing how much it meant to him to have nearly lost one of his dogs. Besides, she'd really missed Derek and was glad to see him. So much for her self-imposed banishment from seeing him. "Imagine my surprise to find her here. I was just coming home from Lexi's place after working on some concepts for the business." She coaxed Foxy into the big bathtub and pulled down the hose to soak her.

"I've been missing you," Derek said.

Spirit sat next to the bathtub, wagging her tail like crazy. She loved baths, but washing one large dog at a time was enough work for the night.

"Yeah, well, I've been missing you too." Kate was constantly thinking of Derek, thinking of what it would be like if she had been with him instead of Lexi or home alone.

He smiled then, and she thought she'd made his night.

"I was just glad we found her here and she's safe and unharmed. She was eager to visit with you," Derek said.

"I was surprised she made it all the way here." Then they both began soaping her up.

Spirit put her paws on the edge of the tub and woofed at Foxy.

Mike came into the dog's bathhouse and handed Derek a pair of board shorts. "The other guys aren't bothering to shift. They're just hanging out by the pool. If you guys need me for anything other than a ride home, you've got it."

"Thanks, Mike," Derek said.

"Is Spirit making a nuisance of herself in here?" Mike asked.

"No, she's fine. She loves the dog company," Kate said.

Then Mike smiled at them and left the bathhouse.

"Sorry about this. I imagine you had other plans for tonight—like a movie or something, not washing a dog." Derek dropped the wet towel and pulled on Mike's spare board shorts.

"I did, but this is okay. I'm glad she's fine. How did she get free?"

"Since walking on the beach with you and Foxy on Saturday, she has been watching for you to show up again. She sits by the door all the time, just waiting. When we put her out in the yard, she sits by the fence observing the driveway, hoping you'll return."

Kate chuckled. "Aww, that's so sweet."

"When I went to take the dogs for a walk tonight, Foxy saw her chance and bolted. I quickly alerted Cliff and Will and put the other dog back in the yard. Then we stripped and shifted to chase Foxy down as wolves. She still had a good head start on us. At first, I didn't know where she was running to. But then it became evident. You had your car top down when you drove to my place, and I smelled your scent. I guessed then that she was going straight to your place!"

"That's really amazing."

"She might not want to leave," he said.

"I don't have a fenced-in yard. Only Lexi does because of the swimming pool, and now she keeps her dog in there."

Kate had changed into her shorts and a shirt after swimming with Lexi, and now she figured she should have just stayed in her bathing suit as wet as she was getting. Washing Lexi and Ryder's wolf dog was one thing she normally didn't have to do. Ryder and Mike always washed her.

Derek was getting just as soaked.

"Do you often wash the dogs?" she asked.

Derek probably had a full-time groomer for the job to keep their fur brushed out and clean when he had a lot of foster dogs.

"We wash the dogs when we need to, but a red wolf takes care of all of them, especially when I have a lot more than just the two. Her son takes care of the dogs when we're gone if Maddie can't." Derek eyed Foxy. "Don't be surprised if Foxy tries to come to your house again."

"Hopefully, she won't. That's dangerous out there for her. She could get hit by a car or picked up by dogcatchers, though I've never seen any come around this area, or just taken in by a family."

After they rinsed her off, they towel-dried her and then used the hair dryer on her fur.

Lexi came out to the bathhouse and smiled. "All cleaned up. Did you want to join us for beers or pink lemonade poolside? Ryder and Mike loaned Cliff and Will some board shorts so we can all have a drink before Mike takes you home."

"Yeah, sure." Derek sounded eager to visit with them for a while after the long run to Lexi's property as a wolf.

Kate was glad Lexi was offering pink lemonade. It always appealed to her in the summertime. "That would be fun." But she wasn't finished with Foxy. She grabbed a brush at the same time that Derek grabbed for it with the same intention, their hands touching, lingering, and they paused to smile at each other. Then he picked up the dog comb.

They all went to the pool, and she and Derek sat on chaise longues with Foxy sitting in the middle of them, Derek's bottle of beer and Kate's glass of pink lemonade sitting on the table between them as they began to brush and comb out Foxy. She was in seventh heaven. It appeared she was being loved on by her two favorite people in the world. Not only was

Foxy sitting with them, so was Spirit, edging up to get some grooming time in as well.

Kate laughed. "Spirit, you're so silly."

Despite Kate's plan to take a break from Derek, it seemed that Foxy had other plans. That made Kate smile.

CHAPTER 16

DEREK HAD REALLY WANTED TO GIVE KATE THE time she needed away from him, so he was worried she'd be annoyed with him once she saw him at her place despite the reason he was there. He couldn't believe it when he saw her cheerfully taking Foxy to the bathhouse to wash her.

He enjoyed washing Foxy with Kate. She was fun to be with. He couldn't imagine being with another woman who would have been eager to help out either. She genuinely cared about dogs, and Foxy had seemed to win her over. He really hadn't intended for her to help brush Foxy out either, but since they were going to be enjoying drinks with the others, he figured he might as well comb her out at the same time. He liked doing things, staying active. He got a kick out of Spirit wanting to join Foxy and get a bath too and then sitting there, waiting to get brushed.

After he and Kate finished brushing Foxy, Kate began to brush out Spirit, and Derek helped comb Spirit out too.

Everyone was talking about the camping trip coming up on Friday afternoon.

"Be sure to bring your favorite fishing gear," Ryder said. "It's going to be perfect for it."

"Yeah, got it planned," Derek said.

"Me too," Kate agreed. "Is Holly going to be all right going camping?"

"Yeah, she says she is. At least if she has the babies at the campsite, Aidan is a doctor, and he can deliver them. Though since Holly is too, I can just imagine her giving Aidan guidance," Lexi said.

Everyone laughed.

"She's going to have them as a wolf, right?" Derek asked, thinking that as a wolf, it would be easier to transport them home if she did deliver during the campout. And easier for her to deliver them too.

"Yeah, so it will be a lot easier for her," Lexi said. "But she said she hasn't been having any contractions and hasn't dilated, so she believes she'll be fine. She's due in a couple of weeks, but they're full term now, so if she has them early, they should be okay. They're taking lots of extra gear for her so she will be comfortable—an air mattress, cotton sheets and sleeping bags, extra fleece blankets and comforters to keep her warm, pillows, and a waterproof tent. She loves to camp and hike, and she's in great shape. They're also bringing old quilts in case she does have the babies at the campout. If she feels uncomfortable, Aidan will take her home."

"She's braver than me," Kate said.

Derek smiled at her.

Kate blushed again.

But Derek did agree. He would have preferred something closer to home if his mate was that far along.

After they finished their drinks, they got ready to go home. Derek wanted to walk Kate back home. It was the gentlemanly thing to do, and he wanted to anyway.

Cliff and Will asked, "Do we return home as wolves or humans?"

"Human. We can return the board shorts to them tomorrow. We won't shed in Mike's car then," Derek said. "Of course, Foxy will, but you won't have three wolves that shed too." Then Derek started walking back with Kate to her house.

"You don't have to come with me," she said.

He hoped she wasn't saying she didn't want him to see her any farther, but he wasn't about to let her walk home alone after all she'd done for Foxy, not to mention he wanted to kiss her goodbye. "I want to. Thanks for taking care of Foxy. She looks great."

Kate smiled. "She needed the bath. I wasn't sure she would want it. Some dogs don't like to be bathed."

"She loves any attention she can get." Since Kate had put on the brakes with him this week, Foxy's bringing them together made him want to remind her of his schedule for next week, just because he wanted to see more of her but had to be out of town and didn't want her to believe he wasn't interested in seeing her during the week. "I'll be going to Colorado Monday through Thursday with Rafe to that business conference. You wouldn't happen to be free and want to join me, would you?"

She chuckled. "I'll be busy. But thanks for the offer. Maybe if I'm on a trip sometime, you can go with me."

"Believe me, I'm all for it."

"If I have more notice on a different trip of yours, I can work it out with Lexi."

He wanted to pump his fist in victory. "Okay, great. Or even better yet, we could skip the business trips altogether and just go somewhere for fun."

"Like that trip to Hawaii?"

"Hell, yeah. Just the two of us. Though the trip is all-inclusive, I'll add a bunch of extra excursions onto it. Like a snorkeling trip to explore the coral reefs and see the marine life, swimming in a pool with the dolphins, and trips to the other islands."

She smiled. "That sounds wonderful. What if you were still with Brenda?"

"I doubt we would have stayed together long enough for me to have taken her on that trip or any other. I might have even gifted it to someone else. Just so you know, I've never offered to take any of my former girlfriends on a business trip with me."

"That's good to know. Truly, I would go with you on the Colorado trip, but I have my own work cut out for me."

"Okay, well, the other thing is I have a roaring twenties ball to go to on Friday night after I return. It's a different charity event."

"How many of these things do you go to?"

"I don't have any more scheduled for a couple of months, but these all seemed to come up at the same time. I would love to take you to it. I know I should have asked you earlier."

She laughed. "You were afraid I would say no, but I love themed dances. I'll go with you."

"Hot damn!" He was so glad he'd asked her, and she'd said yes! "I'll send you the invite as soon as I get home."

"You mean Brenda didn't get it?"

Derek smiled. "Nope. I had planned to give it to her Friday night at the gala, but then she called it quits on me. So that was the end of that. At the time, I thought I hadn't seen the writing on the wall, but thinking back on it, I hadn't given her the invite yet, and normally I would have asked if she would have liked to go. But it sounded like something I would like to do, even if she hadn't wanted to attend it with me. Though I'm sure if I said I was going, she would have gone, just to make sure I wasn't looking for her replacement. For some reason, I just held the invitation back."

"Oh, good, so she won't be there because she won't know you're even going this time."

"Hopefully not." Now he was really glad he hadn't invited Brenda because the invite was truly going to Kate and it wasn't a secondhand invite this time. He knew he would have a great time with her.

"Do you know how to dance the Charleston?" Kate asked. "Lexi and I practiced dancing the period dances with Mike and Ryder while watching YouTube video lessons."

"I sure do. Rafe and his brother and their mates got me involved in doing the same thing—watching videos to learn how to do the dances in anticipation of going to this themed dance. We were sure laughing. Did you learn other dances?"

"Yep, the Lindy Hop and the foxtrot too. We'll dance the night away."

He was so glad, though he would have enjoyed teaching her how to dance to the tunes if she hadn't known how. "We'll have a great time." Yeah, he'd made the right choice that time!

When they reached Kate's house, Derek waited to see if she wanted him to kiss her in case she still needed some distance between them. She smiled up at him, looking like she was expecting him to.

He placed his hands on her shoulders and leaned down and kissed her then.

She kissed him back like she was rethinking

his going home with the dog and his bodyguards tonight. But he figured until the camping trip, he would give her the space she needed.

"I'll try to keep Foxy home. But it might mean you need to visit me more often."

She laughed. "Did you put her up to it?"

He chuckled. "It was well worth the trek here, though I wouldn't want her putting herself in danger. But seeing you tonight? That made the trip here even more worthwhile."

This time, he didn't feel the need to have to see her on Thursday night before the campout. Everything seemed to be fine between them and he couldn't have been more glad for that.

He wondered if she'd seen the tabloids that featured him and Kate kissing when he'd won the trip to Hawaii for two and they were sitting across from a scowling Brenda and her date. "In with the New, Out with the Old," the tabloid had said. He hadn't planned to bring it up if it was something that would bother Kate. He'd told his staff not to mention it to Mike or Kate either! If she brought it up, that was different.

———

It was finally Friday night, and the camping trip was going to be a blast. Just hiking, running as wolves, fishing, and visiting with each other around the campfire telling tales at night. No work. It would drive Kate crazy. Here she thought Lexi was the workaholic and she always—oh, wait, they were going to do a video for a commercial. Kate smiled. She knew Lexi wouldn't stop working.

At Lexi and Ryder's estate, Derek drove up in his Land Rover and parked behind Rafe and Jade's truck and Aidan and Holly's vehicle. They were going in four vehicles because they were each taking their bodyguards with them. Kate was going to ride with Lexi, Ryder, and Mike, but Derek said, "Hey, Kate, since it's just me, Will, and Cliff, we have plenty of room in the Land Rover if you want to join us."

Everyone was casting Kate and Derek glances, not saying anything, thankfully, just loading extra ice chests of food into Lexi's and Derek's vehicles. Kate knew they were all speculating about whether things were getting more serious between her and Derek.

"Um, sure," Kate said. "I'll go with you."

"There goes my tent mate," Mike said, sighing.

"In your dreams," Kate said.

Mike laughed. Derek smiled thankfully.

Kate climbed into Derek's car. It wasn't like she and Derek were taking a private drive to the campsite—not when his two bodyguards were sitting in the Land Rover in the back seat.

Then the caravan of vehicles headed to the Sequoia National Forest to camp.

Four hours later, they arrived at a beautiful campsite surrounded by redwoods that was situated near a river perfect for fishing. They all set up their tents first thing, and Kate was pleased with how much Derek wanted to help her with hers instead of just working on his own tent. She could do this on her own just fine, but she didn't mind the help. She was glad she and he had separate tents for the campout when all their friends were here, watching everything they did and said. No way did she want to make love to Derek while trying to be quiet about it.

After they put up her tent, she went to help him erect his, amused he was setting it right next to hers as if they were together.

Kate heard Rafe and Jade's four-year-old son, Toby, fussing because he had wanted to put up his junior-sized tent next to his parents' so he could sleep there and not in their tent tonight.

Rafe said, "Bears might come into the campsite, so you need to stay safe and sleep in our tent tonight. But tomorrow, if you want to take a nap in your tent, you can."

"I don't need a nap," Toby said.

Kate smiled. She'd been over to Rafe and Jade's house when Toby was taking one of those unnecessary naps!

Still, the mention of bears coming into camp in the middle of the night seemed to convince Toby he didn't want to sleep in his tent alone at night.

After everyone's tents were set up, they began rustling up some sticky chicken with barbecue sauce that Maddie had prepared for them the night before. They grilled the chicken over hot coals for dinner while they relaxed on camp chairs, enjoying the setting sun as it cast yellow, orange, and pink hues against the clouds. Now this was nice, Kate thought, a gathering of the wolf pack on a camping trip.

The last time Kate had been camping with Lexi, it had been in a nice clean cabin. It was interesting to see how everyone would act toward each other on a camping trip. Everyone worked well together, some cooking, some getting more firewood, Rafe starting the fire. Kate thought it was so sweet of Maddie to send dessert with them and to also send breakfast for tomorrow.

"This was a surprise," Rafe said. "It appears Maddie wanted to make an impression. She made a great one."

"Oh, yes," Holly said. "I can't wait to eat the apple and blueberry pies."

"After dinner and the sun sets completely, are we going for a wolf run?" Derek asked.

"Yeah," Rafe said. "I think breaking up the pack would be a good idea, though I imagine no humans will be out and about stumbling around in the dark. But we should limit it to three or four of us in a group."

Everyone agreed with Rafe for safety's sake.

Derek knew who he wanted to be with on the wolf run and glanced at Kate. She smiled at him, and he figured that meant she was agreeable. He pulled out the thermos of mint lemonade Maddie had made for everyone and began pouring it into cups. Maddie had even sent sprigs of mint to garnish the drinks.

"You should have brought Maddie with you," Holly said, "for as much as she prepared the food for our camping trip."

"She doesn't care for camping, but she loves cooking. She has to sleep on an ultrasoft bed at night, doesn't like bugs, and loves the ocean breezes. Besides, when we're gone, she goes swimming in the pool and enjoys relaxing on the patio," Derek said. "She has run of the whole house then, and she loves it. When we're away, she often house-sits and helps take care of the dogs."

"Okay, well, that's good then," Lexi said.

When they went running as wolves after dinner, Derek and Kate went with Cliff and Will and were having a great time, smelling the scent of the red-woods, rabbits, and squirrels. They finally reached a river and drank from it. Then they were off and running again. About an hour later, they saw flash-lights in the woods. Humans weren't supposed to be out here.

Two men were walking off-trail, and the wolves scattered, but not before the one guy said to the other, "Hey, did you just see a pack of wolves over in that direction?" He directed his light at the place where the wolves had been as Kate watched them, hidden in the ferns.

"No. A whole pack? You had too much beer to drink."

"No, really. I know my dogs, and those weren't dogs. There were five or six of them. When they saw us, they took off running."

Five or six of them? There were only the four of them if the man had even seen that many.

"Well, good thing for us," the other guy said, laughing. As if he didn't believe his friend had seen anything. "Come on. Let's do our business and get back to camp before the wolves attack."

"You joke about it, but I know what I saw."

Which meant the one guy might report it. Would anybody believe him? Hopefully not, Kate thought. Actually, if they did report where they'd seen them, they would have to say they hadn't been on the human trails. The wolves were way off the designated trails, so the men could get in trouble with the park rangers.

Kate had lost Derek and his bodyguards when they had all scattered to hide. But once they were out of the men's sight, Kate and the others regrouped. They could still hear them talking in the woods, especially since they were speaking louder than normal. They were probably afraid the wolves were real and would come back to attack them unless they scared them off with their boisterous voices.

Derek checked her over, and she did likewise with him, just a natural instinct, wolf greetings all around with Cliff and Will too. They heard the men noisily moving through the underbrush, headed back to the trail. Then the wolves loped through the ferns to their campsite.

———

The others arrived right after Derek and Kate and his bodyguards did, and they all started going into their tents. Derek licked Kate's face to say he'd had an enjoyable run with her as a wolf, and she rubbed her face against his to tell him she did too. Then they went inside their tents.

After a few minutes, everyone emerged from their tents, dressed and ready to have some hot cocoa by the fire before they said good night— except for Toby, who had retired to his parents' tent and fallen sound asleep.

"We saw people in the woods off-trail," Kate said. "One of them saw us."

"The other guy didn't believe him. He said he'd had too many beers," Derek said.

"True. When we run tomorrow night, we'll have to avoid that area." Kate told them where they had been in relation to one of the trails.

"Well, we didn't run into anything. Too bad we all weren't there to see the guys too. Then they would have really been impressed." Lexi smiled.

Derek got a text and looked at his phone. He was surprised to see it was from Brenda.

Brenda: Hey, Derek, I'm going car shopping on Sunday. Did you want to go with me to check them out? You're so good with getting the best deals on a car.

Derek texted: You just got a car six months ago.

Brenda: Yes, but I found something I really want.

Derek: I'm busy.

Brenda texted: What are you doing?

Didn't Brenda have a clue Derek wasn't seeing her any further? He glanced up at the others, but they were talking about fishing tomorrow and what they could catch.

"You can't catch trout but an hour before sunrise or an hour after sunset." Kate glanced at Derek, though she tried to ignore the texts he was getting.

It had to irk her. It annoyed him for certain.

"Right, so we can fish for the black bass and bullhead," Rafe said.

Derek texted: I'm camping. Got to go.

Brenda: Camping? Where?

Derek didn't respond, turned off his phone, and tucked it into his pocket.

"What did you add to the hot cocoa?" Kate asked Lexi.

"Red wine and double chocolate."

"Hmm, it's good."

"I'll say," Derek said. "Sorry about the texts. Brenda is under the assumption our relationship isn't over or that she can change my mind."

"She's more persistent than the others you have dated," Rafe said.

"Yeah, I agree. But there's no going back to the way it was with her again." Not to mention he totally planned to continue dating Kate after the campout if she was of the same mind.

———————

After drinking their cocoa, they finally said their good nights. Kate kissed Derek briefly and said good night to him like all the others, and then everyone retired to their tents. She didn't invite Derek into her tent though. She didn't know why she felt so vulnerable about showing affection toward him in front of her friends when she could do it at the charity events—except then, she was putting Brenda in her place.

As soon as she pulled off her clothes and put on a pair of sweats, Kate was already thinking about Derek sleeping alone in his tent and how much she wished he was sleeping with her in her tent!

Kate was quickly falling for the wolf. She almost wished she could go with him to Colorado and make wild and passionate love to him the whole time there—after his meetings, of course.

She finally fell asleep, but later that night, she was awakened by the sound of scratching at her tent, and then she heard snuffling. Taking a deep breath, she smelled a raccoon. *Great.* She'd forgotten to spread chili powder outside her tent. She usually slept in a cabin and didn't have any trouble like this. But she'd read that chili powder could help send raccoons packing because they didn't like the strong chili odor.

She knew not to have food in the tent because of the bears. She had to be careful not to have scented stuff, like toothpaste, deodorant, or even scented toilet paper or tissue papers that could attract them. The raccoons could open trash cans, bags, and even ice chests!

All the wolves had left their ice chests in the vehicles just for safekeeping. Their food was in the bear lockers that the raccoons couldn't get into either.

She shined her flashlight at the critter and saw its eyes glowing fluorescent. She could have seen the raccoon anyway with her wolf night vision, but the light was supposed to make them go away. For a minute, it did. But then the raccoon came back as soon as she turned off her light. She couldn't keep this up all night long. She'd read where a camper could growl like a cougar or howl like a coyote, but she didn't want to start howling like a wolf and wake everyone—wait—wouldn't *being* a wolf deter him?

Yep! She pulled off her sweats, shifted into a wolf, but realized she had forgotten to unzip the tent. She shifted back, unzipped the tent, and swore the raccoon was going to come right in as if she were inviting it in. She shifted, bared her teeth, and growled. She'd heard that sometimes humans doing that *wouldn't* be a deterrent though. But as a wolf, even better! As soon as she growled, the raccoon jumped straight in the air and took off running.

Satisfied that her little maneuver seemed to work, she smiled and figured she would sleep as a wolf the rest of the night, just in case the raccoon returned.

Then she heard rustling in the tent next to hers—Derek's—and he came out of it as a wolf and nosed her. He could smell that the raccoon had been there too.

She was glad she wasn't the only one to have heard the raccoon. Or maybe Derek had just heard her growling as a wolf and come to investigate. She nuzzled him, and then she returned to her tent, wanting to get some sleep.

Derek curled up outside her tent, and she

wanted to laugh. Tonight, he was going to be *her* wolf bodyguard. That worked for her. Though she was again thinking she should just invite him in. But if he needed reinforcements, she would be out there with him in a flash.

———————

Derek had heard a raccoon outside Kate's tent trying to get in, and he'd heard her unzip her tent after that. He hadn't expected to her to turn all wolf. But he didn't want her to have to deal with the raccoon the rest of the night. Let the raccoon return to face *him* the next time.

In his warm wolf coat, he was fine sleeping outside her tent. A few times, he heard something moving around in the trees surrounding their tents. One time he saw Rafe leave his tent and smiled when he saw Derek sleeping as a wolf in front of Kate's tent.

Rafe saluted him, went off into the woods toward the toilets, and then returned a few minutes later and waved good night.

Then Derek finally fell asleep. He woke a few times and finally must have fallen asleep for the last time when Kate emerged from her tent and smiled at him. "Thanks so much for protecting me from the raccoon last night."

He gave her a little woof, saying she was welcome,

and then he returned to his tent so he could shift, dress, and join the others for the day's activities, glad he had been the one to protect her last night.

CHAPTER 17

THAT MORNING, THE LADIES WERE PLANNING the breakfast while the guys were building the fire. "We're going to make breakfast burritos, if that's what everybody wants," Kate said. "Maddie was so sweet and sent all the ingredients along." She smiled at Derek.

"Yeah, that would be great," Derek said. "What can we do to help?"

"We've got breakfast if you guys can catch fish for lunch," Lexi said.

"We'll sure do that," Aidan said.

In a large cast-iron pan, Lexi cooked sausage until crisp. Then Lexi and Kate whisked together eggs, salt, and pepper; cooked and then spooned the sausage-and-egg mixture onto the center of each tortilla; and sprinkled cheese on top. Holly and Jade began rolling them up tight and wrapped them in some heavy-duty foil. Twenty minutes later, they were eating the breakfast burritos.

"This is so good," Ryder said.

"Yeah, I agree," Derek said. "We'll have to catch lots of fish for lunch."

Everyone agreed to that.

After they finished breakfast, cleaned up the dishes and cookware, and banked the campfire, some of them had planned to hike two hours out, which would make a four-hour round trip. They would be climbing around two hundred feet on the hike. Holly and Aidan would only take a short hike for as far as she felt comfortable walking, and Mike and Ryder carried any supplies she needed on the trail. Likewise, Rafe and Jade would hike only as far as Toby could make it.

Once everyone had their backpacks and was ready, they headed out together.

The forest was the largest old-growth redwood forest in the entire world—the forest primeval. Fog created a lush carpet of greenery under the lofty, fairy-tale redwoods, sunshine peeking through the treetops. On this hot, sunny day, it was great for a hike for miles with natural shade. Ferns covered the forest floor, and everything was so lush and green. And on the path, a dense carpet of pine needles cushioned and silenced their footfalls.

This was just beautiful, and it was a completely different area than Kate and Lexi had been in before. She would love to go on hikes throughout the redwoods like this.

While they were hiking, they ran into some humans, and Kate recognized two of the men as the ones they had encountered while they were running as wolves. Two more men were with them, but as soon as the one who had observed them as wolves the last time saw them, he said, "Hey, have you been out here for a while?"

"Since yesterday," Kate said.

"Have you seen any sign of wolves out here? We saw a whole pack of them—six or seven at least."

The number of wolves he'd seen was increasing by the day.

"Not me. He did." The friend who had been with him sounded like he didn't want anyone to think he was nuts too.

"I'm a wolf biologist," Kate said, making up a story. "We haven't seen any signs of wolves out here. And they wouldn't have been running along a human trail. They would have avoided it and been far off the beaten path."

The one who had seen them glanced at the other men with him. They shrugged.

"All right. Well, if you see any, I saw them first," he said.

"You had too many beers," his friend said under his breath, looking irritated with his friend that he wouldn't drop the subject of the wolves.

"I'm sure the chance of that would be pretty slim, though I always keep my eye out for them," Kate said. "Now, bears have been spotted in the redwoods, so that's another story."

"Let's go find us some bears," the guy said.

The humans headed down the path in the direction Kate and her friends had come.

Kate and the other wolves were just talking about different topics for a while, but when they were far enough away from the other hikers, Lexi said, "Wolf biologist. Good to know."

"I'm using that line the next time I need to educate someone about the habits of wolves," Rafe said.

Everyone laughed.

When they returned from the hike, Rafe said, "Let's go fishing so we have enough time to catch something for lunch." Toby was so excited to go fishing with his daddy that he was standing there with a pint-sized fishing pole in hand before Rafe had managed to get his gear ready. Toby had long, blond curls. His mother, Jade, hadn't wanted to cut them, though they were going for his first haircut next week, Jade had said. His brown eyes were alight with excitement, and he was ready to dash off to the river as soon as anyone else was ready to go.

"You guys go ahead," Ryder said. "Mike and I will help the ladies get set up for their video."

"I'll also help to make things go more quickly. Are you going to fish with us afterward?" Derek asked Kate, setting up the seating.

"We'll see." Kate loved doing things with the ladies, so this was as much their time to play with each other as it was doing things together as a group.

Before the guys who were going fishing left, they gave their mates kisses, and Toby hurried to give his mom a hug and kiss, nearly hooking her with his fish-hook. Then Toby and the others were off to the river.

Once Derek, Mike, and Ryder finished helping the ladies set things up for the video session, Ryder kissed Lexi before he joined the others to fish. Kate gave Derek a look that said she wasn't his mate and don't even think about it after he helped her set things up.

He winked at her, casting her a sexy smirk, pulled off his T-shirt, slung it over his bare, bronzed, and muscled shoulder, and waved at the ladies on his way out.

As soon as the guys were out of earshot, Lexi fanned herself. "Hot."

"I thought it was comfortable out," Kate said.

Holly and Jade laughed.

"Oh, you mean…" Kate didn't finish what she was going to say, her face flushing with heat instantly as everyone got into position and Lexi readied herself to start talking about the new line.

"Yeah, that's who I mean," Lexi said. "Don't worry about what everyone's thinking concerning the two of you. You just enjoy yourself. If it doesn't work out between you two, no big deal. You'll have dates galore."

Kate didn't want dates galore. She liked some normalcy in her life.

Then they got to the business of filming the video. It was fun hearing the birds chirping and singing to each other in the foliage in the background for the video as Lexi cleaned Jade's face and then Holly's with one of her gentle skin cleansers.

In the middle of the video while Lexi was applying makeup to Jade's face, they heard Rafe shout, "Holy hell!"

Kate stopped the video. She figured Rafe wouldn't have shouted out like that unless it was something bad, knowing it could affect their video.

"Ha! Go away! Get!" Derek said, and the others were yelling too.

Okay, so the situation was serious. The ladies waited. Some of the bodyguards were there with them, but two of them rushed off to check out the problem and let them know what was going on. Then Lexi got a call. She put it on speaker.

"Hey, sorry if we interrupted your video. We have a little bit of a bear issue right now," Ryder said.

"No, no, it's no problem at all. Is everyone all right there?" Lexi asked.

Kate immediately headed for the tent. She couldn't do a very good job as a bodyguard against a bear unless she was a wolf.

For years, Derek had gone fishing with Rafe and Aidan. In all that time, they'd only encountered bears on maybe five separate occasions. They hadn't worried about bears too much because the fish were plentiful and the bears would just go fishing. Even though they were fuzzy and round and cuddly looking, they spent their days climbing steep hillsides and moving about the redwoods, which made them incredibly muscled and strong. He'd even seen one clinging to a dead tree about five feet off the ground while he pulled off tree bark and ate a meal of insects. But this bear had come down to fish where they were fishing, and they had to let him know he was in their territory right now to scare him off upriver or downriver from where they were located.

But first, Derek was trying to get Toby's fishhook out of Rafe's shirt where he'd caught it as soon as they saw the bear. Rafe was more worried about Toby, who was wide-eyed as he watched the bear.

Derek was trying not to tear Rafe's shirt. "Hold still, will you? You're worse than a little kid."

"Not me, Uncle Derek," Toby said.

Smiling at Toby, Derek was glad Cliff and Will had stayed back with the women to make sure they stayed safe. What he hadn't expected was for Kate to join them as a wolf to protect them. He could see she wasn't giving up her bodyguard role no matter what the situation entailed. Her fur was standing on end, bristling, her tail out straight. He admired her protectiveness and dedication.

He finally freed the hook from Rafe's shirt and didn't leave too big a hole. He should have just cut the hook.

Acting as though he didn't have a care in the world, the bear sauntered off.

It was a good thing they had food storage lockers at all the individual sites because of the bear problem the park was having.

Right now, Derek was ready to protect *Kate* if she decided to go after the bear! He was only wearing a pair of shorts and hiking shoes and socks, having dropped his T-shirt on top of the ice chest to fish. He was glad he'd been fishing far enough away from Toby that he hadn't snagged Derek in the shoulder! So it wouldn't take much for Derek to strip off the rest of his clothes and shift into his wolf. The bear gave them a couple of backward glances, but he looked like he was sufficiently deterred from fishing in their spot.

Derek reached down and petted Kate's head, stealing her attention that had been totally focused on the bear. He smiled down at her, her eyes having a hint of blue, amber, and green, her coat shiny and gray on top, a darker saddle on her back, a tan underbelly coat and a tan-and-white face. Really striking.

She peered around at this side of the riverbank,

and he wondered what she was looking for. Then she smiled. Yeah, they hadn't caught any fish yet. They had gotten distracted by one big, old black bear that probably weighed around 250 to 300 pounds.

Kate woofed at them to let them know she was returning to the campsite and then headed back through the woods.

Derek was thinking that he should stay in Kate's tent with her tonight, since she was the only woman who was alone, just in case a bear came into the camp. Two people made a better deterrent than one. Though he didn't want to suggest it while everyone was around in case it embarrassed her. He suspected, from the way she nonverbally had told him she wasn't interesting in having a goodbye kiss when he was about ready to go fishing with the other guys, that she wasn't ready to actually court him. Staying with him in the tent, for her protection as well as his own, probably wasn't going to happen.

He watched her until she disappeared into the woods. When he glanced at the other guys, they quickly switched their attention to the river and fishing.

"She noticed we hadn't caught any fish," Derek said.

"Yeah. I saw that right away," Rafe said. "Kate will tell the other ladies they'll have to help us catch lunch or we won't have any. Not that we don't have plenty of other food. You should offer to stay with her tonight. For protection against the bear if he should return."

"For me or for her?" Derek asked.

The guys all smiled.

"I would but—"

"Hey, Lexi kept turning me down," Ryder said, "until she realized I wasn't trouble. You just have to keep trying. Kate will let you know in no uncertain terms that you need to back off if she's truly not interested."

"Yeah, but I don't want to create a situation between us. We all get along, and I don't want her to feel uncomfortable around me when I'm doing things with you guys and she's also around." Derek cast his fishing line.

"Don't overthink it," Rafe said. "If it's meant to happen, it will."

CHAPTER 18

WHEN KATE RETURNED TO THE CAMPSITE AS A wolf, all eyes were upon her. She smiled and ducked into her tent. Then she shifted, dressed, and left the tent to continue with their video session. "Sorry. I had to help out if I could."

Lexi sighed. "As long as you and the others weren't hurt. I take it the bear moved off?"

"It did. Which is why we're back to this. The guys haven't caught one fish yet between the four of them. Though Toby caught his dad's shirt." Kate chuckled.

The ladies laughed.

Kate began to get ready to video record the session again.

"It's a good thing we brought ice chests full of food then," Lexi said, "just in case."

"Maybe we'll have to go as wolves and show them how it's done," Holly said.

"I'm all for it," Jade said, "as long as no one catches us at it. We don't want anyone to think someone brought a bunch of dogs to the campsite when they're not supposed to be here."

"Nah, if we got caught at it, that wouldn't be

good," Kate said. "If it was dark out, that would be different."

The ladies reluctantly agreed.

"I have some bad news," Holly said, looking at her phone. "It appears we're getting some rain in tonight instead of late tomorrow night like we thought. We'll have to eat dinner and go to bed early."

"Or we could run as wolves. Everyone at the campsites will be tucked inside their tents weathering the storm. But we can run as wolves as long as it's not too bad out—no lightning and thunder," Kate said.

"Yeah, sure, that would be fun," Jade said. "I'm all for it."

"Okay, so the bad weather can be a boon for us as far as running as wolves goes," Lexi said. "Is everyone ready to get back to work on the video?"

Everyone said, "Yes."

Once they had finished recording, Kate asked, "Do you want to compete with the guys at fishing now?"

"And upset the boat if we catch more fish than them?" Lexi asked.

The women all smiled at each other.

"Let's go fishing. At least if we all catch enough fish, we can cook them before the rain comes," Kate said.

"That works for me," Lexi said, and the ladies all

gathered their fishing gear and headed off for the river.

When the guys saw them coming, they smiled.

"Kate said you hadn't caught anything when she came to chase off the bear." Lexi gave Ryder a hug.

"I caught one," Rafe said, hugging Jade.

"Mine's bigger," his brother, Aidan, said.

"I caught Daddy," Toby said.

Everyone laughed.

Kate noticed everyone was keeping their distance from Toby.

Aidan and Holly kissed.

Kate glanced at Derek. He smiled at her. "I was waiting for you to arrive so I would have better luck."

After several of them eventually caught enough black bass and bullhead, they headed back to the campsite, and Kate loved it that the guys cleaned the fish, filleted them, and grilled them in foil packets with potatoes, carrots, and white-wine-and-garlic sauce over the fire. They had apple pie and blueberry pie for dessert, courtesy of Maddie.

After lunch, Holly said, "I don't know about the rest of you, but I'm taking a nap."

Kate couldn't imagine being out here, carrying twins so late in her pregnancy. Holly had to be exhausted, though she looked great.

In the meantime, Rafe was setting up Toby's play tent so he could take a nap too.

"It's daytime," Toby said. "The sun's still out."

"You don't have to close your eyes, but you have to lie down and rest," Jade said. "Come on. Mommy will lie down with you."

"But we don't go to bed until it's dark out."

"I'll race you to the tent." Jade started to move in that direction, and Toby ran for the tent.

Everyone else watched the interaction, learning what they would have to do with a young one to get him or her to nap for a while when they had their own or they had to take care of Toby. Then Toby ducked inside the tent, and Jade joined him.

Kate thought Jade would leave the tent after a while, but she must have fallen asleep.

Kate and the others took a short walk away from the campsite so they could let Holly, Jade, and Toby sleep without disturbing them while Aidan and Holly's bodyguards remained with them to keep them safe.

Later, they sat around the campfire telling stories, real and imagined.

They had Dutch oven mac and cheese for dinner.

Once they finished eating and cleaning up, they ditched their clothes in their tents, shifted, and then bolted out of their tents to run as wolves. The wolves ran mostly in groups of four, so Derek and his bodyguards went off-trail with Kate again. Holly and her mate and bodyguards would only go as far as she felt comfortable running as a wolf, and

Rafe and Jade would return when Toby ran out of steam.

Not long after that, the rain started, and Kate lifted her head and caught the rainwater on her tongue. Derek was beside her in the next instant, brushing up against her as the light rain intensified.

Rain clouds filled the night sky, way up above the giant redwoods. Between the shelter of the trees and their double-fur coats, they were staying relatively dry. Running through the thick coastal fog made it more intriguing too. Being with Derek was enjoyable, better than running with Mike on this journey and serving as bodyguard backup. She enjoyed being with Mike, but he was like a brother to her, not a mate prospect.

She and Derek bumped against each other in playful fun, but then they saw the fluorescent glow of eyes in the woods off to the north. A tawny-colored cougar. When the cougar saw all the wolves, it turned and bounded off.

Wow, first a bear and now a cougar? She'd remembered reading that one hiker had sighted a bear every day for the five days he and his friends were hiking. Yet luckily they hadn't had any face-to-face encounters with them.

After about a half hour of running, they headed back to the campsite. Kate was happily tired and ready to call it a night. It had been a really great day.

Derek was having a blast running with Kate. She was cute, licking at the rain as it fell through the trees, shaking water on him during a heavier downpour. He could have laughed. It was such an automatic reaction as he shook off his excess water back on her and she nipped at him in playful fun.

Again, he wished they could share a tent, his or hers, but he assumed she wasn't ready for that. Certainly not with all her friends here. Now if he'd just come out with her camping alone, then it most likely would have been a different story.

They finally reached their campsite, shifted outside their tents, and then ducked inside before they got too wet. They wouldn't be having hot cocoa with wine at the campfire tonight.

"Night, Kate," Derek said from his tent next to hers.

"Night, Derek."

As if this were the end of one of the episodes of the television series *The Waltons*, everyone began saying good night to the rest of their friends in the different tents, and that had everyone laughing.

Finally, everyone settled down to sleep, but all Derek could think about was what he could come up with to do with Kate for future dates. His life had become more interesting with her in it by leaps and bounds.

The rain was really letting loose now, and he was glad they had erected tarps to help keep the tents dry from the deluge.

He brought out his phone and checked the weather again. It looked like they would be socked in all night, but tomorrow morning it was clearing. Maybe they could go for a swim before sunrise as wolves and then return to their tents to make breakfast when the rain quit.

He got a text from Brenda then: Hey, I've got a luncheon to go to on Monday and we can bring someone with us. Would you like to come with me? I had planned for you to go with me until...well, you know.

Derek: Sorry. I have other plans.

Derek wanted to ask Brenda why she didn't take the guy she had been with at the gala with her, but he didn't want to have any more dialogue with her than what he'd already had. He turned off his phone, set it next to his sleeping bag, and thought about walking Foxy and Red on the beach with Kate; about her taking down the teen who was trying to steal the guy's beach bag; about Kate knocking Derek to the dance floor when she was protecting him from the supposed gunman at the gala. He still couldn't believe she'd been carrying a gun under that beautiful gown the whole time he'd been dancing with her. It was a good thing *she* wasn't dangerous to be around. Taking pictures of the two of them while feeding the giraffe and the kisses and more that they had shared came to mind. He even wanted to give her a decent foot massage again. Several! Then her arriving as a wolf at the river, ready to tackle the bear on her own. Yeah, Kate was definitely fun to be with.

The rain continued to come down, and he closed his eyes. This was the best camping trip ever. He was so glad she had invited him to come.

———

Rainwater continued to pour down during the night, and a stream of it had formed a gully right beneath Kate's tent. She only realized it when the bottom of her tent filled up with water, soaking her sleeping bag and backpack inside the tent. Oh, wet, cold, awful! When they'd set up the tents, they had made sure to watch for drainage, but they hadn't been prepared for the rain to be this severe or to last this long. She stripped off her soaking-wet pajamas, unzipped her tent, and shifted into her wolf to keep dry, her fur coat warming her. Then she left the tent to see what she had to deal with. Like moving her tent in the dead of the night in the pouring rain. But she couldn't do it in her wolf coat. The next best thing was to find someone else's tent to slip into. The other tents were farther away, and no one was stirring, so she assumed they were dry.

The closest tent was Derek's. She noted he'd picked a better spot and the stream of water was only hitting her tent!

She was sure he would let her sleep with him, though her outer coat would be wet, and she would try not to instinctively shake it off once she got inside his tent. Mike's tent was off on the other side of the campsite. What the hell. *You only live once.*

She realized, as she approached Derek's tent, that the flap was zipped closed. She didn't want to disturb anyone else, and she knew if she woofed, even as lightly as she could, she would probably wake most of her friends. She pawed at Derek's tent instead, but she was afraid he might think it was the bear that had come calling. Or a raccoon. Or maybe with the roaring rain, he didn't hear her as he slept.

Her outer guard hairs were getting wetter, and she didn't want to just shift and unzip his tent and barge in, but she had to be a little more aggressive in her approach. Whining and whimpering weren't her style. Even a little woof could be too loud. She opted for a low, soft growl.

She heard stirring and saw a flashlight go on, and then Derek moved around in his tent, his light directed at his tent flap. She waited. He paused. She growled softly again in the event he had only thought he had heard something at his tent. He wouldn't recognize her growl since she'd never growled around him before. But he would know she was a wolf by her growl. Oh, wait, she'd growled at the raccoon, and he'd heard it.

She did have the fleeting concern that he might be a grouch when she woke him, so it would be a test to see how he would react too!

He unzipped the tent flap...*finally*, shining the darn flashlight in her eyes. "Kate?"

She barged into his tent without invitation and fought shaking off her wet fur. He quickly closed his tent and handed her his towel. She shifted and wrapped it around herself, shivering. "Sorry. Your tent was closest. Mine is full of water."

He quickly pulled on a pair of boxer briefs. "Oh, no. Okay. You can have the sleeping bag."

He was trying to be a gentleman about this when she was just cold and wet and wanted his arms around her. "Your sleeping bag is big enough for two. We can share. It's too cold to sleep without a sleeping bag."

"I could shift into my wolf and let you sleep in the sleeping bag by yourself if you would like."

"No way."

"Okay, did you want to wear a pair of my sweats?"

"I think you could warm me up faster if we're skin to skin."

He smiled, rather wolfishly. Yeah, he had her number. "Sure, come on. Get in."

She had never expected to be sharing a tent and a sleeping bag with Derek with all her friends here.

"I thought from the lay of the land our tents were safe, should it rain." She dropped the damp towel and slipped into the bag with him, feeling warmer right away.

"You're shivering." He wrapped his arms around her as she rested her back against him. "I thought the same or I would have suggested locating yours somewhere else. Then again, the rains weren't supposed to come until tomorrow night, well after we were gone. I wasn't expecting this much rainfall."

"Well, every campout can be an adventure. I hope that my tent is the only one that is submerged. Thanks for sharing your tent and sleeping bag with me." She was really grateful he'd let her inside and was willing to share his sleeping bag with her. Especially since she'd let him know she wanted to keep some sense of distance between them.

"That's what friends are for."

She knew without a doubt she wanted to be more than friends. She turned in his arms and kissed him.

He kissed her back.

"You know what they say about imminent danger," she whispered, not wanting to wake anyone up.

"What do they say?" he asked, smiling at her, kissing her temple.

"It's an aphrodisiac."

He chuckled. "I don't know about that, but

being with you like this is certainly an aphrodisiac for me."

"Hmm." She kissed him again, and he cupped her face and kissed her back, his tongue slipping into her mouth and stroking hers with long, deliberate strokes. Now she was really heating up.

His hands moved to her breasts, and he caressed them with a light touch as if waiting for her response; then she kissed him back, hotly, passionately. Oh, yeah, the adrenaline was flowing now. She would never think of camping out in the same way again.

She sighed and gentled her kisses, not wanting to take this too far because she could just imagine the sticky mess in his sleeping bag if they pleasured each other while having unconsummated sex when she was just getting warm and dry. Now if they were mated and could have consummated sex? That was a whole other story.

She settled against him, her head on his chest, her arm draped over his stomach, feeling wonderful like this. In fact, *better* than if she'd been alone in her tent, if her sleeping bag had been dry and she could have slept there. There was something comforting about him, more than just his offer to keep her warm and dry. Something deeper—a personal connection between wolves that was undeniable. An intimacy that she wanted to share. Just with him, no one else. In a way, she wished he didn't need bodyguards, that they could be alone, that he didn't have so much money, that they could just follow their instincts, wolf and otherwise. But when she was with him at social functions, she felt like she had to play a role, and she didn't want that. She wanted to feel totally natural with him. Like she felt right now. She sighed and nuzzled her cheek against his chest. Beautiful. He was beautiful.

He stroked her shoulder and back in a comforting way, and she loved how tender he was with her. She wanted the contact as much as she loved kissing him, but kissing would have led to too much. This was so nice.

Then they got quiet, needing to sleep so they would be ready for the rest of their camping adventure, though tomorrow she would have to try to dry out her tent and sleeping bag before they took them home. She could imagine getting everybody else's stuff wet with her things piled on top of them in the Land Rover otherwise. At least they were leaving tomorrow afternoon after lunch so she wouldn't need to sleep in the tent again this weekend. Though now she didn't want to sleep anywhere else but with Derek, she decided.

She might be warmer, snuggling with Derek like this, but being with him truly wasn't conducive to sleep. He felt good wrapped around her in a loving embrace, and she couldn't quit thinking about where she wanted this to go with him.

Kate was proud of having come this far on her very own. Her parents had drummed into her when she was growing up to be financially independent of men so she never had to feel she had to mate one to survive. And she'd done that.

So why was she wanting something more with Derek? Something like this… God, this was nice. So what if he had money, bodyguards, a body like this, and his tender moves… She sighed. This couldn't have been more perfect.

The rain kept pounding the tarp above his tent, and she couldn't help but worry that the stream that had taken over her tent would widen and encompass his too. That had her on high alert, waiting for the rain to begin to fill his tent, soak his sleeping bag—and them.

But it never did.

CHAPTER 19

DEREK COULDN'T BELIEVE KATE WOULD COME to him in her hour of need. He guessed she didn't want to bother Mike, and his tent was a lot farther away. She couldn't have joined Lexi because she was comfortably sleeping with her mate unless Ryder had given up their tent to the two women and joined Mike. Derek was glad Kate felt comfortable enough to join him in his sleeping bag.

This was so nice—smelling her she-wolf scent, feeling her warm body against his. She'd finally stopped shivering, thankfully. The kissing, he thought, had really heated them both up. He hadn't expected her to kiss him like that, after the cooldown, and he'd wanted a whole hell of a lot more, just like they'd had before. He was glad when she tapered off on her kisses, signaling she wanted to end this before they let things get out of hand. Not that he wouldn't have been ready for it too. He was glad that she hadn't pulled away from him though and continued to snuggle with him. He'd never shared his sleeping bag with anyone before, and this felt just right.

Who wouldn't want the seductive she-wolf

wrapped in his arms like this on a cold and rainy night? He didn't even want to sleep. He just wanted to enjoy the closeness with her the rest of the night through. He did have the fleeting thought that he should wake her early if she wanted to get up before everyone else did, grab some of her clothes from her tent, and dress in his tent. But then he figured her clothes were wet too and she might not have anything dry to wear.

Between her warmth and the sleeping bag and the lulling rain, he finally fell asleep only to wake when he heard the sounds of others waking—low conversation, tent zippers unzipping, some gathering firewood. He realized then that the rain had stopped.

Derek wanted to get up, dress, and try to figure out what to do about Kate's clothes, but she was still sleeping soundly in his arms, and he didn't want to disturb her for anything.

He took a deep breath and let it out. He was courting the wolf for sure—if she was really agreeable to it this time. After a while, he smelled the smoke of the campfire going. His tent was light enough now that he knew it wasn't dusk any longer. He figured the others had decided not to go for a wolf run earlier this morning in the rain.

Since both Derek and Kate were absent, he assumed they all thought he and Kate were sleeping but still in their own tents, so everyone kept their voices low as they talked about the wild rainy night they'd had.

Finally, Kate stirred and lightly groaned. "I dreamed I'd ended up in your sleeping bag with you. I didn't think it had happened for real," she said softly.

"I hope it was a good dream, not a nightmare." He lightly kissed her forehead. Hadn't she remembered kissing him?

"As cold and wet as I was in my sleeping bag last night until I joined you and got warm and dry, it turned out to be a good dream." She didn't say anything more as they both listened to the conversation over the fire. "Ugh," she finally whispered. "It sounds like everyone is already up except for us."

"Yeah, sorry, Kate. I meant to get up early before everyone was awake and see if I could salvage any of your clothes."

"Everyone is going to know I slept in your tent." She sighed.

"I guess that means it's time to officially court each other."

"Yeah, I agree."

He was thrilled. He kissed her then, to seal the bargain, and she kissed him back.

"I have to admit that kissing you last night was nice. Really nice. So was snuggling, and if we wouldn't have made a mess of things in the sleeping bag, we could have done more." She took a deep breath and let it out. "I guess no one's going to leave the camp until after breakfast."

"I would have been all for doing more… And about the others leaving the campfire, I doubt it."

They could smell coffee, cocoa, eggs, bacon, and potatoes cooking over the campfire.

She sighed again. "All right, do you have anything for me to wear so I can try to get something out of my sopping-wet tent?"

"Yeah, the pair of sweats I mentioned to you last night, and I'll get your backpack out of your tent and bring it to mine to see if anything stayed dry."

"Thanks, Derek. I had packed clothes in plastic bags inside my backpack, but I was rummaging around in them during the day and might not have resealed them properly."

"If you had, that would be good." He left the warmth of his sleeping bag, but Kate didn't begin to get dressed. She had closed her eyes, and she looked perfectly happy to stay away from everyone else for the moment. He smiled, thinking he would love to keep her in his sleeping bag with him the rest of the day. "I'll be right back."

He unzipped his tent, and everyone looked in his direction and saluted him with mugs of coffee or hot cocoa. "Morning," he said. Then he walked the short distance to Kate's tent, saw the stream of water still coming down under her tent, and unzipped it. All conversation had stopped behind him. He ducked inside her tent, found her backpack sitting in water, and brought it out of the tent. He shook the water off it.

Lexi hurried over. "Kate's tent flooded last night?"

"Yeah. We need to dry out her tent and sleeping bag. I'm hoping she has something dry to wear in her backpack. She was going to wear a pair of my sweats for now."

"I have an extra pair of hiking shoes she can wear if she needs them. I always bring a couple of pairs in case one pair gets wet," Lexi said.

"I've got extra clothes too," Jade said.

"Me too," Holly said. "Well, maternity clothes."

Everyone laughed. But in a pinch, they were better than nothing, unless Kate wanted to be a wolf this morning.

Rafe and Ryder began pulling all Kate's things out of her tent to dry them. Aidan and Mike started to take down the tent.

Except for Jade, who was cooking the breakfast, Derek, who was delivering Kate's backpack to her, and Toby, who was still sleeping in his parents' tent, everyone pitched in to start laying out Kate's things to dry in the sun. It was still early morning, but hopefully everything would dry out before they left.

When Derek slipped back inside his tent carrying Kate's wet backpack, she was still naked in his sleeping bag.

"Are you okay?" He worried she might have gotten sick from being so chilled last night.

She gave him a warm smile. "Yeah, just feeling relaxed and lazy. Can you pull out the plastic bags of clothes in my backpack and see if any of my clothes are dry?"

Relieved she was okay, he unzipped her backpack and reached inside. "Your backpack is all wet inside, but the plastic bags that you packed your clothes in seem to have kept everything dry. I'll empty your plastic bags in here and take your backpack and everything that got wet out to dry."

"Thanks, Derek."

"You're welcome. If you didn't hear them already, everyone's offered you clothes, so if you need anything else, they've got you covered. Everyone's taking care of your wet tent and other items."

"Oh, good. I figured that was my next chore this morning."

"Nope, we're taking care of it." Then Derek left to help the others either cook breakfast or dry out Kate's things while she got dressed.

"Does she have shoes?" Lexi asked.

"Yes! She does," Kate said from inside Derek's tent. "Thank you!"

Lexi laughed.

Before long, Kate was leaving Derek's tent as everyone was just settling down to have breakfast and Toby had finally wiped the sleep out of his eyes, having smelled breakfast and joined them. He was cuddling against Jade.

"What a night," Kate said. "I didn't realize I would have a river running through my tent. It would have been better if I'd at least been sleeping on a cot. That'll teach me not to bring one next time. Poor Derek, since he'd pitched his tent so close to mine, I shifted into a wolf and bugged him. I didn't want to wake everyone else while I was trying to get his attention."

"I thought I heard a light scratching at my tent door. All I heard after that was the sound of the rain, and I figured I'd just imagined it." Derek ate a slice of bacon.

"I was afraid a low growl might have worried you, but I wasn't about to whimper or whine. Then you finally let this big wet wolf into your tent. Believe me, I had to really quash the urge to shake the water clinging to my fur off all over your tent," Kate said.

Everyone chuckled. They all knew how difficult that inborn habit was to break.

"I'm glad you didn't," Derek said.

"At least your tent was out of the path of the stream of water. I was afraid the stream would expand and fill your tent with water too, and we would have to join someone else in their tent," Kate said.

"I could have doubled up with someone else," Mike said, as if Derek and Kate were a couple and hadn't wanted to be split up.

"Everything will be dried out well before you know it," Lexi said. "But if you need anything, just let one of us know."

"I guess we missed our wolf run this morning." Kate sounded disappointed.

"It was still raining at dawn this morning. No one was feeling like leaving their tents, or we would have run anyway," Rafe said, assuring Kate she and Derek's getting up late hadn't had anything to do with them not running.

Aidan was smiling. "We were being a bunch of lazy wolves."

Holly said, "I needed the rest, truly."

"I'm glad you got it," Kate said.

They had done so much hiking and fishing and then running as wolves yesterday, Derek was glad they'd just chilled out this morning. Particularly since he got to stay with Kate longer in the sleeping bag.

Derek got a text message and pulled his phone out of his pocket. *Brenda.*

Brenda texted: I hope you stayed dry enough on your campout.

He felt she was rubbing it in that he'd gone camping, it had poured rain, and he probably was having a miserable time. But she didn't know anything about wolves.

He texted: I'm seeing someone else. I enjoyed our time together, but it's time for us to both move on.

He waited a moment, but Brenda didn't respond. Good. Maybe now she had gotten the message. He was about to pocket his phone when she texted again.

Brenda: Kate Hanover?

Derek turned off his phone and tucked it in his pocket.

"Brenda?" Kate asked and then ate some more of her eggs.

"Yeah. I told her I was seeing someone."

Kate raised a brow. He smiled.

"Okay, Derek asked me if he could court me, and I said yes. But he has to ditch the human first," Kate said.

Everyone chuckled.

Derek sighed. "Okay, I didn't want to tell Brenda I was going with you for sure until you were ready for us to tell our friends first."

"Good. You're free to tell her anytime."

Derek smiled. "Good." He was thrilled. Everyone else smiled and looked happy to hear the news too. "So are we still going on a hike this morning?" Derek asked.

"Yep, sounds good to me," Lexi said. "I need to get all the exercise I can in before I can't exercise because of carrying twins."

"Ha!" Holly said. "You can continue to exercise as you have done before. You do lots as a wolf already."

"What did your parents say about your babies, Lexi?" Kate asked.

"They'll both be here when the babies come, but they won't deliver them. Holly will. I'm having the babies as a wolf, so it really shouldn't be an issue," Lexi said.

Since Lexi's parents lived in Silver Town, Colorado, both doctors, but so far away, it was a good thing that Holly and Aidan were doctors too, who lived where they all did. If she had the babies as a wolf, even the new wolf vet could be there to ensure everything worked out for her.

Rafe said, "I'll send my private jet for your parents when you need them to come see you."

That was one thing Derek loved about his wolf friends. He didn't have his own jet, but if he ever needed to use one, Rafe would let him.

Derek was glad no one made a big deal about him dating Kate. Now that he'd shared with everyone, he would tell Brenda that he was indeed dating Kate and hopefully that would be the end of her pestering him about it. He was glad Kate had wanted to officially court him too.

He hoped Brenda didn't find someone to take her to the roaring twenties party. She had enough money to attend these functions on her own, but she preferred showing up on her date's dollar. He just didn't want to have to deal with her if she turned up there too.

"So is everyone up for a hike now?" Rafe asked.

"Yeah, we sure are," Holly said. "I'm sorry about your business with the flooded tent, Kate. Are you okay?"

"Oh, yeah, I'm fine," Kate said. "It's an adventure. That has never happened to me before, but it all worked out." She smiled at Derek. "He saved me from the cold and wet."

"I was glad to do my part." Derek smiled back at her.

Then they cleaned up the cooking ware and put the rest of the food away, packed their backpacks, and started their hike.

A couple of bodyguards led the group on the trail, while Holly and Aidan followed behind them to set the pace. Rafe, Jade, and Toby followed them; they would end up walking as slowly as Holly, especially since Toby kept checking out things on the trail—rocks, a banana slug, twigs, a snail—which they knew about because he was calling out all his finds.

Lexi and Ryder stayed back at the camp with Mike because she was tired and feeling nauseous.

Kate and Derek brought up the rear. She decided there was no way she was going camping if she were pregnant until she was through her first trimester and she would just stay in a cabin instead of the whole tent routine, especially after hers had flooded.

Holly suddenly stopped on the trail, and everyone behind her stopped. She was holding her belly, and Kate worried the babies were coming.

"Are you okay, honey?" Aidan's hand was on her back, rubbing gently.

"Um, I think it's time for me to return to the campsite."

"Can you walk okay?" he asked.

At least they had only just begun the hike and hadn't gone very far.

"Yeah, just—more slowly."

All of them turned around and headed back to camp because they wanted to be there to help out if the babies were coming.

"Do you want to shift into your wolf?" Aidan asked Holly.

She glanced up at him and frowned.

"I mean when we get back to camp."

"Yes. That would probably be the best idea."

"Are you having labor pains?"

"Yes, but they're far apart and not regular." Holly didn't sound concerned in the least.

"I think we should head home." Aidan sounded worried.

Kate suspected everyone felt the same way as Aidan did about Holly. Kate sure did.

"It's a four-hour trip," Holly reminded her mate.

"Right, but the babies might not come for hours." Aidan had his arm around Holly because she looked like she was afraid she was going to have the babies right on the path if she moved too quickly.

Toby raced ahead with Mike to reach the camp.

After that, they saw Ryder running to meet up with them. He looked as worried as everyone else did. "Toby said the babies are coming."

"Not yet," Holly said. "I'll shift into my wolf and hang around camp until we're ready to leave."

Kate thought Holly didn't want to ruin the campout for the others if she should go home now and everyone else felt they had to as well. They would want to make sure Holly was all right, and they would want to see the babies soonest. They'd had enough fun at the campout already.

"Do we need to carry you?" Ryder asked.

"No, I'm fine, truly." Holly's cheeks were a little flushed, and she appeared embarrassed that she had caused such a ruckus. "How's Lexi doing?"

"She's sleeping. I didn't want to wake her. Mike and Toby stayed back in the camp."

"Toby's excited about having some cousins," Rafe said. "We keep telling him that the babies will be little and he can't really play with them for quite a while."

That was a hard concept for little ones to learn. Especially when his cousins would be wolf pups first.

Then they finally reached camp and Lexi came out of her tent to hug Holly. "I heard all the excitement. Are you okay?"

"Oh, uh, my water just broke."

That seemed to put everyone into a panic as some of the guys asked if they could pack up the camp.

"I'm shifting into my wolf. You know that it helps to walk when you're in labor, so I was perfectly all right walking," Holly said.

Then she went inside her tent, and everyone was just watching it as if they were expecting her to have the babies any second. Aidan joined her inside the tent.

"Should we prepare lunch then before we go, like we had planned?" Rafe asked.

"Sure. Do we catch fish for the meal or cook what we brought with us?" Derek asked.

"It's not raining right now," Kate said. "We can eat the other food at any time later."

"Well, I guess we could go fishing." Running his hands through his hair, Rafe looked the part of an anxious brother-in-law.

"Let's go fishing," Jade agreed. "This could take hours, and Holly would probably be more comfortable knowing we're all not just sitting around waiting for the babies to come. Though that's just what wolves would do. We'll have a couple of bodyguards watching her, and someone can let us know if she's having them."

Toby already had his fishing pole in hand. Kate smiled at him.

"All right, let's do that." Ryder glanced at Lexi to see if *she* was feeling well enough to join them.

"I'm fine. I had a really nice nap," Lexi said. "Let's go."

Inside the tent, Holly told Aidan, "You join them to go fishing."

"No way. I'm staying right here with you. If our bodyguards had to help with a delivery instead of me, they would both expire on the spot."

Mike and Ryder laughed because they had been Aidan's bodyguards before they started to work for Lexi.

Holly sighed. "Okay, but you know what, I'm going to sit with you all on the riverbank for a while. I don't want to be cooped up in the tent for hours as a wolf. I'll be out in a minute."

They all headed to the river, and Holly joined them as a wolf. Kate was glad she was not going to be left behind in the tent like that, though she knew Aidan would stay with her the whole time.

This would be the wildest camping trip Kate had ever been on.

She cast out her line, and Derek smiled at her. They were actually officially dating, and she was thrilled.

Then Toby snagged a twig and was laughing. Rafe told him it was a special kind of fish but they couldn't eat it.

Everyone glanced at Holly as she rested on the

bank watching them fish. No one was catching anything. Which was fine. They still had plenty of food
to eat in the event they couldn't catch anything.

Aidan left after a while, returned with a water
dish, and set it next to Holly. She didn't even get up,
just poked her head into the water dish and lapped
up the water. She was panting. Aidan started timing
Holly's contractions.

Except for Toby, everyone was watching Aidan
to see what he had to say. They could carry Holly
back to their tent if they needed to. They didn't
want her to have the wolf pups out here.

"I've already prepared your nest in the tent,"
Aidan said.

Kate realized then that he hadn't just left the riverbank to get Holly some water. Of course wolves
made dens, but when they were *lupus garous*? Nests
worked.

Holly sighed.

Kate guessed the contractions were far enough
apart that Holly didn't feel the need to return to the
campsite right away.

Rafe caught a bass, and Ryder finally did too.
Everyone else was still trying to catch something,
but Kate figured if they didn't, they could have the
two fish they caught as a side dish.

Holly suddenly woofed at Aidan, and he checked
her contractions again. "Let's get you back to the
tent."

He helped her up, and then they headed back along the path to the campsite. Rafe and Jade went with them because they were family.

The others fished a while longer, keeping an eye on Toby.

Then Kate couldn't put off the inevitable any longer and wanted to offer help if Holly or Aidan needed it. "I'm going back to camp."

"Me too," Lexi said.

"Are you okay?" Kate asked, worried about her too.

Lexi laughed. "Yes. I'm just getting started on this journey. I just want to check on things and offer my assistance if it's needed, just like you do."

CHAPTER 20

DEREK FELT IMPOTENT TO HELP WITH ANYTHING as far as Holly was concerned. He wanted to do whatever anyone needed him to do, but waiting on the outcome of Holly's babies? He didn't think he'd ever been this stressed out. If he were mated to a wolf and she insisted she wanted to go on a camping trip, he and she would stay in a cabin, *if* he had any say in the matter! Though he supposed if his mate was adamant about it and they had a doctor along, he could be fine with it.

Then he thought about Kate joining him in his tent after being flooded out. He loved how she was so resilient. Not once had she complained about anything. He didn't think he would have been that nonplussed had he been drenched in the middle of the night. Of course, if he had joined Kate in her tent instead, he hoped she would have been just as accommodating. Still, he suspected he would have joined Mike instead, not wanting to disturb Kate or to force her to have to decide if she would let him stay.

Derek and the other guys and Toby stayed at the river and continued to fish. If they were needed, someone in camp would let them know right away. Still, he kept worrying about Holly and the babies.

Toby had put his fishing pole down on the ground, tired of fishing already. It didn't take him long to wear out on an activity. A couple of the bodyguards helped him stack rocks nearby, keeping him entertained.

"All right," Derek finally said. "I don't think our minds are on fishing. At least I know mine isn't. I'm going back to camp."

"Me too," Mike said.

They all carried their fishing gear and the ice chest back to the campsite and found that someone had started the campfire. Derek and Ryder began cleaning the fish—the whole three that they'd finally caught.

"How about having nachos for lunch?" Lexi asked. "That really appeals to me. Holly can't eat anything heavy, just broth or water. Popsicles if we could have had them out here."

"Okay, remind me not to go camping unless I can bring Popsicles if I'm getting ready to deliver a couple of babies," Kate said.

"You and me both," Lexi agreed.

"Are you taking notes?" Mike asked Ryder.

"Hell, no camping trips period when it gets close to Lexi's due date. This has been way too stressful—for me!" Ryder said. "Then she can have all the Popsicles she wants—at home, safe and sound, with Aidan and Holly nearby to help out."

Everyone laughed.

After eating lunch, they began to pack up some of the tents. As a wolf, Holly wandered around the campsite and then returned to the "nest" that Aidan had made for her in their tent, restless, ill at ease. Derek thought everyone else looked that way too. The rest of Holly and Aidan's bedding had already been loaded in their vehicle, except for the old quilts they were using for her nest.

Aidan came out of the tent to get her some more water.

Jade was trying to get Toby down for a nap. He would probably sleep in the vehicle on the way home, but they didn't know how long this would take.

"But it's not nighttime yet," Toby said. "The sun's still out."

Derek smiled. He wondered if Toby used the same excuse every time.

"Right, but we always take a nap about this time of day. Do you want to sleep with me in the big tent or the little tent?" Jade asked her son.

Toby considered both the tents. "The big tent."

"Race you there," Jade said, and Toby took off running. Jade let him beat her—again.

As soon as they were inside the tent, some of the others continued to pack up things. Kate and Lexi were making Dutch oven apple cobbler—cinna-mon-and-brown-sugar-coated apples with a biscuit dough—the perfect dessert for the end of their stay.

Derek just wished Holly could have had some!

After their nap, Jade and Toby joined Lexi and Kate while they finished the cobbler.

They sat down to eat some of it. With half the tents packed away, the campsite was beginning to look a bit barren when Aidan came out of the tent all flushed, smiling. "Number one son!"

They all whooped, whistled, and hollered heart-felt congratulations to both Holly and Aidan. He was the first baby actually born to the pack, and that was something wolves really celebrated. Toby was Rafe's adopted son, and Jade had Toby before she'd met Rafe, though he treated Toby like he was his son through and through.

Aidan ducked inside their tent to wait for the birth of the other twin. They all continued to eat their cobbler.

"This is really great, ladies," Derek said.

"We didn't realize Maddie was sending desserts with you, and we had planned to make one of our own," Lexi said.

Everyone agreed it was delicious. They were saving some for Aidan and Holly though. Derek wondered what he and Holly wanted to do next. Leave the campsite quickly after the second baby was born? Or give Holly some time to recover?

They finished their dessert and then began packing Jade and Rafe's tent and some of the bodyguards' tents. They left Toby's up in case he wanted to play in it before they actually finished packing up the campsite. They still had to take down Aidan and Holly's tent once she birthed her second twin and was ready to go home.

Once everyone was about done, they had tea and coffee.

Aidan finally came out of the tent, smiling broadly, wiping his sweaty brow. "Number two son!"

They all cheered the whole family.

"What now?" Derek asked.

"Holly wants to leave. She's hot and tired, and she wants to ride in the air-conditioned vehicle on the way home. I've already made her a nest of clean, old bedding in the back seat for when we drive home, either for if she had them on the drive or after she'd already had them. So we're ready to leave."

"All right, let's get everything else packed up then," Lexi said. "Oh, Aidan, here's your cobbler."

"Thanks, I can't eat it right now." Aidan smiled. "I have an upset stomach. But save some for Holly and me if you have enough. We'll both enjoy it tonight after we get home."

"We saved some for both of you," Lexi said. "You will need some energy food when you get settled in."

Aidan went back into the tent, and everyone got to work packing up the rest of the camping gear, including Toby's tent.

"Hey, we're ready," Derek finally told Aidan.

Aidan came out of the tent carrying both newborn wolf pups. Jade and Kate hurried to take the pups from him. Both pups were sound asleep.

Aidan went back into the tent to get Holly.

As a wolf, Holly came out of the tent looking anxious, and then she poked her nose at Jade and Kate's legs, and they crouched to show her the pups were safe. They waited with her until all the bedding used for Holly's nest that had been in Aidan's and her tent could be put in plastic bags, taken home, and washed. Then the others took down the tent.

Kate couldn't have been happier to cuddle the sleeping wolf pup while Jade was loving on the other. The boys would know that all the wolves here were their family.

Toby was trying to check on the wolf pups and saying, "Let me see! Let me see!"

"Just pet them gently," Jade said, guiding him on how to do it. "Later, you can see them as babies. For now, they're your little wolf cousins."

Everyone greeted the pups, Miles and Emmett, though they were still sound asleep. Wolves in a pack treasured the offspring of their wolf couples. All of them would be nannies!

All of the rest of the gear was packed, and everyone began loading into the vehicles.

Jade went with Aidan to help Holly in the back seat with the pups. One of their bodyguards was driving, the other sitting in the passenger seat.

Derek hadn't really thought Holly would birth her twins on the campout. He suspected she hadn't really believed she would either, unless she had wanted the whole pack together for the momentous event. If that was so, it had been ideal planning.

———

"That was a great campout," Kate said on the drive home. "It couldn't have turned out any more special than it did when Aidan and Holly's babies came. It was the perfect time to leave before it rains tonight—no more bears, cougars, or hikers to go off-trail to see us either."

"Yeah, I would say that was a great campout. Except for your tent flooding."

Though she thought that had turned out well too. *In the end.* She stretched and yawned. "It worked out. I have to admit I will enjoy sleeping in my own bed tonight though." Kate was glad all her gear had dried out before they began packing up, but she would wash everything when she got home.

"Remember Friday is the 1920s dinner and dance," Derek told her.

Kate felt like such a mess and really needed to get cleaned up. "I will be a new woman by then. It's a good thing it's at the end of the workweek."

He chuckled. "Yeah, I know how you feel. A nice hot shower tonight, a shave, clean clothes, and I'll feel like a new man."

"I'll be wearing a dress I wore to a costume party that had a roaring twenties theme that I attended last year with Lexi. Hopefully, I won't have any big issues with it."

Derek shook his head. "I can't believe women can be that petty. I wear the same suit or tuxes all the time to these events. I can't imagine tossing them out and getting new ones every year."

"Me either," Kate said. "It's wasteful. And I can't afford it. Nor would I want to just so I could do that."

He glanced at her.

"Seriously. I mean, I *could* afford to do it now, but I wouldn't waste that much money on a single-use gown. It's not worth it."

"I agree."

———

They all stopped for bathroom breaks and gas a couple of times on the way home, everyone checking on Holly and the pups. Aidan had to walk Holly as a wolf on a leash while the others cuddled the pups in the car. There wouldn't be any lack of loving on them in the pack.

After the long drive, Derek finally reached Kate's home. Lexi and Ryder parked up at their house right after that. Derek walked Kate to her door while Cliff and Will hauled her camping gear and her backpack into her garage for her. Derek wanted to help her clean up her equipment, and he wished he could stay the night with her since he was leaving for several days with Rafe on a business trip and he wouldn't get to see her again until Friday.

"Did you need any help cleaning up your camping equipment?" Derek knew what a chore it was, but all the guys cleaned theirs together, making short work of it.

"Yeah, I mean, I'll deal with it later, but we could use it as an excuse for you staying overnight." Kate wrapped her arms around Derek's neck.

He smiled. "We'll clean it up, take a shower, and—"

"You will stay the night?"

"Hell, yeah."

She sighed. "But don't you have to fly to Colorado tomorrow?"

"Yeah, but my bag's packed. Cliff can bring it with him when he picks me up at your house and takes me to the airport."

"What time is your flight?"

"Ten thirty." Smiling, Derek raised his brows.

"All right. We'll do it. I'm going to run into the house and get us some water to drink." Then she went inside.

"We kind of screwed things up for you," Cliff said as Derek walked back to the Land Rover, the guys both waiting for him to return to the vehicle.

"I'm staying the night." Derek explained what he wanted Cliff to do for him tomorrow morning. He grabbed his toiletry kit and a pair of clean boxer briefs from his bag in the Land Rover. Cliff would have to bring his clothes tomorrow so Derek could dress in something nicer for the plane trip, though they were going in Rafe's jet, so they could wear whatever they wanted. "I just need you to bring my packed bag sitting in the bedroom and the clothes I had set out for tomorrow's flight when you take me to the airport in the morning."

Both of his bodyguards smiled. Cliff said, "You got it, boss."

Then Cliff and Will drove off in the Land Rover to leave them in peace.

This was the perfect end to a great camping trip.

Kate had propped open the door for Derek. "Hey, I guess I need to give you the key code to the front door," she called out to him from the kitchen as he entered the house and shut the door.

He suspected this was only the beginning of their blossoming relationship. Then he got a call from Aidan, joined her in the kitchen where she'd poured them glasses of water, and put the call on speaker for both of them to hear.

Aidan said, "Hey, I'm just making a conference call with all of you. We're home, tuckered out, and Holly wants to thank all of you for making this the best camping trip ever! She had abhorred the notion that she would be sitting around the house all by herself—well, with me there too—when the time to have the babies came, so she was thrilled we could all be with her, sweating it out."

Derek laughed. "Yeah, well, we were all doing just that, that's for sure. I'm glad the new momma, daddy, and the babies are home and doing just fine." Derek and Rafe had bought the twins cribs that made up into daybeds when the kids were bigger. But he figured the babies would be in bassinets for a while, at least when momma wolf wanted to change back into her human form.

"I'll let you all go. I'm taking care of the little ones while Holly's in the shower. They're babies now and they're already awake and hungry," Aidan said.

Everyone congratulated them again and then ended the call.

"Okay, I wanted to take a shower first, but I guess the best way to go about this is we clean the camping gear first and *then* take our shower. There's no sense in getting dirty all over again," Kate said to Derek.

Kate said *shower*, not *showers*, he noted, which meant she wanted to take the shower with him too. He wanted to tell her to get cleaned up and he'd take care of the camping equipment, but he didn't want to miss showering with her, and he suspected she didn't want to leave the job to him either.

It didn't take long for Kate and Derek to hose down her tent and the rest of the items, though she kept turning the hose on him and he chased her around her backyard for it a time or two. They were laughing and having a blast. He'd never expected to have this kind of fun while cleaning up after a camping trip.

He caught her and kissed her and got her all wet. "We don't even need to take a shower now," she said.

"Oh, yeah, we do. Thinking about all that soap sliding down your body is enough to make me want to toss you over my shoulder and haul you inside right now."

She laughed and got him with the hose again. Then it was time to go inside, sopping wet, no towels out here, and they raced each other to the master bath. She slipped on the tile floor in the kitchen, her expression mischievous, and he grabbed her up, and then he did just what he said he wanted to do, tossed her over his shoulder and walked triumphantly to the bathroom. He had caught her, and she was his.

Chuckling, she said, "Reminiscent of your cave-man days?"

"You bet." He set her down on the bathroom floor, and he removed her hiking shoes and then his own, ready to make love to Kate.

———

Kate slid Derek's zipper down on his sopping-wet jeans shorts molded to his cock and felt his erection fully aroused after all that sexy playful fun they'd had with the garden hose. She slid her hand down his arousal, still covered in navy-blue boxer briefs. She pulled his shorts off his hips as he captured her mouth, his hands cupping her face, kissing her with passion.

He stirred a need in her that was nothing like anyone else had ever done for her. She was glad they were dating each other exclusively now.

He kicked off his shorts and then worked on the fastener on hers, unzipped them, and slid them down her hips. Once she'd stepped out of them, she slipped her hands up his wet T-shirt, marveling at the feel of his soft skin stretched over hard pecs, and felt his nipples peaking as she swept her fingers over them. They would need to wash their clothes—but later.

Then he was pulling her hard against his body again. She wrapped her arms around him and rested her head against his soft, wet T-shirt and hard abs.

"Hmm, what a campout." She was so glad she had asked him to come with them! He had been a great camping mate.

"I'll say." He pressed a kiss on top of her head.

She pulled off his T-shirt, and he unfastened her bra. Then he slid her bra straps slowly down her arms as he kissed her breastbone. He dropped the bra and began kissing her breasts, licking one nipple and then the other, molding his hands to her breasts, and kissing her mouth again.

Being with him felt so right. She ran her hands up his chest, grazing his nipples with her fingernails. Then she reached down to pull off his boxer briefs. She slid them down his legs until he could step out of them. He slipped her panties down her hips until she was completely bared to him like he was to her.

They kissed again, his erection hard against her, and she felt real satisfaction in having him here with her tonight.

She started the shower and stepped into it. He joined her, closing the glass shower door behind him. Then she squirted shampoo on her hands and began to soap up his hair, and he did the same with hers.

This was just too nice. They started soaping each other's bodies after that, and she was thinking how much she liked this routine and how she didn't really want to give it up. She moved her soapy hands all over his body, his chest, his shoulders and arms, and his back and then lower to stroke his rigid erection, and he groaned. He reciprocated by sliding his soapy fingers all over her at the same time, the same places. Then he slipped a hand between her legs and began his slow seduction of rubbing her nubbin. She thought they were going to move this to the bed, but he didn't seem to be in any hurry to rinse off.

So she went with the flow and began stroking him in earnest, her hands just as soapy on his flesh as his hands were on hers. He was kissing her at the same time, his free arm wrapped around her as if he had to keep her on her feet or she would melt right into the floor. The way his eyes were smoky with desire and his breathing shallow, she thought he might be holding on to her for the same reason as she suddenly stroked him to completion and he erupted all over her. She came in the same instant, crying out.

"Oh, Derek" was all she could get out before they were kissing again and soaping and washing.

They finally rinsed off and dried off, and Derek got the hair dryer out this time and began blow-drying her hair in that amazing way that he had while gently massaging her scalp before. She couldn't believe he would do this for her again. She felt heavenly, satiated, ready to join him in bed to cuddle the rest of the night. Once her hair was dry, she grabbed her lotion and took him into the bedroom. She figured with all the hiking through the woods they'd done, it would be nice to massage their feet again.

They climbed into bed and she had him lie on his back first as she applied lotion to his feet and began massaging them. He was lying with his head on her spare pillow, his arms behind the back of his head, smiling, his arousal growing—again—and his beautiful body on full display. Just from showering and thinking of their hands running all over each other's soapy body, his drying her hair had all been enough to prep her for making love to him—again.

"I meant to give you some lotion to take home with you the last time we did this."

"I would need the masseuse to go along with the experience like the last time—and this time. That's what makes it ultra-special."

She smiled while working on his feet with slow deliberate massages.

He moaned. "Man, does that feel great."

"Yeah, I know, just like when you did it with me."

When they switched places, Derek not only massaged her feet but started working on her legs, up her thighs, and that felt heavenly, sensual as he moved closer to her nether region. She was primed to lose herself in his lovemaking all over again.

It didn't take long before he was moving up her

whole body, kissing her tummy and her breasts, licking her nipples. Then he caressed her open mouth with his, lips brushing eagerly, tongues tangled.

She pressed her mouth against his, loving the sensuous seduction.

He kissed her with tenderness, the heat intensifying, the kisses harder now, scorching. She savored the sensual exploration as his tongue swept over hers. He intoxicated her with his kisses, made her want him rocking inside her with fervor, completing her, completing him, uniting them.

Their hearts were pounding hard and fast when he began to work on her nubbin with slow, deliberate strokes. The ache between her legs demanded desperate fulfillment, and she arched against him, hungry for his affections and savoring his touch. She groaned under his ministrations, loving the way he was stroking her. She wanted to reach the sweet peak of climax again, to experience the pleasure only he had ever given her.

Then she was coming unglued. She cried out as the orgasm hit, and she closed her eyes, welcoming the ripples of climax that filled her with satisfaction. She wanted desperately to tell him she loved him, but she wasn't sure of it herself yet. She did love making love to him. That she had no doubt about!

But would she lose herself if she mated him? Would she no longer be her own person, having more of a normal life, not being in the spotlight? As the billionaire's wife—would others believe she was marrying him for his money and the prestige? She had trouble with wanting to be independent when she'd been only dependent on herself for so long. And being seen as dependent on Derek for everything.

───────────

Derek enjoyed the way Kate made love to him. Here, he'd thought of just drying her hair, getting into bed, and giving her a foot massage too. But just smelling the she-wolf's turned-on scent and bringing her to climax in the shower had worked him up all over again.

He just had to pleasure her and make her come to prove to her he had what it took to make her collide with heaven and earth and shatter into a million pieces of ecstasy. But she was stroking him again too, and he felt overwhelmed with bliss when she made him come as well.

Now all he would think about tomorrow was being with Kate in the throes of passion, and he wished he could cancel the conference. He and Rafe had so much wheeling and dealing to do, he couldn't leave his friend in the lurch, but Kate was the first woman who had ever made him want to skip out on the whole thing and spend the time with her instead.

He knew he was in trouble now.

CHAPTER 21

THIS TIME WHEN DEREK WOKE WITH KATE snuggled in his arms in her bed—though he was conscious of having to get up and get ready for Cliff to pick him up and take him to the airport—she didn't seem to be in a big hurry to leave him to go to work with Lexi. Kate kissed his chest and smiled at him. He really could get used to this.

"I'm going to miss you while you're gone," she said. "Don't pick up any stray women while you're out there."

He chuckled. "All I will think about is getting back to you." Seriously, he knew he would too. But this was such a change for them from the last time they were together like this, and he figured the camping trip had been a success. Who would have thought a rainstorm would have thrown them together in an unexpected way and he would be staying with her again overnight, making love, twice last night even? Instead of pulling away this morning, she didn't seem to want to give up the intimacy between them. He was thrilled.

Thankfully, Derek had packed his things for the trip before he left on the camping excursion, so

Cliff dutifully arrived with his bag in hand and his change of clothes. While Derek went back to the bedroom to change, Kate made Cliff a cup of coffee.

"I don't think I've ever been on that wild a camping trip before." Cliff drank some of his coffee. "Bear, cougar, flooding, wolf giving birth at the campsite?"

Kate smiled. "Oh, and Toby hooking his dad's shirt."

Cliff laughed.

Then Derek came out of the bedroom wearing his suit, ready to leave.

"Wow, you look like a first-class executive." She kissed Derek.

"Thanks, Kate." He kissed her back. "I'll see you soon."

"I can't wait." She gave him one more hug, which he warmly returned, and then he had to leave. She went outside to see them off with a wave of her hand and a smile.

She'd made his day and night asking him to stay with her last evening.

———————

Once Derek left in the Land Rover with Cliff to go to the airport, Kate didn't want to do anything. She missed him already! She really had fallen for the wolf—*hard*.

She'd had a supersized crush on him in the beginning, but the more she got to know him, the more she really cared about him. She loved the way he was with others, with animals, and especially with her. He was genuine. Protecting her as a wolf from the raccoon the one night on the camping trip and then taking her into his tent and his sleeping bag proved he could be her hero too. Just like she wanted to keep him safe.

She loved how Derek had helped her clean up her camping gear, and she'd had fun doing it while hosing him down. She loved how he'd played along when it would normally have been a chore. That was one of the drudgeries of camping: cleaning up after the fact. Especially when she had been tired. But boy, when it came to making love to him, all that tiredness sure had gone away.

There was no doubt in her mind now that he was the one for her. She was excited about the roaring twenties party they were going to, and she already had it in mind that she was going to stay at his house afterward. She wanted to see the dogs—they had found a place in her heart—and she wanted to swim in his pool and take a walk on the beach.

She headed over to Lexi's a little late, but she'd texted her that she was seeing Derek off. She wasn't keeping that a secret, even though she suspected Mike wouldn't know this time because Derek's bodyguards left in the Land Rover and Mike could have assumed Derek went home with them.

Lexi greeted her with a hug. "So spill."

Kate smiled at her inquisitive friend. "Yes, he spent the night. Yes, I miss him already, and we're going to the roaring twenties dinner and dance party on Friday night when he gets home." She showed her a picture of the fancy dinner invitation he had sent her featuring a dancing couple dressed in flapper-era clothes.

"I knew this would happen."

Kate chuckled. "Yeah, yeah. We'll probably go out this weekend to someplace."

"The weekend is yours. All weekends are yours. We were working all the time because we had fun doing it and because you were my bodyguard anyway. Now with me being mated to Ryder and the little ones coming and you having dates with Derek, your evenings and weekends are free to do as you like. Besides, you're my partner, and you can take off whenever you need to. Like taking that trip to Hawaii?" Smiling, Lexi raised her brows.

"Yeah. We're going to have a ball with that. I'll make sure I won't leave you in a lurch."

"Just don't wait until the babies are ready to come."

"Oh, I am going to be here for that!"

Lexi laughed. Then they got to work.

That night after working with Lexi on designing

new labels for the cosmetic line, Kate headed for the grocery store to restock her fridge when she swore someone was following her on the coastal road. A black pickup like the one she had seen when she returned from Derek's house after having grilled hamburgers and a swim that one night was following her and harassing her. So many black pickups were on the road at any given time that she couldn't be certain. She kept an eye on it and drove into the grocery store parking lot. The truck hurried on past. She sighed. She was just imagining things.

She went inside and picked up all the groceries she needed, and then she headed home. As soon as she was on the main road, she saw a black pickup following her again. Okay, this was not a coincidence. When the vehicle's high beams came on, she was certain it was the same pickup truck that had hassled her before. She pulled off onto the shoulder, and the pickup drove past her car; then she got on the road and saw that his license plate was covered up so she couldn't even report him to the police. *Bastard.*

Then she got a call from Derek, and she was so glad to hear from him. "Hey, you."

─────

"Hey, I've been missing you." Derek was calling Kate from the hotel in Denver, Colorado, to let her know he was thinking about her. "How's the business going?"

"Great! How's your trip?"

"I wish you were here, and it would be so much greater."

"I'm sure you are busy."

"During the day, but you could have come to the dinners and luncheons, and I would have taken you out if we had wanted to skip them."

"Just keep me in mind for future business trips."

He laughed. "If you don't have any plans this weekend, I thought we might go pedal boating on Saturday."

"Sure, I would love that. Lexi had been working on the weekends, but she said now that she's going to have twins, she wants to keep our weekends free. She wants to make sure I have dating time too."

"With me though, right? Am I glad for that!"

Kate laughed. "Why don't we just stay at your place on Friday night after the roaring twenties party and take off to the lake from there the next morning? I'll pack an overnight bag."

"That would be great. We'll be getting in from the party after two in the morning, so we'll have to skip the dog walk."

"And a moon-lit swim and a wolf run too. But maybe after the pedal boat ride on Saturday we can do those things?"

"All right, that certainly works." He was so glad

he'd called Kate and she was all for making further plans. At least Brenda hadn't bothered him again after he told her he was seeing someone else. He wondered if she would learn he was going to the 1920s party and find a date for it. Seats had sold out a long time ago, so unless she found someone who was willing to give up their seat or she found someone dateless who was willing to take her, she wouldn't be there. At least he hoped.

"Uh, I've got to watch my driving. I have a pickup truck harassing me."

"Where are you?" He was ready to fly home to protect her!

"I just left the grocery store that's located between your place and Lexi's. I'm on my way home."

"I'm on it."

"You're in Colorado."

"Yeah, but I'm sending my muscle."

"If you're sending Will and Cliff to come to my aid, who's watching over you?"

"Rafe's at the conference with me, and two of his bodyguards are there. We didn't need that many on this trip, and I'm damn glad I left them home."

"Well, me too, and thanks."

"I'll call you back in a minute." Furious that anyone would be giving Kate trouble and he couldn't be there physically to help her out, Derek immediately got hold of Cliff. "I need you and Will to take separate vehicles—the Land Rover and your truck—to chase down a black pickup on the coast road. The truck is harassing Kate."

"On our way," Cliff said.

Then Derek called Kate back anxiously, hating that he couldn't be there for her in person. "Okay, can you get the license number of the vehicle?"

"No, he has covered it up, and if it's the same one who did this before, then it's not just a one-time road-rage issue."

"He did it before?" That sounded a lot more sinister, and he wanted to ask why she hadn't told him about the other instance, but he didn't want to upset her any more than she probably already was.

"If it's the same guy," she said.

"Okay. Does he know where you live?"

"Uh, yeah. He drove on past Lexi's place as soon as I reached the property the last time."

"Call Ryder or Mike and get them on it, and then call me back. Maybe between all of us, we can nail the bastard and learn what's going on and stop him from doing this in the future with you or anyone else."

"Okay." A few minutes later, Kate called Derek back and said, "He's doing the same thing as before, slowing down, speeding up, pulling off on the side of the road, then when I drive past, he's following me the whole time with his high-beam lights on."

"Did you get ahold of Mike or Ryder?"

"Ryder. He's having Mike come to intercept him from the house and your guys will be behind the black pickup."

"Good. Damn, I wish I was there with you."

"I do too. I see Mike. He's in his pickup, and he's got a big grill too. The truck is in front of me now. Mike flashed his lights at the black pickup to turn off his high beams. The driver just flashed them on and off as if to say he was keeping them on so what are you going to do about it? Someone's coming up behind me going a hundred miles an hour. Oh, I think it's your Land Rover. I'm slowing down. He's going around, and he and Mike—"

Derek heard the sound of a crashing vehicle and prayed Kate and the others were okay.

"They ran him off the road. He slammed into a tree. Mike and Cliff pulled off on the side of the road," she told Derek.

"Keep driving home." Derek didn't want her anywhere near the guy if he turned out to be armed and wanting to harm her.

"Okay. I'm driving past them. They're checking on the driver. He's going to have to get a tow truck. Serves him right. I can't see the driver, so I don't know who it was or how he fared."

"The guys will get an ID on him if they can."

"What if he tries to sue them for wrecking his truck?"

"All of you were eyewitnesses. The guy was driving recklessly."

"Well, that's for sure. I have a navy-blue pickup following me home now."

"That would be Will."

"Okay, good. I'm pulling into the driveway now, and Will's parking behind me. Ryder's outside already. I'm going to go so you can find out what's going on with Cliff and Mike."

"All right. Miss you, Kate." Derek wished he could give her a big hug. He knew, though she was trying to sound calm and fine, that she had been rattled.

"Miss you too, and thanks for all the help!"

Then they ended the call, and Derek called Cliff. "What's going on?"

"We're calling an ambulance to take this ass to the hospital. It would have served him right if he'd broken his damn neck. He pulled a gun on us, but he isn't in any shape to use it, though he tried firing at us. He hit his already-shattered window. The police are on their way. He'll get cited for covering up his license plate and any number of moving violations. Not to mention he was armed and firing at us. We all witnessed his pulling around Kate and slamming on his brakes, nearly making her run into his back end, which would have totaled her car and could have injured her badly."

"Did you get his license and learn who he is?"

"Lars Gnoffo. But he's not really in any shape to answer questions. Mike and I will talk to the police, and they'll have to talk to Kate about this once they're finished here. The police and ambulance are just down the road from the accident. I hear them coming now. His truck is totaled. We still don't know why he was targeting Kate. Maybe he learned his lesson. We didn't try to take the gun from him. It looks like he has a broken arm, and he can't really aim at anything, he's in so much pain. But we figured we would let the police deal with him."

"Okay, good, that's just how I would have handled it. I'll call one of Rafe's PIs and have him check into the guy. He's a wolf, discreet and fast," Derek said.

Then they ended the call, and Derek called one of Rafe's PIs, Callahan Rutherford. Derek had used him before for background investigations and even to check out Kate before he interviewed her for the bodyguard position. Though Callahan hadn't told him she'd worked as a lifeguard before.

"Hey, it's Derek Spencer. I need you to look into a Lars Gnoffo for me. I want to know every detail of his life." Then Derek explained the situation to him.

"Yes, sir. Does Kate have any enemies?"

Brenda came to mind, but there might be others he had no idea about. "Let me get back with you on that."

Derek knew if there was anything shady on Lars, Callahan would learn of it.

CHAPTER 22

When Derek called Kate to ask if she had any enemies, immediately she thought of Brenda. Sure, Kate might have made other enemies. But since she'd had trouble with stalker exes and ex-girlfriend stalkers, it was on her mind. Brenda could definitely be a stalker ex-girlfriend. What if Brenda had hired the guy to harass Kate?

Now, Ryder and Lexi were giving Kate grief for not telling them about the first incident—if this black pickup was the same one involved the last time. Crazy drivers were on the road all the time, so she really hadn't believed he had targeted her. She hadn't looked for his license plate that time, but the two incidents were so similar, she imagined it could be the same driver.

"Maybe you need a bodyguard to be with you twenty-four seven," Ryder said, sounding serious.

"*I* am a bodyguard," Kate reminded them.

Tilting her head to the side, her chin down, Lexi looked exasperated with her.

"Derek said he has hired a PI and he'll learn who the guy is and what his involvement in any of this is." Kate hoped that would make everyone chill.

Though she had to admit she'd been shaken by the event, as much as she was trying to put on that she was fine.

"You had this happen to you with stalker exes before," Lexi reminded her.

"I know. That's why I took up martial arts."

Then Mike and Cliff arrived. The police were right behind them. Kate sighed and told everyone the story all over again about how this guy, if he was the same one, had harassed her before. And no, she didn't know any Lars Gnoffo.

After the police left, Cliff said, "We don't need to safeguard Derek's house while he's gone if you could use us here. Or at least one of us can stay."

"No, thanks, I'll be fine," Kate said.

"Why don't you all join us for dinner," Lexi said, "since you're here now? Mike and Ryder were going to put some hamburgers on the grill."

"I need to put my groceries away," Kate said.

"We'll stay for dinner, thanks, Lexi, and we'll go with Kate for now and help her with her groceries," Will said.

"Thanks." She really didn't feel she needed them to, but she knew everyone would feel better if she took them up on their offer.

"Are you sure you don't want us to stay the night?" Cliff asked as they unloaded the groceries from Kate's car.

She was glad she had insulated grocery bags for

the foods she needed to keep cold for all the delay in putting them in the fridge. "Yeah, really. Mike and Ryder are so close by, they'll be here in a jiffy if I need them." She wasn't reminding them again that she was a trained bodyguard herself. Though it was nice having the guys' help with unloading her groceries, and then they walked back to Lexi and Ryder's house.

"What about tomorrow?" Will asked.

"I'll be at Lexi's house all day working."

Then they had an enjoyable dinner with Lexi and Ryder and Mike, and she finally headed home, with an escort, naturally. After Cliff and Will checked out her house to make sure it was safe, they looked reluctant to leave her alone. She gave them both hugs. "Thanks, guys. I'll be fine."

"Call us if anything happens," Cliff said, and then they finally took off.

Once Kate had settled down at her place for the night, she called Derek. "Hey, I just wanted to let you know I'm home and getting ready for bed. If you were here, it would be so much better. Not just because of this incident, by the way."

"Is Mike with you?" Derek asked, skipping the part about her wanting him in her bed. He sounded more concerned for her safety.

She appreciated Derek for that. "No. He offered, but he's only a skip and a hop away from my place. Cliff and Will offered too. I'm fine. They have

Gnoffo locked up anyway. At least I hope he's not getting out anytime soon."

"You call everyone at any hint of trouble. I wish I was in your bed with you too."

She smiled. "Yeah, I think I'm falling for you."

He chuckled. "Good, because you're taking me with you."

After talking forever, they ended the call and she tried to sleep, but she kept seeing the events of tonight repeat in her mind—the bright lights in her rearview mirror, the black truck bearing down on her and then sailing past her, his red brake lights coming on and Kate slamming on her own brakes. Then it was morning again.

All Tuesday, Derek checked up on Kate too. She didn't find his concern suffocating, like she might have thought, but endearing. "Lexi won't let me leave the property until you've returned home," Kate said, giving Lexi a wicked smile as they sat down to have lunch with Ryder and Mike.

Lexi was so lucky that Mike and Ryder were always trying to outdo each other at making the most astounding dishes. They were having honey-garlic shrimp over rice. She wished Derek was here with them having a lovely lunch poolside.

"Good. I hope I'm not bugging you too much with all the texting and phone calls."

"Not at all. It shows you care." She suspected he would have done just as much texting and calling even if Lars hadn't been an issue, and that was nice too. She welcomed his attention. Besides, she was sending animated GIFs to him throughout the day too.

———

Wednesday afternoon while Derek and Rafe were at a luncheon, Derek got a call from the PI concerning Lars Gnoffo and said, "Hey, Rafe is here with me at a luncheon. We'll move this to someplace more private."

"Okay, do you want me to call you back?" Callahan asked.

"I'll call you as soon as we're in my room."

Then they ended the call. "That was Callahan," Derek told Rafe as they made it up to Derek's room.

"Hopefully he has news about Gnoffo."

"Yeah, I hope we can learn if there's something more sinister going on with regard to Kate."

When they arrived at Derek's room, Rafe took a seat in the living area of the suite while Derek called Callahan back. "I'm putting this on speaker so Rafe can hear you too. What do you have?"

"Lars Gnoffo has been in trouble with the law for several years on several different counts of B & E, burglary of stores and homes, possession of a stolen car and other property, all kinds of moving violations. Seems he has a bit of a drug addiction. Anyway, he's on probation for the last stunt he pulled. I dug into the family background, and lo and behold, the name both you and Kate gave me—Brenda Connors—came up. She's Lars's sister-in-law."

"I'll be damned." Derek was certain that was no coincidence.

"It sounds to me like Brenda put Lars up to it," Rafe said.

"Yeah. That's what I figured right away. I went to talk to him in the holding cell, and he told me she hired him to scare Kate Hanover off," Callahan said.

"Scare her off from what?" Derek asked, knowing Callahan meant that Lars tried to scare her off from seeing Derek further, but how would harassing her on the road convince her of that?

"Dating you. I asked him how threatening her on the road with his truck would have thwarted her from seeing you," Callahan said. "He said Brenda told him to take more drastic measures if that didn't work."

"Did he give you any details?" Derek would ruin Brenda.

"He said Brenda wanted Kate out of the way. Gone. Permanently. By any means necessary. If Lars hadn't already confessed, they record everything in the holding area, so he's confessed now. Brenda gave him Kate's address and told him to watch her at all times and, whenever the opportunity availed itself, to take it. He wanted more money for the job because he was spending a lot of time just waiting for the perfect moment to go after Kate. He said most of the time you were with her or she wasn't going anywhere, but it meant he had to sit around watching for her to make a move all the time."

"Was he paid any money for the job?" Derek asked.

"A thousand down and nineteen thousand when Kate stopped seeing you. I'm sending you a photo of him that you can share with Kate and see if she recognizes him."

"Okay, thanks. He seems familiar, but I can't place where I've seen him before."

"Let me know what else you need me for. I have a detective friend at the police station, and he said he and his partner are going to question Brenda within the hour. He knows I'm discreet and wouldn't share it with anyone but you and Kate, not realizing we're wolves and protecting one of our own takes priority. I'll let you know if I learn anything from him. You probably want to wring her neck, but let the police handle this. If they don't take care of it like they should because she has more influence, then it's your call."

"Thanks, Callahan." They ended the call, and Derek got ahold of Kate and shared the picture of Lars and other details he'd learned with her.

"Ohmigod, that's the waiter who shot the

chandelier with the champagne cork! And I thought I saw him at the zoo watching us in the restaurant. He was wearing mirrored sunglasses, so I couldn't be sure. Now I think that was him."

"Hell, I never noticed him."

"You were paying too much attention to me."

He smiled. Yeah, everything about Kate fascinated him. "I thought I recognized him from somewhere though. I should have connected him with the champagne incident."

"The comments Brenda made to friends on social media showed she was willing to do something more than just talk about it." Kate sent Derek the screenshots she had taken.

Frowning, he read through the messages Brenda and her friends had posted to Facebook. "You didn't tell me about this."

"I didn't think anything would come of it. In the posts, she's not really threatening to take action, but her friends are goading her on to do it," Kate said.

"Which could be enough to push someone over the edge to do it who was teetering there already. It's good you took screenshots of her conversation to show to police if anything more happens and she decides to delete them. The police can still get them from someone else, but this makes it easier. I might have been able to convince her to give up this notion of us getting back together had I known what she was capable of."

"If you said something, she might have reacted worse. Who knows her frame of mind and what she could be capable of?"

"You're right. I'll let you know what I learn as soon as I discover anything more."

"Thanks, I appreciate it."

"Rafe is here with me," Derek said.

"Okay, I'll let the two of you get back to work on whatever the two of you were doing."

He was still worried about Kate. "Are you all right?"

"Yeah, thanks, Derek. I can't wait to see you on Friday."

"Earlier, if I can get in on time Thursday night. I won't be in until ten, but if you're still up…"

"Oh, if you're coming in, I'll be up."

He smiled. "Good. I'll let you know if we have trouble getting in on time."

When they finally ended the call, Derek told Rafe what was going on as far as what Kate had also seen on social media and showed him the messages she had shared with Derek.

"If Brenda wants to play hardball, I have a whole team of black ops wolves at my beck and call, and they can make life difficult for her without her even knowing what hit her," Rafe said.

Derek knew he would too to protect one of their own. "Yeah, I was thinking of that and also of ruining Brenda's social standing in the community. That might have even more of an impact on her."

"For someone like Brenda who is all about making an impression to show her in a good light, I agree. That's what she lives for. It appears that you and Kate are headed in the right direction though."

Derek smiled. "I sure hope so." Then he frowned. "But no way did I want to put her life in danger because of an ex-girlfriend."

"It's happened to Kate before, but I'm sure it's not something anyone would ever get used to," Rafe said.

"Oh, she hadn't told me that." Now Derek felt worse for having put her in that position.

"She didn't tell me, but she talks to all the ladies, and Jade told me what had happened. I was ready to take care of the problem people in her life, but it was a nonissue for her at that point."

"Good." Because Derek was ready to do the same for Kate. "Did you want to return to the luncheon?"

"Yeah, let's go."

After their busy day was over, Derek talked to Kate until they both went to bed. He wanted this connection between them always.

Thursday, he called Kate early before they both were busy, and throughout the day, he texted her, and she texted him just as much whenever she had a free moment before he had to leave with Rafe to return home.

Then Derek finally called her when he was ready

to leave. "Hey, honey, we're at the airport, and we were getting ready to leave, but thunderstorms are over the area, so we may be delayed."

"Okay, don't take any risks just to get home to see us."

"All right." Though he felt the same as Rafe, that they wanted to see their significant others tonight if they could, to make love and enjoy the rest of the night with them.

CHAPTER 23

THE NEXT MORNING, KATE WAS GETTING READY to go to work, but she wanted to check in with Derek to see that he had arrived home okay. She found a text on her phone that said he'd gotten in at two in the morning. Relieved, she called him, hoping he wasn't still sleeping because he'd arrived so late.

"Were you still sleeping?" she asked.

"No, I've been up for a little bit."

"I'm glad you got in okay," she said to him.

"Yeah, it was wild last night. We were afraid the storms would never blow out of the area and we'd be stuck there until morning. But we finally had a clearing that was supposed to last for a brief time and got the okay to take off. I texted you as soon as we got in to let you know we made it in safely."

"I must have been sleeping so soundly, I didn't even hear the text notification. You could have come by. Though I'm sure you were as busy as me all day, and I know if you had come over, we wouldn't have gotten much sleep."

"I didn't want to disturb you. We have a long night ahead of us what with the 1920s party, and I want to thoroughly enjoy that with you."

"Same with me. I'm going to let you go. I need to run to Lexi's house to get started on our day. You probably need more sleep."

He chuckled. "To talk with you, I would happily give it up. I'll text you later."

Which of course he did, and he had Lexi laughing every time Kate received a text that day.

"You're going to have to just mate him," Lexi said.

That was exactly what Kate planned to do.

That night, Kate was so excited. She'd missed seeing Derek, even though they'd talked daily, several times a day, amusing Lexi when he checked in with Kate while she was working. That was one thing about working with Lexi. She didn't mind at all.

Tonight, Kate was wearing a gold flapper-era gown, the fringe bouncing off her legs as she walked. She also had a gold jeweled headband adorned with feathers. Her faux-pearl necklaces hung down her front between her breasts. She loved the idea of this themed dinner dance.

She had decided tonight that she would ask Derek to mate her. She had already packed her bag with changes of clothes for the whole weekend. She wanted to stay with Derek the whole time. She wanted to mate him. But she wasn't sure he was ready. She would just play it by ear. It really depended on how he was feeling about her and making a permanent commitment to her. But she didn't want to presume anything. She wondered if Brenda would finally give up her quest to cause trouble for her if they announced their engagement. Kate was almost nervous about asking Derek to mate her, afraid he would turn her down. Her hands were clammy, and she wasn't even going to ask him yet. Not until after the party. Then she was going home with him and mating him if he was agreeable.

"You look beautiful in your flapper-era gown. I love it."

"You look most dapper in your dark-gray pin-striped suit. Very handsome."

He was wearing a black Homburg hat, a dark-gray striped suit, a silk vest, suspenders, and a white shirt. He was so cute. He was so much fun to be with. His black-and-white two-tone shoes, dark-gray leather gloves, and smart-looking walking cane finished the look.

"Does that have a weapon?" she asked, pointing at his cane.

Derek smiled. "Naturally, though I doubt I would ever have to use it."

"Well, you look really great. This is exciting. I couldn't wait to do this. And to be with you, of course. I was surprised Lexi didn't want to go to it because she's usually always eager for themed parties. She just wanted to chill with Ryder, and I can understand that too."

"Maybe next time they have a themed dinner dance, we can convince her and Ryder to go with us."

"We'll have to. How was the rest of your conference?"

"I worried about you. The rest of the conference was boring compared to being with you. You make everything an adventure."

She smiled. "Well, Lexi and Ryder, and Mike too, had me eat dinner with them *every* night, just to make sure I remained safe. Once during the night, I had to get up to get some water because we'd had pizza for dinner and it always makes me thirsty. Anyway, I looked out the window and saw Ryder walking around the property as a wolf, keeping an eye out for anything that looked suspicious. Then he curled up to sleep on my front doorstep. I wanted to tell him he didn't have to do that, but knowing him, he did it for his own peace of mind."

"I'm glad he did, though I wish I had been there with you instead."

"It was all good. Have you heard anything more about Brenda?"

"They took her in for questioning at the police station. That must have hurt her ego. If her brother-in-law wasn't lying and she truly did pay him to go after you, she'll be in a worse situation. So I'm sure she's sweating it out. They'll be looking for a cash withdrawal in the amount she allegedly paid him. Unfortunately,

Lars didn't have the money she supposedly paid him because he was too busy spending it."

"Oh, great. And if she has large sums of cash in a safe or something, she might have been able to pay him off the record," Kate said.

"Exactly."

Kate let out her breath. "I've been following the social media, but I haven't seen anything on it. You would think a news reporter would have heard about it and wanted to do a story. I'm afraid with her wealth, she'll be able to get away with it. You know how it is. The wealthier people are, the more they can get away with crime—even murder."

"I agree with you," Derek said.

"Okay, enough about her and all of that. I just want to enjoy the dance with you. I'm so excited about it. I was thinking we all should go to a mystery murder dinner sometime. All of us wolves. Wouldn't that be fun?"

He laughed. "We'll have to make you our party coordinator."

"I can do that. I'm very good at organizing things."

"That's why Lexi made you a partner in the business."

"Yep!"

Then they arrived at the restaurant and found their way to the ballroom that made her feel as though she was immersed in the 1920s—the music, the costumes everyone was wearing, the decorations. The only thing they didn't have was a smoke-filled room, and she was glad for that. No one was smoking, but several were holding props to appear like they were.

She knew none of their friends were going to be here, but if they had been, it would have made it even more fun.

Then they moved through the ballroom and looked around at everything the event had to offer. Pickup poker, gin rummy, blackjack, roulette, and craps seemed to be the favorites of the partygoers. The organizers for the party had even hired real dealers and gaming tables to use for the games. Kate was more interested in dancing than gambling, but she still wanted to take home some of the chocolate prizes. Dealers had made sure the guests had plenty of chips to gamble with when they arrived so they could win bottles of liquor, wine, six packs of beer, chocolate cigars, chocolate guns, strands of faux pearls, and a few disposable cameras.

Men and women were busy playing the games, some dancing, others just nibbling at a table of appetizers and enjoying alcoholic beverages. Some of the people who talked to Derek and Kate had purchased from Clair de Lune Cosmetics.

"Congratulations," one woman said to Kate. "I'm sure you're happy about the partnership with Lexi."

"I am, thanks."

"Well, Lexi has done nothing but praise you for all your hard work. It's well deserved. Oh, and as to Brenda Connors, a lot of her closest friends are distancing themselves from her for what she allegedly pulled," the woman said.

Good. Kate hoped they would all dump her. "Well, there wasn't any reason for it."

"She says there was, but we know she was just bitter. You know she has been married and divorced and has two kids by the marriage? She has to support them, and she wants to snag herself a much wealthier man so she can still have tons of money to play around with. That's why she wanted to marry you so badly, Derek. But it sort of backfired."

Another woman listening in said, "Yeah, everyone knew it. She was really vocal about wanting to marry you. I hadn't known about the ex-husband and kids. I don't know if she just thought no one would ever mention it to you or that you didn't care, but with threats to Kate's life, people are really backing away from Brenda. If her brother-in-law didn't lie about it to get himself out of hot water, then she's not going to be welcome at any of these functions anymore."

A third woman was holding a long, tapered faux cigarette in her hand and shaking her head, her feathers dancing around on her hat. "She cooked her goose on that one. The paparazzi finally got word about the whole sordid affair. I heard they're going after her. They'll also be featuring the two of you, I'm sure."

As long as Kate and Derek were seen in a good light and they didn't portray Brenda as the poor woman who had been everything to Derek until Kate broke them up. It would be hard to explain how they meshed so well so soon after dating because in truth, they were wolves and had a lot more in common than most people they knew.

After that, it seemed the ice was broken, and several others came over to offer their support and condolences for the repugnant affair. Kate was surprised but glad. She had worried that being out in public might have been uncomfortable if anyone had learned what had gone on. She wasn't sure that the press had really captured anything on it. Though she hadn't been looking at the news either and Lexi hadn't mentioned anything to her about it.

Then the small crowd of people moved off to enjoy themselves, and Kate and Derek kissed. "I was a little worried about everyone's reaction over this whole business with Brenda and her brother-in-law," Derek admitted.

"Oh, me too, but I hadn't wanted to mention it and ruin this for us."

"Me either." He smiled at her and took her around the room to see what else the event offered "If you wondered, I didn't know Brenda had an ex-husband and kids."

"I wonder why she didn't get custody of the kids."

"Maybe it cramped her style too much. I'm having my PI check into it for me." Derek took a moment to text someone and then pocketed his phone. "Done."

A large dance floor was surrounded by tables trimmed in gold fringe and a band dressed in period costume playing ragtime and swing tunes for the entire night.

"What do you want to do first?" Derek asked.

Kate immediately led him to the dance floor. "Let's dance." She hoped she remembered the dances well enough from when she had danced them last year.

An instructor was there to give lessons on the various roaring twenties dances for anyone who didn't know the steps. But Derek was a marvelous dance partner, and Kate was having the best time with him.

They did the Charleston, and then they danced the foxtrot, the Texas Tommy, and the Black Bottom.

After that, she got a Brandy Alexander and he got a Hanky Panky, drinks that had been invented in the 1920s. It had been a toss-up between those and a Grasshopper and a Blue Hawaiian, and they snacked on the appetizers—egg rolls, meatballs, deviled eggs, and lobster Newberg.

Then they were off to play roulette, and they won her coveted chocolate gun. They headed over to the booth to take pictures, though they were also taking pictures of themselves all over the place.

When the band took breaks, the sound system filled in the gaps. That meant between playing games, eating, drinking, and picture taking, they spent the rest of the night shimmying to the music like there was no tomorrow. They were dancing to the Brazilian samba and then doing the shimmy, slow waltz, and tango and loving it.

Even though Derek and Kate took a number of pictures of themselves participating in the activities, a professional photographer was on hand taking photos too. They had their pictures professionally taken in front of a gold-and-black city backdrop to take home as souvenir photos in their costumes. It was just too much fun. The event even provided a few disposable cameras in case someone hadn't brought a smartphone with them and hadn't won a camera at one of the games.

Kate kept thinking about Brenda and how peeved she might be if she saw the pictures of Derek and herself plastered all over the place on social media and in the tabloids, particularly if she was being questioned for wrongdoing in Kate's case.

Kate and Derek were having so much fun dancing to the songs that she felt Derek needed to be her lifelong dance partner, pedal boat partner, camping partner, swimming partner, walking-the-dogs partner, and running-as-wolves partner. She didn't know for sure if he was feeling the same way or he wanted to continue to date her for longer to see if the magic wore off, but she knew she'd never find another wolf she cared about or enjoyed sharing so many similar interests with as much as she did with Derek.

She'd never met another wolf like him, who charged up her day and made her want to do more things than she normally would because she loved doing them with him. Even the social events and dinners she attended as a means of promoting Clair de Lune's products were better with a hot wolf date. That was a whole new experience for her, and she loved it—she felt empowered, not alone.

She'd known she'd have a blast at the roaring twenties party with him. No more trying to decide about this. She loved how protective he'd been of her when he hadn't even been there to take care of her. That was above and beyond being a hero for her.

Being in his arms for one final waltz of the night, feeling his hard body against her, smelling his interest, the heat of him warming her, she envisioned being with him like this always.

The party was ending at 2:00 a.m., and the dance music was still playing. About ten minutes before the party ended and still in the middle of their dance, men in old police uniforms rushed into the ballroom, shaking billy clubs, shouting, "This is a raid!" Several of the coppers were blowing whistles, adding to the chaos.

CHAPTER 24

KATE'S HEART SKIPPED A BEAT WHEN THE FAKE old-time cops raced into the ballroom, and she was thinking she needed her gun out and readied before she realized what was going on. Then she saw Cliff and Will were some of the ones wearing the vintage police costumes—based on the navy-blue uniforms that had been surplus United States army uniforms left over from the Civil War and used by the police in the 1920s. They were wearing wool stovepipe hats, similar to a top hat but not as tall.

Everyone began laughing and grabbing up their party favors and other belongings, the jazz band immediately stopping in the middle of the "raid," signaling it was time to leave.

What a delightful way to end the party. She would never forget how much fun she'd had with Derek, and she was so glad he had asked her to go with him. She couldn't believe that Will and Cliff had been coppers taking part in the raid either!

"Did you know your bodyguards were going to chase us out of the party tonight?" she asked Derek as he led her outside and a valet got his car.

"No. I'm glad they appeared to have as much fun

as we did. Will and Cliff dressing up and chasing us off appeared to be the highlight of the evening's events for them," Derek said.

"Do you blame them? We employ them, and suddenly, they're the ones in charge?" Kate laughed.

By the time they arrived at Derek's place, it was so late, she knew they wouldn't be doing anything but going to bed.

"I'm going to give you my event schedule for the rest of the year," he said, surprising her.

She smiled at him as they got out of the car and went inside the house. Immediately the dogs greeted them. They both petted the dogs, and Derek's comment made her think they were headed in the right direction.

"I don't know when I've had such a wonderful time other than the time I've spent with you." Derek grabbed some glasses of water for them to take to his bedroom, seeing Cliff and Will coming inside about that time.

"Oh, me too with you," she said. "You can be my dance partner always." As soon as Cliff and Will joined them in the kitchen, she said to them, "I loved your stunning performance."

The guys both laughed. "We were trying not to let our little secret slip before the big night," Will said.

"So you knew about it all along?" Derek asked.

"Yeah. Half of the bodyguards who wanted to

play the game left to get dressed and the other half stayed focused on their mission," Cliff said. "The rest of us waited out of sight while the other guys dressed in costume. We all had a blast playing the cops."

"Well, you did a good job keeping the secret. It was a real surprise to us," Kate said, "and it added so much fun."

Then Derek and Kate said their good nights. The dogs would stay with whoever would be pulling guard duty.

Derek swept her up in his arms and carried her into the bedroom, while the guys decided on who was staying up tonight to serve as a bodyguard and who would relieve him after a few hours.

Derek set her down on the floor, where she breathed in the leather scent in the room. The king-size bed featured a camel-colored leather headboard and footboard, and the mattress wore a light-gray comforter. Very stylish for an alpha male wolf.

"I love your king-size bed. Lots of room for romping and loving."

"Oh, yeah."

One wall featured paintings of the ocean, seagulls, and porpoises. A large dark oak dresser and mirrors took up another wall, and the other had large glass windows and doors that viewed the pool and, beyond, the Pacific Ocean. The bathroom was huge and perfect for pampering oneself.

She suspected Derek didn't use it for that purpose, but if she lived here, she sure would.

The bathroom had a large whirlpool tub, which she wanted to enjoy with him too. The countertops were gray-and-white marble, and the toilet had its own little room. Kate's was like that too, but her bathroom was all in tan and white and had white cabinets. His were dark gray. She liked the differences between them.

He smiled at her when she came out of the bathroom. "Do you like it?"

"I love it. Okay, so do I have any say in these outings we'll be going to?" Kate asked as Derek closed the bedroom door and then pulled her into his arms.

"Yeah, absolutely. I've already signed up for them, so if there's anything you don't want to go to, like the pirate party at Halloween—"

"Oh, I'm going to that."

"Or the Christmas dance—"

"Count me in for that."

"Or the New Year's Eve party..."

She sighed and wrapped her arms around his neck. "It sounds like I'm all booked up now."

He smiled down at her. "That's what I wanted to hear."

"After tonight, I wouldn't give you up for anything. There are so many things I want to do with you. You are definitely my go-to dance partner. But we need to be mated."

"Hell, yeah. At first, I was in denial. Everyone told me what a wonderful friend you were, and I could see it too. I wanted to really meet up with you in the worst way, but I just knew it would be a disaster," Derek said. "I was afraid you would want to wait longer before I proposed a mating."

"No way. I already know what I want, and that's you. To be with you as your mate, and I will still serve as your bodyguard if you need me to, only I'll get a lot more perks."

"Only if you allow me to protect you when you need me to. Ditto on the perks."

"That's a deal."

"Good. I love you more than anything in the world," Derek told Kate. "I hadn't thought I would ever feel this completely in love with anyone."

"Oh, me too. I love you, Derek. It started out as a huge crush on you. I never thought it would lead to this. I couldn't be any more thrilled about the way things worked out between us. No pressure—just fun and real. What we have is totally genuine."

"I agree." He moved her onto the bed and began removing her high heels. Then he ran his hands up the gold fringe of her dress and the gold and pearl beads in interesting patterns across the dress and caressed her legs. "I love this dress."

She chuckled. "I was whipping you with my fringe half the time I was dancing with you."

"Hmm, yeah. I loved the way your fringe caressed my legs. You're a terrific dancer."

"You too. That's a lot of why I want to mate you."

He smiled, the dimples in his chiseled face dazzling. His smiles warmed her, made her want to do anything for him, made her want to smile in return.

She stood and ran her hands over his pin-striped suit coat and then peeled it off his broad shoulders and down his arms and tossed it on the chest at the foot of the bed. She touched his silk vest—the fabric soft to the touch, his pecs hard beneath it—and began to unbutton it.

Distracting her, he caressed her breasts through her pearl-decorated dress, making her panties wet, her body already throbbing with need in anticipation of mating him. She couldn't imagine being with anyone else like this. He was the only one for her.

Once she removed his vest and tossed it aside, she began working on his cuff links. His thumbs stroked her nipples through the fabric, and she worked faster on his cuff links, finally removing them and setting them on his jacket, not wanting to toss them aside and lose them.

He leaned down and kissed her temple, his mouth caressing her skin with a gentle touch that made her insides melt. He closed his arms around her and pressed a kiss against her lips. She loved his tenderness and hotness all in one.

He removed her headband and then slid the pearl necklaces over her head, dropped them on the bench, turned her around, and unfastened her dress in the back. The dress fell to the floor, and he cupped her lace-covered breasts with his large hands.

Then he turned her again to face him. He settled his mouth on hers, and they were kissing and hugging, sharing the heat and passion with each other. He knew just how to rev up her motor, and he made her feel like a real winner.

She unbuttoned his shirt and then pulled it off his shoulders and tossed it. Neither of them had worn an undershirt or a slip like they would have in the '20s, but she realized she hadn't removed his shoes or socks yet. She pushed him back on the bed, making him sit. She untied his shoes, pulled one off and then the other, and set them aside. She briefly thought of a lotion foot massage after all the dancing they'd done, but she didn't want to take the time to do it right now. Instead, she pulled off his socks and then pushed him back against the bed to unfasten his belt. He was smiling at her, seeing a side of her that he hadn't before. She was in charge.

She slid his suspenders off his shoulders, pulled down his zipper, and then began to take off his pants. He helped her, and then she pressed her body against his aroused one. He felt divine beneath her. "God, I love you," she said.

"I don't know how I managed without you," Derek said, his voice husky with desire.

"Me either," she said, smiling before she kissed him again on the mouth.

He chuckled. "I love you with all my heart." Then he slid his arms around her back and unfastened her bra. She felt free of confinement until he moved her onto her back, and he covered her breasts with his hands, placed a knee between her legs, and kissed her mouth.

He started to kiss her breasts. And she loved the way he licked her nipples, making both tingle and ache, and that made her nether region throb even more for his intimate touch. She reached down to relieve him of his boxer briefs. Then he was slipping the scrap of lace and silk panties off her bottom.

His beautiful eyes were filled with lust, looking at her with love and admiration and hunger—definitely hunger, as if he wanted to memorize this moment for all time and didn't want to rush this. He slid his hand over her belly and then lower, through her short curly hairs, and then he connected with her nubbin. He began to rub her in the most pleasing way.

Oh, sweet, yes! She was so glad she was keeping him for her own! His finger was working magic on her when he speared her mouth with his tongue and deepened the kiss. She moaned softly, loving the way he was stroking her, the way he was kissing her.

Then she kissed him back, combing her fingers through his silky hair. He stole her thoughts with his heady strokes on her nubbin, and she felt the climax coming, climbing, peaking, and then it hit hard.

"Are you ready?" he asked, his voice thick with lust.

"Yeah. I am." She was so glad to do it.

He pressed his stiff erection between her legs and pushed home. He forged forward, and she loved how he filled her to the max. Her heart and his were pounding like crazy, the blood rushing to her head. He captured her mouth, his body moving against hers in a mating dance.

He was so well built, his body perfect against hers, and she rubbed her foot against the back of his thigh, her hands sweeping down his arms. Then he was coming in a heavy groan, releasing, pumping, kissing her. He drove into her harder, faster, and continued to thrust into her until he was spent.

"Oh, baby, I love you," he said, hugging her tight against him.

"I love you, Derek." He was too good to be true.

He sighed. "You're amazing."

"So. Are. You."

He finally pulled out of her and cuddled her in his arms. "Life will never be the same again."

"That's a good thing. A wonderful thing." Now

they had to tell everyone, and she needed to move in. Whoever would have thought she would mate the wolf who had taken her to the gala because he'd been dumped by his human date!

CHAPTER 25

SNUGGLING WITH KATE THAT NIGHT, DEREK couldn't believe that he and she were mated wolves now, and he couldn't love her more. He had been hoping for this ever since he took her out to their first social engagement. He'd loved how she had shown her wolfish possessiveness over him, kissing him to claim him in front of Brenda, showing a natural instinct when a wolf was intrigued with another, just like he had been intrigued with her and had been from the start.

He had known beyond a doubt that Kate was the wolf for him. He was afraid he would have had to work for months to convince her of it, but when she said she had wanted to mate tonight, he couldn't have been more ecstatic. He hoped she didn't mind telling the world first thing tomorrow morning about it because he wanted everyone to know they were getting married. In the wolf way, they would be lifetime mates after they had consummated love, but humans wouldn't understand it was a forever deal with them, no marriage license needed. So they mated, or to the humans' way of thinking, were engaged to be married, and when they had time, they'd plan their wedding.

"Let's get married in Hawaii," she said.

"You mean use our free excursion trip for that?"

"Sure, but we'll be there for longer, for a honeymoon too. Everyone we would want to attend can afford it. We'll just try to plan it for when Aidan and Holly's babies can travel and before Lexi is too far along to fly and everyone else can plan some time off to do it," Kate said.

"Rafe has a plane we can use to take the lot of us," Derek said.

Kate smiled. "That's perfect. And if anyone wants to shift while en route, they can."

"Yeah, like Holly, if she's still nursing her babies."

For a little bit, they were quiet. She was running her hand over Derek's stomach in a gentle caress, and he was running his hand over her bare arm.

"Love you." She kissed his chest and then nestled her head against him.

"Love you too." He kissed the top of her head. He felt on top of the world, and he knew just what it was like for his good friends who were all mated wolves.

They finally fell asleep in each other's arms.

The next morning, Derek found a wolf nuzzling his back instead of a woman cuddling up to his backside. He chuckled, turned, and ran his hand over Kate's furry head. He was always amazed how pretty she was whether she was ready for the beach, swimming in his pool, or hiking in a park. When she dressed up for the social events, she was gorgeous. In her fur coat, she was just as beautiful.

"Man, you're beautiful." He kissed her. "All right, wolf run now." He could take a hint.

He shifted, and she jumped out of bed. He leapt off the bed on her side and raced after her, expecting her to go to the dog door in his bedroom.

She raced out of the bedroom instead, heading for the only dog door she knew about in the kitchen!

Will waved at them from the living room. "Morning."

They both woofed at him, low woofs though because they knew if Will was up, Cliff was sleeping.

Then Derek and Kate were outside and racing across the pool patio and down the steps. Derek shifted so he could unlock the gate, open it, and then stepped outside the gate while she ran into the sand. He locked the gate and shifted. They ran down the beach, the wind in their fur, the sound of the waves lapping at the shore. It was dark out still, the sand and white caps on the waves seemingly illuminated with their wolf vision. He never saw anyone on the beach this early, and he hoped he never would.

It was the perfect place to get a wolf workout in the evenings after it closed or early in the morning—or both.

He usually ran with one of the guys, but running with Kate was even better. Her tongue was hanging out, and so was his.

They had run on the sand in the cool early morning sea air for about two miles when they saw a patrol officer on the beach with a flashlight.

Great! Derek and Kate did a swift turnaround and raced as fast as they could back toward his home and safety. They were so far away from the officer that Derek didn't think he could see them in the dark when the beam of the flashlight didn't carry that far. But he didn't want the officer to see where Kate and he ended up either—opening the gate to his estate. Especially when he had to get naked to do it. Then he could be charged with being on the beach after it was closed, being naked on the beach, and having a dog on the beach, and the dog wasn't even a dog but a wolf.

He unlocked the gate, they headed inside, and he shut it, the lock clicking automatically. Then he shifted into his wolf and ran up the stairs with Kate.

He was glad they hadn't gotten caught. He and she rested their paws on the wall and looked down at the beach. They could see the patrol officer way off down the beach, his flashlight poking into the darkness. He couldn't have seen them, and Derek was glad for that.

Kate turned and licked Derek's face. Then she went over to the outdoor shower, and he joined her, shifted, and turned on the water. She shifted, and they washed in the shower and then both went for a dip in the pool.

Now this was the life. A good wolf run—they hadn't been caught—and a swim with a naked woman in the pool? Yeah, it couldn't get better.

"I wonder if someone alerted the police that they'd seen dogs running on the beach," Kate said, her arms wrapped around Derek's neck while he treaded the warm pool water.

The stars were beginning to fade, the moon still full, clinging to the early morning sky.

"Anything's possible. Or someone just started to patrol the beach, maybe to catch fishermen trying to set up before first morning light. Other beaches are open twenty-four hours for that purpose, but not this one."

"That's good for us—as wolves."

"I agree. We'll have to see about running at night though."

They swam for a bit, got out of the pool, and grabbed terrycloth robes out of an outdoor closet, and she smiled. "Wow, now this is living."

He smiled at her. "I never expected to be wrapping up my wolf mate in a terrycloth robe here anytime soon." He helped her into hers and cinched the tie for her and then put one on too. They went through the bedroom door, and he pointed to the wolf door there.

She laughed. "Here I went all the way through the house to the kitchen door to go outside."

"Yeah, I was surprised when you tore through the house. Then I realized I forgot to tell you about the one in my bedroom."

She laughed again. "I'm sure Will got a kick out of it." She hurried to dress in a shirt, shorts, and tennis shoes, ready for him to take her to the lake on a pedal boat ride. She was always a ray of sunlight.

He sat on the bed, ready to make love to her again—skip the trip to the lake and pedal boating.

"Time to go." She came over and kissed him on the cheek, but he pulled her into his arms and hugged her tight.

"We could go just a little later." He raised his brows and smiled.

"No way." She squirmed out of his arms, hurried off down the hall, and then returned with a beach bag in hand, floppy hat on her head, and wearing a pair of sunglasses. She always looked so bouncy and eager to try out something new with him. "We need to tell everyone we're mated." She looked like she wanted to howl it to the world!

He pulled on his board shorts and then sat on the bed again. "I'm all for it." He reached out his arms for her. "Let's call everyone on speakerphone." She sat on his lap, and then he made a conference call to the whole pack.

"Hey, hope everyone is up for the news"—though Kate suspected Aidan and Holly might have had a sleepless night with the new babies—"but Derek and I are mated."

Whoops and hollers—the loudest from Derek's staff since Will, Cliff, and Maddie were just down the hall from them in the living room—sounded over the phone. A few howls rent the air, and then that was all they heard.

Kate and Derek laughed, then added their own howls to the mix.

"We all told you so, Derek. That Kate was the one for you," Rafe said.

Derek kissed Kate.

"Yeah, I knew more would come of this," Lexi said. "Then there will be jet-setting all over the world—"

Kate laughed and snuggled against Derek. "I'll be there for the business, Lexi. Don't you worry."

"In your capable hands, I'm worry free."

"We'll take out the yacht and celebrate," Rafe said. "It's comfortable enough for Aidan and Holly and the babies, if they think they can manage, and we'll have a whole staff to cater to our needs."

"Ohmigod, yes!" Kate said, and Derek agreed.

Holly and Aidan said they would love it. Even Maddie piped in and said she was coming. She might not like camping in the woods, but she loved to boat!

With a few more congratulations, they ended the call to have breakfast before heading out to the lake.

Will and Cliff would follow them and would sit on shore while they pedaled about the lake.

"You're doing all the pedaling, right?" she asked as Derek pulled on a T-shirt and some waterproof sandals.

He laughed. "Yeah, sure."

She figured he would too. Anything to make her happy. She was so glad she had chosen him to be her mate.

After he was dressed, they headed to the kitchen where Maddie was making them breakfast.

The dogs were outside after having eaten their breakfast and were chasing each other around the yard.

Maddie gave Kate a hug. "I told Derek he should have hired you as his bodyguard, and then when this happened, he could have hired Will."

Everyone chuckled. Kate loved Maddie and hugged her back. Then Maddie hugged Derek. Will and Cliff hugged them too. It really was a family affair.

"Because you are going boating this morning, I baked egg boats for breakfast. I didn't realize it would be a celebratory feast, but just having you here, Kate, makes it so anyway. You'll love the quiche, baked into a crusty, toasted baguette instead of a pie crust. The egg filling made of eggs, cream, cheese, pancetta, and green onions is poured into the hollowed-out baguette and baked until the eggs have set and the baguette is toasted. Salt and pepper to taste. Mimosas are the drink of the morning in addition to coffee and tea," Maddie said, serving up the food while Cliff made the mimosas.

"Wow, that looks divine," Kate said, thinking she was going to have to do a lot more exercising to wear off the extra calories if Maddie kept making such delicious meals.

Once Derek and Kate finished breakfast, they headed to the lake.

"I brought us chilled bottles of water and suntan lotion in my bag," Kate said.

"Maddie packed us a picnic lunch while you were grabbing a couple more things. I told her we were eating at the marina for lunch, but she thought I should take you there tonight and so"—Derek motioned to the back seat—"we have lunch we can eat at the park if you would like."

"Oh, that will be super!"

He smiled. "Good. I didn't expect her to take over my dating plans."

Kate laughed. "Well, they were both good plans."

CHAPTER 26

DEREK LOVED HOW ENTHUSIASTIC KATE WAS about doing anything different. He wouldn't have even suggested it with any of the girlfriends he had dated before. He actually hadn't done anything like this since his youth. Which was part of the reason he loved her and had wanted to mate her. Her passion was contagious.

After they arrived and parked at the boat rental at the lake, they checked in. Will and Cliff parked nearby.

"I'm sorry," the boat rental manager said, "but the two-person pedal boat you had reserved had to be pulled out of service. A four-person pedal boat is available instead. The family who had reserved this one called to say they couldn't make it, so we kept this one for you, if that's all right with you."

"Oh, sure," Kate quickly said, taking Derek's hand to tell him that she was fine with it.

He was glad she was so easygoing. He could imagine Brenda having a conniption if she had even wanted to do this. Brenda had thrown a fit before when he couldn't get preferred seating at a restaurant one night, and he never took her there again.

Wearing life jackets and with Kate's bag containing sunscreen and bottled waters in hand, they climbed aboard the pedal boat and began pedaling out. She was pedaling just as much as he was, and they were a good way across part of the lake where others were paddling in kayaks and canoes in the expanse when they saw three people riding on an electric pedal boat. What was the fun in that? At least Derek thought the whole point of riding on a pedal boat was to self-propel it and get some exercise.

But as he and Kate watched the electric boat pass them by, he thought the stern where the younger woman was sitting was starting to sink lower and lower into the water.

"That doesn't look good," Kate said, confirming what he suspected.

"No, it doesn't. Let's pedal faster if we can and get as close to them as possible so if anyone's injured, we won't have as far to reach them. If the boat sinks, we'll be saving them." Normally, he would have kept his distance from another boater, but it looked like this could be turning into a rescue mission.

"I agree. If they can't swim, we'll need to bring them to our boat and fish them out of the water." She looked back at the electric boat and frowned. "It's really sinking. There's no doubt about that."

The woman sitting at the stern started to move portside before she ended up sitting in the water as the bottom continued to fill up with water.

"She's going to capsize the boat. She's tipping it on the port side already because of the older gentleman sitting there already. They're losing their balance," Derek warned.

Then what he worried would happen did. The whole boat flipped over, sending Derek's adrenaline into overdrive. "Stay with our pedal boat," Derek said before Kate dove off their boat to rescue the people herself. He stripped off his T-shirt and kicked off his sandals, leaving his cell phone and car keys with Kate. "Keep pedaling toward the capsized boat. I'll try to rescue anyone who needs my help."

He dove into the water and swam toward the boat, where he couldn't see anyone emerging from the water. He was afraid they might have been knocked unconscious by the boat when it flipped over. Then he recalled what Kate had done as a living earlier—she had been a lifeguard. Maybe he should have continued pedaling to draw closer to the sinking boat while *she* rescued the survivors!

He reached the boat just as one of the people came out from under the boat coughing. At least all three of the victims had been wearing life jackets like Kate and Derek were.

Kate pedaled up closer to the capsized boat so Derek didn't have to swim too far to ferry the victims to the manpowered pedal boat. Derek reached the elderly man first and told him, "Grab hold of the strap on my life jacket, and I'll pull you to our boat." The man did as he was told, and once Derek reached their pedal boat, he and Kate helped him onto the stern of the boat. The older man sat on the seating for two more people who wouldn't be pedaling, just along for the ride.

"Did you want me to help with the other two victims? Wait, here comes one of the women," Kate said.

She was the younger of the two women and looked to be the daughter of the older couple, maybe in her thirties while they appeared to be in their sixties.

"Yeah, I'll go back for the other woman. See if you can help this one." Then Derek swam back to the overturned boat and found the older woman clinging to the other side of the boat where they hadn't been able to see her. "Okay, ma'am, I'm going to help you over to our pedal boat." He was afraid the five adults would weigh too much if they all tried to climb aboard. He could just envision their boat sinking too.

He would help the older woman onto the pedal boat and stay in the water until help reached them. Hopefully someone on shore had seen the mishap and called it in. Derek figured Kate might have been too busy taking care of the survivors to call 911 herself. Would they even have cell reception out here?

"Just hold on to the strap of my life jacket," he

told the older woman, and then once she had hold, he headed toward the pedal boat. Luckily, Kate had managed to pull the younger woman aboard. "Let's get this woman onto the boat, and then I'll wait in the water until we get a rescue," Derek told Kate as he continued to swim toward the boat.

"All right. I already called 911 for help. I hear the siren of an ambulance on its way." Kate pointed toward the other side of the lake. "A lake patrol boat is also headed this way."

"Okay, good." While in the water, Derek hadn't been able to see it coming with the capsized boat blocking his view in that direction. He'd been concentrating on helping the woman to their pedal boat, or he would have heard the sound of a boat engine drawing closer. He wondered if the three people's combined weight had been too much for the electric boat.

When he reached the pedal boat, he and Kate helped the older woman onto it, the other two people sitting in the back. "Judy says that's her mom and dad," Kate said.

The lake patrol boat was speeding to their location, and Derek was glad for that. He thought the dad looked pale, and the daughter had a goose egg on the side of her forehead. The mom looked all right, except she appeared exhausted from the ordeal. At least the water was warm, or they could have some cases of hypothermia.

Kate was giving the dad and daughter bottles of water as the mom collapsed on Derek's seat.

When the lake patrol reached them, they tossed Kate a towline, and she tied it to the pedal boat.

"Is everyone okay?" one of the officers called out.

"Yes, I am," the older man weakly said.

The older woman nodded, and her daughter said, "I got hit in the head by the boat when it flipped, but I'm okay. I just have a horrible headache."

"Okay, we're towing you in to get medical attention on the shore," the officer said.

Another was helping Derek into the patrol boat, though he wanted to be on the pedal boat with Kate. He knew that logistically, trying to transfer the older couple and their daughter from the pedal boat to the patrol boat could prove disastrous.

Once Derek was onboard, the patrol boat began to tug the pedal boat in while another vessel came out to take care of the flipped boat.

"Thanks for taking care of the victims," the officer told Derek. "On her 911 call, Kate said you both witnessed the electric boat sinking and then the daughter moving portside and that tipped the boat."

"Yeah, she was trying to keep from being in the water since the stern was sinking so fast. We were just trying to reach them as quickly as we could in case anyone was in danger of drowning."

"Well, thanks. Without your help, someone might have."

When they finally reached the shore, the paramedics helped the three people from the pedal boat and started checking them over.

"I think my dad might have suffered a mild heart attack," the daughter said, and they rushed him in the ambulance—where they could do an EKG and provide treatment if he was having one—on the way to the hospital.

Another ambulance had arrived, and the EMTs were looking over the mother and daughter. The mother appeared fine, but the daughter needed some more care because of the mild concussion she might have suffered.

One of the lake patrol officers asked Derek and Kate, "Do you want us to tow you to the other side of the lake to the boat rentals?"

"Thanks for the offer, but no," Kate said. "We'll pedal back there on our own."

"Yeah," Derek agreed. Though he knew they would be late in arriving by about an hour.

"I called to let the boat rental place know we were rescuing people on the water. They said our trip was free and to get in when we could," Kate told Derek.

"Good show!" Derek loved how quickly Kate had taken care of the situation in a crisis. "You know, I hadn't really thought about the businesses that I manage, but I know who I'm going to rely on if I need help with them."

She gave him a brilliant smile. "I'm going to be running everyone's business before long."

He laughed. "And then rule the world."

Then the officers thanked them again, and so did the mother and the daughter before the ambulance took the daughter to the hospital to be checked over.

Kate and Derek got on their pedal boat and headed across the lake at a more leisurely pace this time.

"You know, after I dove into the water, I realized I should have asked if you wanted to use your lifeguard training instead." Derek sure hoped his actions hadn't annoyed Kate.

Kate had thought the same, but she had assumed that Derek hadn't remembered that about her and that, being an alpha male wolf, he had been too concerned with saving lives right away instead. "It didn't matter. You did a great job, and everyone survived. Hopefully, the father and the daughter will be all right after they run tests on them."

"I hope so. Thanks for the quick thinking about calling 911 and the boat rental company."

"I was worried about the people we rescued. The

man appeared so gray and seemed out of it. I asked his name and where he lived, but he didn't respond. His daughter seemed a bit out of it too. At least we had our cell phones and could call it in. They lost their bags, wallets, cell phones, and keys, all at the bottom of the lake."

"I hadn't even thought of that."

"Yeah, that was the first thing the mother said to me. As to the boat rental company, I was afraid we would be charged a huge amount for not bringing the pedal boat in on time. I knew we had a good reason, but I wasn't sure they realized we were involved in the rescue. I wanted to let them know that we weren't at fault. I know you could afford the fine, but it just wouldn't have been right."

"I agree. Though I'm afraid whoever was waiting on our pedal boat would have to wait way longer or just give up and do it another time. It's summer and the place was booked, but when lives are involved, I'm sure they'll understand."

They had pedaled out a lot farther than they had planned to and then the lake patrol had pulled them to a different landing site, so they had a lot farther to go. Kate didn't mind the exercise. She figured she'd be worn out though by the time they got back in.

"Hmm, love all your muscles dripping with water," she said.

He smiled.

It was a good thing he'd been wearing board shorts.

"I guess we'll have our picnic lunch when we get in," Derek said.

"Yeah, I'm starving already." Kate reached into her bag and brought out a couple of fresh bottles of water. "It's a good thing I brought a lot of chilled water bottles since I ended up giving some to the family. We were supposed to have these in case we drank the others up."

"I was going to grab some, but Maddie said she packed us some in the ice chest."

"What did she send with you for us to eat?" Kate hoped it was something she would like.

"No telling. But for you? Something good, I'm sure. I've never seen her go all out for any of my other dinner guests. Not that any girlfriends ever came to the house. I'm sure they wanted to, but that was my way of maintaining my privacy. Two of them didn't like dogs, so I told them I had a whole houseful of them, and that was a great deterrent."

"Even for Brenda?"

"Especially for Brenda. She said she would come over if I would kennel the dogs. As if I would ever do that for a date."

"I guess she didn't realize that the relationship wouldn't ever have gotten anywhere if she didn't like dogs."

"Nope. A person who doesn't care for pets—she didn't like cats either—wouldn't have been the one for me. It wasn't like she was allergic to them or anything. She just felt they were dirty and shouldn't be kept in a house with humans."

Kate smiled. "Imagine if she knew you were a wolf living among humans."

Derek chuckled. "Yeah. You know, you would think that a woman who was interested in marrying me for my money would at least put on a show to like something that really meant something important to me just to convince me to marry her. I can't imagine how terrible that would have been— had I not been a wolf and married her."

"She would have made you get rid of the dogs or at least kept them in kennels."

"Yeah, it wouldn't have worked out at all."

They finally reached the landing for the pedal boats, and Derek asked the rental manager, "Who was delayed because we didn't return the pedal boat on time?"

"We were," a man said, standing with a woman and a couple of kids—aged about six and eight, Derek thought. Both kids were dripping wet and must have been swimming in the meantime.

Derek went ahead and paid for the family's two-hour trip on the lake to make up for the delay.

"You didn't have to do that," the man said. "We know you saved those people out there. The manager had quickly told us. And there wasn't another pedal boat available."

"It's my treat."

"Well, thanks, man."

Then Derek and Kate left to return to their car and find a picnic spot.

"That was nice of you," Kate said.

"That's one nice thing about being able to afford it."

"That's true. And you did several good deeds for the day, so what's one more? You made their day. Hey, over there, a table is freeing up." Kate pointed to a picnic table where a family was just packing up their supplies. "I'll grab it." The park was so busy, she knew someone else would if she didn't right away.

"Okay, I'll bring the ice chest and picnic basket." Derek headed for the car.

Kate raced to the picnic table and set her bag down on it, a she-wolf claiming her territory.

She saw Derek coming with the ice chest and the picnic basket, and she smiled. She wondered just what goodies Maddie had made for them. After the camping trip, she suspected it would be really good.

He set the ice chest on one of the benches, and then he opened the picnic basket next to it. Inside the picnic basket was a tablecloth, silverware, and porcelain plates. She had expected plasticware and paper plates, but this was really nice.

Kate smiled. "Now this is what I call a classy picnic."

"I've had picnics with the guys, but Maddie never fixed anything like this for us. It was strictly sandwiches, packages of chips, and some paper napkins, no tablecloth, dinnerware, silverware, freshly made lemonade, or salads." Derek smiled. "Maddie really likes you."

Kate chuckled. "Well, she's a really sweet lady, and I like her too."

He and Kate both spread out the white linen tablecloth. After that, Kate began to set out the silverware and plates, and while she was doing that, he opened the ice chest and started to bring out the food.

"Hmm, that looks good."

Maddie had made them Cornish pasties filled with steak, potatoes, and onions, a lemon and kale salad with a buttermilk dressing in sealed jars, and blueberry bars for dessert. Pink lemonade, frozen water bottles, and a freezer pack helped keep everything cold.

Then Derek and Kate sat down next to each other to eat and watch the people on the lake.

"This is nice, sitting by the lake, having a world-class lunch, watching everyone having fun on the water." She noticed the electric pedal boat being pulled into shore. "Except for the family who rode that boat. The daughter said the boat was brand-new, and the rental manager told them they met the maximum recommended weight limit."

"Well, obviously it wasn't seaworthy for one reason or another."

"True. Hmm, this food is delicious. So what will we do after this? We're going to the marina for dinner now, but—"

"What would you like to do, Kate? You always come up with great plans. I'm so used to doing fancy affairs with women, but you're not like other women I've dated."

"Even the two she-wolves you dated before?"

"Except for them. Still, you keep coming up with things I didn't do with either of them."

"I like to do all kinds of things. But I'm fine with just swimming this afternoon at your pool. I know you've already had your swim, but—"

"Saving people, right."

"Sure, and we can walk the dogs."

"That's all?"

"I think we might grab a quick nap"—though she was thinking the nap might be a bit delayed—"and then we can have an early dinner at the marina."

"All right. We can do that. And tomorrow?" he asked.

"Hmm." She sipped on her lemonade. "A run as wolves on the beach first thing in the morning way before the beach is open. We can enjoy the sunrise. We could take a swim in the pool before breakfast."

"And then?"

"Your decision. You have to come up with something that isn't a society-related ball or something."

He laughed.

"Oh, wait! We were going to go to the botanical gardens," she said. "Sorry. But if you had thought of something else first, we could have done it."

"I can't wait to see all the flowers."

She smiled at him. She wasn't sure he really wanted to, but at least he was willing to do something she loved to do.

She then noticed a dark-haired man watching them. Maybe he thought it was nice that she and Derek appeared to be on a date and were having a good time, or maybe he was waiting for them to give up their picnic table. Which reminded her they probably needed to give it up at some point so that others could use it. She always thought it was mean when people would hog a table from first thing in the morning through the park closing, just to keep it in the family, as if they'd paid a rental fee for the goods.

She glanced back at the man, but he was gone, and she was relieved. She did have the notion he was a reporter, but he would have had a camera to document his "find," and he hadn't appeared to have one. She relaxed a little. She didn't like it when people watched her as if she were a specimen in a petri dish. She smiled at Derek.

"Yeah, that was a reporter," Derek said.

"He didn't take pictures. Or at least that I saw." She was having so much fun with Derek. She loved how he had helped her save the family in the water. She'd had the notion he might be a little pampered, but seeing him like this and after he lost his board shorts in the ocean last time, he was totally human and, well, of course, all wolf.

"Maybe he didn't realize who we were."

She sipped some more of the drink Maddie had sent with them. So much better than just plain water for their whole dining experience.

They watched the swans swimming across the lake and a couple of geese soaring in to land on the shore. It was the perfect day, breezy enough to make it cool so that they were perfectly comfortable, not sweltering in the heat. She wanted to snuggle against Derek. Kiss him. But he was eating his meal and enjoying the sights with her, and she didn't want to intrude on his thoughts at the moment. It was just too perfect.

He glanced at her and smiled. "A penny for your thoughts."

"This couldn't be any more perfect today, don't you think?"

"No. I don't know when I've enjoyed a day at the lake like this. Not since I was a kid, playing in the lake with Rafe and Aidan. I guess we began to get stuck in our routines and don't do any of the other things we enjoyed when we were younger. You've really made me appreciate all the things there are to do and not get stuck in such a rut."

"Good. I have to admit I'm the same way. I work all the time, go home, eat, watch a movie, run as a wolf, go to sleep, next day, repeat. This has been so nice for me. Especially since Lexi has a mate now and they need time to themselves. Before, Lexi and I would do lots of things together. She loved that I could enjoy them with her, and I could feel satisfied that I was still serving as her bodyguard. It was the perfect arrangement. This is just as nice."

"I'm glad you're enjoying it with *me*. I couldn't think of anyone I would rather be with like this."

They finished their drinks and their food, and then they began to pack up the picnic basket. She still couldn't believe how fancy their picnic had been.

"I guess I'll need to move my things over to your place and then Lexi can have her house back. Mike might end up staying there," Kate said.

"I'll get everyone together to help move your things. When do you want to do it?"

"We could do some of it tomorrow night. Just my clothes. That way, I can have my clothes at your place and then we can really clean my house out next weekend."

He smiled. "Sure thing." He got on his phone.

"Hey, tell Will we're going to move some of Kate's things to my house—um, our house—tomorrow night. So can you get some packing boxes when you have a chance?"

CHAPTER 27

When they arrived at Derek's house, Maddie was there, all smiles to greet them. "Did you enjoy your picnic lunch?"

"Yes, and thanks for the beautiful lunch," Kate said. "It was just wonderful."

"Are you going to the marina for dinner then?" Maddie removed the used dishes and silverware from the picnic basket.

"We are. Your suggestions were perfect."

"I'm glad you liked them."

"You should have seen what Kate and Derek went through on their date," Cliff said, he and Will just coming inside after following them home.

"Oh?" Maddie asked. "What happened at the lake?"

"Derek and Kate saved some people from a capsized boat. Here Will and I were stuck on shore, watching the whole scene play out way off in the distance, and we couldn't help one little bit," Cliff said. "Though we tried to rent a rowboat to go out to assist."

"We managed, but thanks for trying to come to our aid," Derek said. "We're going swimming."

"I'll set out some cold drinks for you," Maddie said.

"Thanks, Maddie." Derek hadn't expected her to be at his house all the time, but she loved it there, and she was welcome to stay there as much as she wanted to. He was thinking of building her a cottage on the property so she could just live there.

Kate had already headed for the bedroom, and he realized they were planning to take a "nap" first. When he reached the bedroom, she had tossed her shorts and shirt on a chair and was just wearing her bathing suit.

She kissed him, but as soon he started to kiss her, she smiled. "You told everyone we are going swimming and Maddie's putting cold drinks out for us."

He chuckled. "Yeah, I goofed on that."

"Let's swim, play in the water, and come back in for our nap."

He was already yanking his T-shirt off, wanting to do this. Though they would have fun, he wanted to get back to the bedroom business.

"See you," she said.

He kicked off his sandals and raced out the back patio to the swimming pool.

She jumped into the swimming pool, and he jumped into the pool after her.

At least here, Cliff and Will didn't have to watch them. The estate was secure, high walls and locked gates keeping out anyone who they didn't want in. No one could see them in the pool area unless someone flew over in a plane or helicopter. A couple of times, aerial drones had flown over the estate, trying to capture videos of his property. It wasn't legal to take pictures of property or people without their permission, but paparazzi or curious people had been known to attempt to see what was going on where Derek lived, and Will was a great marksman and would quickly take them down. If they didn't like it that their property had been destroyed, too bad. They shouldn't have been trying to spy on private property.

"Tomorrow we can just fall out of bed and run as wolves and then go to the botanical gardens." Derek pulled Kate into his arms in the pool. "About tonight… We can watch the sunset and run as wolves if you would like."

Then he leaned down and kissed her, loving that this was her home now and he could swim with her in the pool or hug and kiss her like this anytime. She was made for kissing, he thought. *His* kissing, not anyone else's.

She slid her arms around his waist in the silky, heated water. The warm ocean breeze caressed their skin and tossed her hair about as the waves rolled in down below his estate and crashed on the beach, over and over again.

Seagulls cried out overhead, and he realized he'd never enjoyed being here as much as he did with Kate.

She kissed him back, slowly, pressuring, building, seeking entrance with her tongue, and then exploring him. He quickly took advantage to do the same with her. She was addictive.

He slid his hand down her buttocks and pulled her against his burgeoning arousal.

"Hmm." She finally broke off the kiss and smiled. "Let's play some basketball and swim. I think I'm going to be just a little sore from all that pedaling on the pedal boat today. What about you?"

He got out of the pool to get the basketball hoop and ball. "Yeah. Even though I run and walk all the time, that pedaling worked some different muscles."

He tossed the ball to her and set the hoop in the water. Then he dove in, and they began playing basketball. He tried to keep her from making a basket, but she tackled him under the water; then he was laughing so hard, she scored.

Everything was different between them now. The first time they did this, they were just tossing the ball and talking to each other. This time, they were playing hard, playing to win, but deterring each other in an intimate, sexy way. Instead of trying to block her from making the basket, he wrapped his body around her and kissed her. This was fun before-bed play too.

She missed the basket because he was taller than her and she couldn't see the target.

The next time he had the ball and tried to make

a basket, she jumped up and kissed his nose, and he lost the ball to her. He swore he heard Will and Cliff laughing inside and figured they were either watching a comedy or them.

After they finished playing, they swam a little, not laps, but just floated around each other talking.

"You know I regret not having dated you before."

Kate treaded water near him and smiled. "I totally understand. You were having a good time with Brenda, no strings attached, as far as you were concerned."

"Yeah, but with you, I quickly realized I wanted strings attached."

She smiled. "I'm so glad for that."

He drew close and pulled her into his arms. "You are so worth it." He smiled and kissed her.

She wrapped her arms around his neck. "At least I didn't need to give you an ultimatum to mate me or else I was dumping you."

"I wouldn't have needed you to give me an ultimatum. Ever."

———

Kate smiled and kissed him again. "Hey, would you mind walking the dogs on the beach before we lie down and then go to the marina for dinner?"

"Sure, let's do that."

Kate loved him for letting her decide what they

were going to do next. She figured he wanted to make love, and she did too. Afterward.

They left the pool to walk along the beach in their bathing suits so they would dry out. It was late enough that she didn't care to take a dip in the ocean this time. What if they had a repeat of Derek losing his board shorts? And she did have the notion that the sharks fed at night.

Cliff went with them this time, wanting to see if Kate tackled any more would-be thieves on the beach.

"Yeah, you really missed out last time," Will told Cliff before they left for their walk. "Not to say that Kate is going to go after anyone else this afternoon, but you never know."

Of course she was going to be watching for would-be thieves again this time. She was sort of programmed that way. "You know we could just set up a sting operation and pretend that we're enjoying the beach and let them think we're clueless that they're out to rob us."

Derek laughed.

"I'm serious."

"I know you are. Hey, if you want to do it, we can set it up. And the guys can tackle them."

"Cliff and Will have to look like they're beachcombers and not like they're ready to grab would-be thieves," Kate said.

"Oh, we can get the look down next time.

Mirrored glasses," Will said. "Board shorts, flip-flops, shirtless, sunning on towels behind you, but far enough away that it wouldn't look like we're together and watching out for you."

"I'm all for it," Cliff said. "An entertaining day spent on the beach for sure."

Kate thought the guys were funny and they really needed a good mission to show off their skills. "Okay, well, we'll have to do it one of these days. Let's walk the dogs for now and then we can shower and rest before we go to the marina for dinner."

Will told Cliff, "Just you take down the thieves this time. Kate caught me off guard when she tackled the other guy."

"I'll certainly do that," Cliff said.

But if Kate saw the guy first, she was taking the thief down before he got away with it.

Then they headed down to the beach.

———

Truthfully, Derek hoped for just a fun walk on the beach with Kate, though if it made her feel right with the world while apprehending thieves and making it safer for beachgoers to enjoy the beach, he would back her all the way. But he was thinking that if that happened, they would have to wait for the police to get there, and they could miss their dinner date since he had already made a reservation. Though if that made her night, they could just grill steaks tonight. He was up for anything she wanted to do.

Foxy saw a crab on the beach, stopped them in their tracks, and barked at it. Red watched, but he left it alone—good boy.

"No bothering the crab," Kate said and pulled Foxy away to walk her farther down the beach. "How much time do we have?"

"If we walk to that man's blue chaise longue under the red-and-white-striped umbrella and then turn around and head back, we should have enough time to clean up, nap, dress, and then head over to the marina."

"Okay, that sounds good to me."

Thankfully, they hadn't seen anyone who was causing any mischief. Even if Cliff took care of anyone like that, Derek and Kate still wouldn't leave to have their dinner on time because they would have to give their statements to the police too.

They turned around at the man's umbrella and started to walk back to the house. "I wonder if the police officer was down on the beach last night because he'd had word someone had been out there. If a complaint was made about dogs running loose, he would have called animal control," Kate said.

"Yeah, I suspect you're right." Derek glanced

back at Cliff. "Hey, I was thinking only one of you needs to come to the marina restaurant tonight with us, but I imagine you'll get into a fight over it, so both of you can come unless one of you wants to chill out at home."

Cliff smiled. "I'll go for sure and text Will to see what he wants to do."

Derek always paid for their meals out, and they ordered whatever they liked. But in a case where he felt he only needed one of them, if that, he wanted to give them the option. Will might even want to go on a date! Derek realized he should make sure both Cliff and Will had time enough off to do whatever they wanted to. He really didn't feel like he was in any danger.

They hadn't walked very much farther when Cliff said, "Will is coming. The food's too good, and he doesn't want to miss out."

"Okay, good." Derek had already made reservations for both Will and Cliff too, just in case they both had wanted to come. Derek knew that if there was any action to be had, Will would want to be there in the thick of it to protect him and Kate as well.

They finally reached the gate to his place, and Derek was glad that they hadn't had any incidents on the beach. Then they headed up to the house, showered off the sand in the outdoor shower, and then rinsed off the dogs' paws. Cliff took the dogs back to the yard to play, while Kate and Derek went inside to shower and nap.

After making love and napping, Kate slipped on an aqua sundress featuring pink roses. She wasn't wearing a bra under the smocked bodice that embraced her breasts, and Derek was thinking about slipping it off her tonight when they got home. She looked pretty and summery, and she made for the perfect date. She was wearing slip-on sandals, not high heels, and that made her appear dressy casual. Not that he didn't like sexy heels on her, but he loved the more casual look on her too.

Once they were driving to the restaurant, she said, "I bet you're glad we didn't have to catch any more thieves tonight."

"Yes, for two reasons. We didn't see any, and that's a good sign, and because I just wanted to have a good time with you and have more time to love on you."

"Cliff would have had a great time of it though."

Derek smiled. "Yeah, he would have."

Kate was so glad Derek had brought her to the marina at night for dinner instead of for lunch as they had originally planned. The whole marina was decorated in lights that reflected off the water. Ripples of water made the boats rise and fall in a gentle dance while rigging on sailboat masts clinked and clanked against the metal. Derek had gotten them one of the best seats by the water. Everyone knew Derek here, and she wondered if he often brought his dates here. Even Brenda, since she'd wanted him to take her here for lunch.

Kate looked over the seafood menu, and everything looked great. But the king salmon really appealed. "I'll have that and a salad." She pointed to the salmon on her menu, showing it to Derek.

"Okay, that looks good." Then Derek pointed to the appetizer he thought would be good.

Kate agreed. A nice sampling of seafood. They had hamburgers and steaks too, but why eat anything but seafood at a restaurant at the marina? Unless of course someone hated seafood or was allergic to it. But wolves loved fish.

When the server dropped off glasses of water and came to take their orders, Kate got the salmon, rice, and peas while Derek asked for the lobster, rice, and broccoli and for an appetizer for the both of them: mussels, squid, shrimp, oysters, tomato, celery, fennel, and grilled bread.

They heard a loud party across the bay, music playing and laughter. It sounded like the people there were having a blast.

"We'll be taking Rafe's yacht out and having that party and sounding like that soon enough," Derek said.

"That will really be nice. I would love it. Did you ever take Brenda out on the yacht?"

"Nope. Rafe only has parties for us. His staff are wolves too, and he wants to keep it free for everyone to do their own thing. Which means lying around as a wolf or in a bikini."

She chuckled. She thought that would really be entertaining.

After they finished eating dinner, she ordered the devil's food cake with hazelnut butter cream, cocoa nibs, and whipped cream topping. Derek had the banana cream pie trifle made with butterscotch and chocolate graham crackers and topped with whipped cream.

"Now that looks good too," she said, thinking she would try it the next time they came to the marina because this was too much fun not to come here again.

They were eating their meals and loving the food. Kate didn't know why she'd never been here before when she got a call. Thinking it was Lexi, she checked her phone. She didn't recognize the number and set her phone down on the table.

"No one you know?" Derek asked.

"No. I've been getting a lot of random calls since Lexi made me part owner of Clair de Lune Cosmetics—everyone from financial advisors, insurance agents, real estate agents. I guess they think I'm now in the market for an expensive sports car, but I would rather just ride with you in your car."

Derek chuckled. "I'll get you your own anytime you would like."

"Oh, I would love that. Thanks!"

Then they saw Brenda and a couple of her gal pals headed for the entrance to the restaurant. Brenda immediately saw Derek and Kate, and her jaw dropped. Good. Kate was glad Brenda was surprised, which would indicate she wasn't stalking her and Derek now. Kate wanted to turn into a wolf to scare Brenda away from her man—who happened to be a hot wolf and her mate now.

Kate guessed the police didn't have enough cause to put Brenda in jail, though she was hoping something more had happened to her so Brenda couldn't be out with her friends having a great time. Kate didn't want to have to deal with what she'd dealt with before when it came to an ex-girlfriend who wouldn't move on.

CHAPTER 28

WHEN DEREK SAW BRENDA ARRIVE AT THE marina restaurant with her two friends, he shook his head. "I guess we should have gone somewhere else."

"No. Way. It was my choice. Brenda doesn't own the restaurant, does she?" Kate asked.

"Nope."

"Okay, then we're good. Even if she did own the restaurant, she wouldn't dare piss me off any more than she already has."

Smiling, Derek raised a brow, waiting for clarification.

"I have a lot of friends through Lexi's business. After what has already happened, I wouldn't hesitate to do something about it."

"Well, she's on *my* bad side already too," Derek said. "I'm surprised any of her friends would even be seen with her."

"I suspected some would be despite what some of her former friends said to us at the roaring twenties party."

"Well, she's not going to cause any more trouble for you. We'll make sure of it. Now that you're

with me permanently, she has to face reality. I have
a lot more influence than she does. She's more
one to just hang on to other's coattails. Oh, and
we need to list our engagement announcement on
all the sites."

Kate smiled. "Yeah, let's do it. But for now, can I
have a bite of your dessert?"

He laughed. "Priorities, priorities. Yeah, sure."

"It looks so good, I figure the next time we come
here, I'll get it if I really like it."

He moved his plate over so she could scoop up
as much as she wanted.

She took a spoonful and ate it. "Hmm, yeah,
definitely worth a try. Do you want some of mine?"

"Sure." She offered her plate to him, and he
spooned up a portion and then ate it. "Yeah, this is
really good too."

Then Derek saw the reporter who had been at
the lake near their picnic table coming into the
restaurant. The guy didn't seem to see him and
Kate. The reporter disappeared somewhere in the
back of the restaurant in the direction that Brenda
had gone. Maybe he would give her a hard time.
Derek could only hope.

"That's the same guy I saw at the lake," Kate
whispered to Derek.

"Yeah."

"Hey, well, I'm done, if you're ready to leave,"
Kate said. "We could walk along the marina."

"Let's do it." He paid for their meals, and they left the restaurant. He noticed that Cliff and Will were also finished with their meals, and then the two bodyguards joined them outside. "We're just going for a walk along the marina," Derek said.

"Did you see the reporter?" Will asked.

"Yeah, he had to be after someone else," Derek said.

"Brenda. No telling what she'll say," Cliff said.

"He writes for a tabloid. No telling what the reporter will say either," Derek said.

They were walking along the water, listening to the boats moving in their slips, the water slapping against them, the rigging on the masts clinking in the breeze. It was really lovely, doing this with Kate. Then he saw the reporter who had been in the restaurant, and he was headed their way.

"Do you want me to head him off?" Cliff asked.

"No. Thanks though." Derek wanted to be with Kate tonight without anyone harassing them, but he did think this might be the perfect opportunity to get the word out that he and Kate were engaged and would be married as soon as they came up with a date.

"We could tell him we're getting married," Kate said.

"I was considering that too." He was glad that she was thinking along the same lines as he was.

She squeezed his hand and smiled up at him. "Let's do it."

Cliff stepped back to allow the reporter to talk to them.

When he approached them, he said, "Do you care to comment on Brenda Connors's situation with her brother-in-law?"

"That is an ongoing investigation, but I can tell you that Kate and I are engaged and shortly to be married," Derek said.

The reporter smiled. "Congratulations to the both of you. Do we have a wedding date?"

"No, not yet, but thanks," Kate said.

"So is what Brenda claims—that you and Kate had been seeing each other while you were dating Brenda—true?"

"Derek and I've known each other for a year," Kate said, "but no, we never dated each other during that time. Then he asked me to the gala when Brenda gave him up, and we just hit it off. It might sound cliché, but it truly was love at first sight."

"I agree with Kate there," Derek said, kissing her.

The reporter snapped a couple of shots. "What do you think will happen when Brenda learns of this?"

"I don't even want to speculate," Derek said. "But I hope she's mature enough to realize that I've moved on and she needs to as well."

"Like Derek, I'm hoping she realizes it's over between her and Derek now and she'll peaceably get on with her life." Kate smiled sweetly.

Derek was glad Kate said what she did. Though he hoped it wouldn't further antagonize Brenda.

To their surprise, Brenda and her girlfriends headed their way. Cliff and Will were tense, ready to intercept them, though Derek couldn't imagine Brenda would pull anything herself—not in front of so many onlookers and a reporter. If she hired her brother-in-law to cause trouble for Kate, that was a much sneakier way of dealing with her competition.

"For the record, if I even cared about the two of you screwing each other, I would have said something to your face, not gone behind your back," Brenda said, her girlfriends standing on either side of her, glowering just as much at Kate.

"Like in your social media where you said I had been seeing Derek behind your back? It isn't true, *for the record*," Kate said. "You wanted him to marry you. He didn't want to. Then we fell in love."

Brenda scoffed.

"We're engaged to be married. You'll hear about it soon enough. It might as well be now," Kate said.

Brenda's face reddened. She glanced at Derek as if she couldn't believe Kate could be telling the truth.

He shrugged. "Love at first sight, whirlwind romance. Kate's right. Once we started dating, I knew she was the one and only one for me. I wasn't letting a good thing go."

Brenda rushed forward and shoved him hard before

anyone realized she would react so violently. Derek was shocked! He was close to the edge of the cement walk next to the water and thrown off-balance. Kate quickly grabbed his arm and pulled him away from the edge before he fell into the water.

Cliff and Will grabbed Brenda. Their mouths agape, her girlfriends looked horrified that Brenda would do that while the reporter was happily taking videos and snapping photos.

"Oh, did you see what she did?" someone in a gathering crowd of onlookers asked.

Derek hadn't even realized they'd gathered a crowd and some of the people were taking videos, naturally. Two celebs fighting it out in public—the perfect storm.

Then a police officer arrived. Derek normally wouldn't have pressed charges over something so benign, but he was worried this would escalate with Brenda and she would attempt to hurt Kate. He and the others told the officer what had happened and about the business of Brenda and her brother-in-law. The officer took Brenda into custody. Her girlfriends looked on horrified.

"Can we have your car keys?" one of her girl-friends asked Brenda before she was hauled away for questioning.

The police waited to see if Brenda wanted to give them her keys. She cast them a look like they had to be kidding.

The woman shook her head as if she couldn't believe Brenda would strand them. Served them right for sticking with her through this whole sordid mess.

Derek would get a restraining order against Brenda first thing. He could handle himself, but he didn't want Kate harmed. Several more police officers arrived, and bystanders were sharing videos of the confrontation with the police.

Derek thought of offering to have one of his bodyguards take the women to their places, but he figured they would be back to being friends with Brenda as soon as she returned home. He was certain being nice to her friends wouldn't influence them to change their mind about her.

The police had enough evidence to charge Brenda with battery, and if Kate hadn't reacted so quickly and grabbed Derek, he would have fallen into the water and might have suffered some injuries. He tightened his arm around her shoulders, hugging her. She made a hell of a bodyguard, and she was all his.

Then the police took Brenda away while her two friends were texting away. Spreading the story to other friends? Trying to get a ride? Derek took Kate's hand and continued to walk through the marina. But then he took her to a security gate and unlocked it. He and she and Will and Cliff walked down to one of the slips where Rafe's yacht was moored.

"This is amazing," Kate said.

"*You* are amazing." Derek pulled her into his arms and kissed her again. "Thanks for saving me back there."

"Hell, yeah, boss," Cliff said. "I would never have reached you in time."

"Me either," Will said. "She was as quick as a big cat. And her instincts were right on."

"I couldn't believe anyone wouldn't have seen that coming." Kate smiled.

They all chuckled.

Derek loved her. Man, had he made the right decision to mate her. He just wished he hadn't put her in the middle of all this drama. He should have known Brenda would be a pill about all this, given the way she had acted when she didn't get her way before when they were dating. He realized just how spoiled she was and how Kate really wasn't. She was happy to do anything with him and just as eager to foot the bill. Of course, now, his money was hers. He needed to get a will drawn up that stated that too.

Then they headed back to their vehicles, and it was time to go home and make love to his she-wolf.

"Well, I don't know if Brenda finally got the message that it's not in her best interests to mess with us any longer, but I sure hope she rethinks things," Kate said.

"I think this last fiasco will be the end of it." At least he hoped it would.

When they arrived home, she and Derek said good night to the guys, and then they retired to the bedroom. "Did you want to do anything else tonight first? Swim? Walk the dogs? It's too early to run as wolves," he said.

She began unbuttoning his dress shirt. "This is all I want to do for now."

He smiled. That was just what he was hoping for. He slipped the smocked bodice of her summer dress down, revealing her creamy breasts. He leaned down and kissed them. Then he pulled her dress off the rest of the way. He liked this setup. She heeled off her sandals, and all she was wearing was a pair of white bikini panties.

She quickly began working on his belt buckle. He ran his hands over her breasts. She felt heavenly to his touch. She unzipped his pants and slid her hand over his boxer briefs that melded to his full-blown erection, making it jump against her exquisite touch.

"Hmm, someone's ready for me," she whispered.

"Hell, yeah, always." He nuzzled her cheek, slipped his hand between her legs, and smiled when he found the crotch of her panties was wet. "Someone's ready for *me*."

"*Always.*"

Kate felt Derek's arousal jump against her hand and knew he was as ready for her as she was for him. She slid his trousers down his legs, and he hurried to push off his shoes so he could remove his pants the rest of the way. She slipped her hand down the waistband of his boxer briefs and touched his hot erection. He was such a wolf.

He caressed her breasts with his hands, his warm flesh against hers feeling so divine. He leaned over and kissed her breasts.

Then she was sliding his boxer briefs down his hips, and he kicked them aside. Before he removed her panties, he cupped her buttocks, pulled her close, and kissed her mouth again, his searing kiss sending a torrent of heat hurtling through her. Her bare breasts were pressed against his hard chest, and she felt heavenly. What a lovely way to end the beautiful day she'd spent with him.

He slid his hands down her panties and held onto her buttocks in a possessive, endearing way, his hands warming her, and then he removed her panties, and they were both perfectly naked. They quickly moved this to the bed.

He just held her close for a moment, their mouths kissing again. She was enjoying the nakedness of their bodies pressed together, the heat, the passion between them. Then he slid his hand down to begin stroking her feminine nub, and she was caught up in the moment, the way his fingers caressed her, the way he kissed her forehead, her mouth, her chin, her throat. She soaked in the heady feeling as he continued to stroke her. She caressed his arms, the muscles taut as he smiled down at her, his eyes lust-filled, the musky scent of their sex adding to the intimacy. Pheromones were busy at work, telling them to boldly take this all the way again.

His questing fingers continued to stroke her nubbin, and his mouth sought the pleasure of kissing hers deeply, stirring the compulsion to take him into her fully. She thrust her pelvis at him, wanting him to stroke her harder, faster. He quickly obliged. She loved how he was always so eager to please. He sucked on her lower lip, and she felt the hurtle of climax coming. "Inside me now," she urged him.

She spread her legs farther, and he plunged his erection deep inside her, shattering her composure, and she cried out with joy and relief, the ripples of climax washing through her. Her inner muscles clenched around him as he continued to pound inside her. She loved how they had gone all the way, to consummate the love they had for each other as *lupus garous*. She had never felt this way about another wolf as he danced with her in the intimate throes of passion, connected to her in body and soul, maybe even making little wolf babies when they made love.

He was gorgeous—a consummate lover,

respectful of her needs as she was of his—and life couldn't get any better now that he was her mate. He dipped his head to kiss her mouth again, and she wrapped her arms around his neck, welcoming him.

———————

Every time Derek made love to Kate, it was like the first time. A new experience and as hot and loving and passionate as the last. He loved her with all his heart and kissed her pliant mouth again, her lips parted to take him in, and he thrust his tongue into her mouth. She stroked his tongue with hers in seductive caresses. He loved how receptive she was, the way she tightened her sheath around his shaft, thrust her hips to connect with him, moved her legs to give him deeper penetration. She ran her hands over his biceps with silky caresses, her mouth on his again, kissing with reverence. She drew him deeper, and he couldn't hold off any longer. Then he thrust and gave way to the elation of completion. He continued to plunge into her until he was spent, sinking against her, hugging her, kissing her chin, her throat, and then moving off her so he could pull her against him and snuggle with her until they were ready for this again. "I love you."

She smiled at him, her blue eyes soft with a dreamy quality, her arm and leg thrown over him in a way that said he was her conquest. "I'm so glad you didn't hire me."

He chuckled. "Because you much prefer working for Lexi."

"And making love with you. I love you."

CHAPTER 29

I<small>N THE MORNING WAY BEFORE DAWN</small>, D<small>EREK AND</small> Kate snuggled in bed. He figured she was awake, but her eyes were still closed, and she didn't appear to want to leave the bed. It reminded him of when they had camped out and she had ended up in his sleeping bag. This was really nice. It was still dark out, so they could go out and run as wolves, but she might be worried about a police officer patrolling the beaches again. Or maybe she just enjoyed cuddling with him longer. He fell asleep with her wrapped in his arms, and when he woke, a new day had dawned.

"I guess we missed running as wolves this morning," he said.

"We'll make up for it with a whole day spent at the botanical gardens. We can eat lunch at the tea gardens. They have soups and sandwiches and desserts," Kate said.

Will and Cliff followed them in the Land Rover to the gardens. When they arrived, she said, "Oh, the gardens are just beautiful, aren't they?"

"They sure are." Derek had never been to the botanical gardens, and he realized just how much Kate was opening his world up to doing new things. He really was enjoying them, but she was what made them so special.

They checked out some of the fountains and water sculptures. The exhibits here were of statues created from waterproof origami—one of birds flying, another of a horse standing among flowers, and another of a sailor's folded hat sitting in a pond surrounded by koi. Inside the museum, there were more artistic origami creations, from unicorns to dragons to flowers.

They went back outside and walked through the rose gardens to the area that had lily ponds and waterfalls. Brass statues of running horses, fish jumping out of the pond, and geese taking flight filled the space. Real geese enjoyed the shaded trees by a pond, and ducks and swans floated on the water. In one of the gardens, they even saw a wild turkey roaming about.

The next garden, a Japanese garden, featured curved pathways covered with crushed stone similar to moonstone. Crape myrtle trees were filled with red, white, and pink blossoms. Pink granite stepping-stones made their way through the crushed stone, and a stone bridge crossed over waterways filled with koi. Boulders, bamboo, and stone lanterns made Derek feel he had been transported to Japan. It was so pretty, and he was thinking how beautiful it would be to create something like that in the entryway to his home.

"Wouldn't it be great to create a Japanese garden like this? The front yard just has a lawn, a couple of trees, and several shrubs, but it could be really spectacular," Derek said.

"Oh, like having the boulders and a little waterway? A trellis? Koi? And a bridge to cross it? A little waterfall? Oh, absolutely," Kate said. "It would give the front of your home more privacy as well."

"It would be wonderful for parties too. Right now, no one even uses the front yard. We all end up in the back because of the swimming pool and the beach."

"Yeah, that would be great."

The botanical gardens stretched forever with little garden rooms with benches to sit awhile. He and Kate were getting quite a workout too on the hilly acreage.

They finally went to the tearoom to have sandwiches and tea for lunch while Cliff and Will took seats at a nearby table and placed their orders.

Kate and Derek ordered grilled ham and cheese sandwiches and potato chips—she went for sour cream, he went for the lime chips—and both of them had water.

A shop filled with paintings of flowers and wildlife was situated near where they were seated by one of the windows. They could look out on the butterfly gardens and watch the myriad of butterflies flitting about the flowers here.

"I really have enjoyed coming here," Derek said.

"Oh, me too. Between some of the things you suggested doing and some of the things I've come up with, our outings have been so much fun."

Their lunch was soon served, and they began to eat. Several people were stopping to see the butterflies on the flowers, some taking photos right outside the windows Derek and Kate were sitting at. Then Derek saw Randall Roberts—the guy Kate had dated before—making his way to their table. He wondered if Randall thought he could persuade Derek to use him as his investment advisor.

"Your friend Randall is headed this way."

Kate turned around and saw him smiling at her. "Ugh." She turned back to eat more of her sandwich and chips.

When Randall finally reached them, he offered his hand to Derek. "Congratulations are in order. You ended up with a beautiful she-wolf."

Before Derek could say anything, Kate asked Randall, "What are you doing here?" Her tone of voice was biting.

Derek saw a paparazzo taking photos of them through the window. He figured they wouldn't have bothered them here, since it wasn't all that exciting for a news story, not when he and Kate were now engaged and there wasn't any drama.

"I came with a friend. She wants to make me

her financial advisor. You might know her. Brenda Connors?" Randall asked.

Either Randall was clueless, or he knew all about what was going on, and Derek suspected the latter was true.

Derek was out of his seat in an instant. "Where is she?"

"In the rose gardens. She said she'd meet me here for lunch." Randall smiled, as if he had made the greatest deal in the world. If he couldn't solicit Kate's business, he was going to work with her enemy.

Which made Derek wonder if Brenda knew Kate had been seeing Randall before. Sure. Brenda must have seen the tabloid showing Randall with Kate at her house.

Out of his peripheral vision, Derek saw Lars move around the reporter near the butterfly bush, a gun in Lars's hand. Kate must have seen him at the same time, and she and Derek grabbed each other and dropped to the floor of the restaurant as the gun went off and the window shattered.

Randall fell to the floor nearby. Cliff and Will bolted out of their seats, upsetting their table, their chairs clattering to the floor, and Will raced out of the restaurant. Cliff hurried to join Derek and Kate when a guy as muscular and hefty as a football offensive lineman knocked him down, trying to get out of the building before he got shot.

"Are you all right?" Derek asked Kate as Lars tore off across the gardens, people scattering in his wake at the sight of the gun in his hand.

Kate was ashen. "Uh, yeah, I thought that criminal was supposed to be in jail! Sorry, I didn't bring my gun with me too. I figured Will and Cliff were with us and I didn't need to bring it."

Derek saw Cliff was lying on the floor cradling his arm, not jumping to his feet like he thought he would be after being shoved to the floor. "Are you okay, Cliff?"

"Yeah." Cliff sat up, his forehead sporting a red abrasion—rug burn, Derek thought. And he still wasn't jumping to his feet. "I sprained my wrist badly, I think."

"Are you sure?" Derek asked.

"No. I heard a crack."

Derek rubbed Kate's shoulder. "Okay, not good." Derek glanced at Randall, and he was holding a bloody shoulder. "Randall, hold on, I'll get help for you." He yanked out his phone, called for an ambulance, and mentioned Cliff's possible injury.

Kate grabbed some linen napkins off the table and pressed them against Randall's wound while Derek called the police, but several other guests had already alerted them.

Lars was running away. The reporter had dropped into the butterfly bushes when the shooting took place, but he was running after Lars, video recording the whole show. So much for going to a safe place, Lars being locked up, and nothing exciting going on for a news story.

The restaurant manager hurried over to them with a first aid kit. "Is everyone else all right?"

"Yeah, thanks." Kate took the first aid kit and found elastic bandages and wrapped them around the napkins pressed against Randall's wound.

As much as Derek didn't like the guy, he hoped he would be okay.

Derek ran his hand over Kate's back while she ministered to Randall, and he felt her tremble a little, but that was to be expected because of the adrenaline shooting through their bloodstreams from the concern about being shot and that Randall had been. That was when Derek remembered Randall had said he was supposed to meet Brenda here. Then again, it could have all been a ploy.

"Did Brenda come with you?" Derek asked to confirm if she had actually been here or she'd just said she was going to meet him.

"She met me here and said she wanted to see the rose gardens first. I was going to go with her, but... Oh, hell!"

Derek turned to see Brenda running up to the shattered restaurant window, gun in hand. Derek took Kate to the floor again. The manager tore off. Being around Kate was a dangerous proposition. With the window frame in the way and Derek and

Kate below the table, Brenda couldn't get a shot that way. But it didn't deter her. She shoved her way through the shrubs, the butterflies still fluttering about the flowers as if they hadn't a care in the world.

Derek knew rushing her could be deadly, but then Kate said, "Let's do it."

"Rush her?" he asked, to clarify that was what Kate meant.

"Yeah. We're sitting ducks here. If we run away from her, she'll shoot us in the backs. You go to the left of the tables, I'll go to the right, and we'll tackle her."

"I'll slide my gun to you," Cliff said, but he did it with his left hand without enough force, and it was too far away to reach without Derek exposing himself to Brenda.

"I'll stand up and get her attention in the center," Randall said.

"No," Kate said. "You're already wounded."

"We were meeting here. I'll set it up, you two take her down. I know you can do it, Kate," Randall said.

Kate's eyes were filled with tears. She quickly brushed them away.

They really didn't have much of a choice. Once Brenda was inside, she would have a clear shot at them. Derek gave the signal, and he and Kate moved around the tables, low, keeping out of Brenda's sight. Randall stood up. "It's just me."

Kate and Derek lunged for Brenda as her attention was on Randall. At least until she saw Kate and Derek rush her. They grabbed her arms. Both her hands had been holding the 9mm, and they shoved them up in the air. Bullets smacked into the ceiling, plaster raining down on them. Cliff moved in by that time too, slamming his body into Brenda.

The restaurant was deathly quiet as Derek broke Brenda's grip on the gun and Cliff and Kate took Brenda to the floor.

"I should have had zip ties on me," Kate said, pinning Brenda to the floor, Brenda's hands behind her back. "Of all the people who have stalked me in the past over broken-up relationships, *you* are the worst. Here you have money and could have had most any guy you would ever want but Derek. He's all mine. I play for keeps. Now you've thrown your life away for what?"

Derek took over Kate's role, handing her Brenda's gun for safekeeping so she could minister to Randall, who appeared to be fading fast.

"Not me," Randall said, sounding as though he was afraid Kate was including him in her list of previous exes who had stalked her. "I wasn't stalking you." He had slumped down on the floor, looking pale. But he didn't seem to be in pain yet. The adrenaline pumping through his bloodstream was probably keeping him from feeling it.

As a wolf, he would heal faster, but he still

needed medical attention right away. They needed to check out Cliff too.

Then they heard all the sirens—police cars and an ambulance. Derek wanted to call Will to ensure he was safe. About that time, his phone rang. With one hand, he held both Brenda's wrists, and then he fetched his phone.

"Let me go," Brenda said, growling. "If you had just continued to date me like you were supposed to, none of this would have happened."

He shook his head and saw the call was from Will. "Hey, are you okay?"

"Yeah, I'm a little wet. We had to tackle Lars before he could get away and all ended up in one of the koi ponds. What about you guys?"

"Kate's ex-boyfriend, Randall Roberts, was shot, Cliff took a nasty fall, and Brenda came after us."

"I was after Kate, not you," Brenda grumbled.

But Derek wasn't so sure about her claim. He figured if he and Kate hadn't stopped her, Brenda might have shot both of them.

Then the police were rushing into the restaurant, guns drawn. Kate had already set Brenda's gun on the chair next to her while she continued to keep pressure on Randall's wound.

"Brenda Connors, one of the shooters," Derek said, releasing her to them. "Lars Gnoffo was the one who shot Randall Roberts, but Lars was aiming to hit Kate Hanover."

Then the officers took Brenda into custody and the EMTs arrived to transport Randall out of the restaurant and to the waiting ambulance. Another was securing Cliff's arm in a splint to protect it until he could get it x-rayed.

The police had everyone's statements and had taken Brenda's weapon for evidence. The detective in charge of the investigation of Lars's earlier stalking charges confirmed Lars was again in custody after he had slipped out of the hospital while under observation for the car accident. Brenda and Lars were hauled off to the police station. Randall was taken away by ambulance.

Derek hugged Kate. "Are you okay?"

"Yeah, I need to get washed up though." She was wearing Randall's blood on her hands. "I hope Randall will be okay. And you, Cliff."

"Both will be. They're like us. I doubt Randall will go chasing after anyone who has any vendetta against you again," Derek said.

Smiling a little, she gave Derek a kiss but wouldn't hug him because of her bloody hands. "I'm going to get washed up."

"And then I can take you home."

She frowned at him. "No. Way. We have a ton of gardens to see still, and I'm not letting Lars or Brenda ruin this for us."

That was what Derek loved about Kate. She didn't crumble under pressure.

"Sorry about being out of commission when Brenda was still an issue," Cliff said, looking guilty about their mission.

"We had it well in hand," Derek said. Though things could have turned out a lot differently than they had. But he had felt confident in Kate's ability to work with him to get Brenda under control. "We didn't realize Brenda was here too when Lars took off, and we needed to apprehend him before he had a chance to shoot at Kate again. Besides, I saw that guy who knocked you down, Cliff. He was a mass of muscles."

Cliff and Derek escorted Kate to the ladies' room, and Will arrived to make sure it was all clear, just in case. Though the restaurant itself was empty; everyone had cleared out as soon as the shooting began. Then Will, Derek, and Cliff, cradling his arm in a sling, stood outside the restroom while Kate cleaned up—all of them serving as her bodyguard for a change.

When she finally came out of the restroom, she gave Derek a big hug and kiss. Then she hugged Cliff gently, careful of his arm, and Will. "Did you all get enough to eat?" Kate motioned to the spilled drinks and sandwiches knocked on the floor in the patrons' haste to dodge bullets.

"Yeah," Cliff said. "We're thinking of making burgers for tonight. Our treat."

Kate frowned at him. "You need to get your arm checked out."

"I'm going to get an x-ray and see if I just badly sprained it or actually broke it. But I'll be there for helping with the dinner."

Smiling, Will shook his head. "Cliff will be directing me while I grill."

Kate laughed, and then she took hold of Derek's hand. "Let's finish our walk through the gardens."

He squeezed her hand and smiled down at her. "You are a treasure, and I love you." He wrapped his arm around her, glad that she was so resilient and that despite what had happened, she was ready to enjoy the rest of the day with him. He would have taken her home in a heartbeat if she hadn't been. Luckily, the gardens were huge, and only the actual crime scene areas—the pond where Lars was stopped, the secondary crime scene, and the restaurant, the primary crime scene—were closed to conduct a criminal investigation.

"So are you, and I love you right back." She smiled up at him. Then as they walked by one of the koi ponds, they saw all the footprints in the mud. "Is that where you went swimming?"

Will sighed. "Yeah. I'll need a shower when we return home."

Then they finally saw the police coming to tape off the area, and Derek and Kate, Will and Cliff headed off to explore more of the gardens.

Derek and Kate needed to shower too. He wasn't sure what she wanted to do after they returned home, but it was up to her. He realized with her in his life, that was how he wanted it to be, no longer a single male winging it on his own but having her for his companion and enjoying life with her as a wolf couple now.

Kate loved Derek for believing in her when she went to tackle Brenda. She had prayed Brenda wouldn't shoot Randall fatally when he stole Brenda's attention to give them time to take her down. Kate would have to do something about Randall. To thank him for risking his life for them. Maybe he really had cared for Kate more than she'd thought he had. Or maybe it was because he was a wolf and wanted to protect his own kind from harm. In any event, she wanted to do something for him. She glanced back at Cliff and hoped his arm was just sprained. "You know, you can leave us and get that checked out."

"No way. What if you needed me to be the fall guy again?"

Everyone chuckled, Will shaking his head.

For now, she wanted to forget all that had just happened, take in the serenity of the gardens, and enjoy her time with Derek—her wolf—and no one was taking her from him.

And then—they would return home and take it from there.

EPILOGUE

DEREK WAS GLAD HE HADN'T HIRED KATE TO BE his bodyguard because he wanted her just like this, his mate. Oh, sure, she was still a bodyguard because she wouldn't give up protecting him for anything, but he wanted her for so much more. She was truly the light of his life.

Holly and Aidan's babies were a couple of months old now, and Lexi and Ryder's babies were two months closer to being here. Derek couldn't be more glad he had a mate and was no longer the odd man out. Though he and Kate were the only couple without kids or expecting kids.

It would soon be Halloween, so no one was lying around on the beach tanning for would-be thieves to fleece. And the project of the Japanese gardens was nearly completed. Both he and Kate loved it, and even Maddie, Cliff, and Will did too. Derek and Kate's friends all had come by to see it, and Lexi was ready to put in a water feature in front of her place with boulders and koi but a completely different setup.

Derek and Kate had started a trend.

Cliff's broken arm had healed in three weeks,

and Will was still giving him a hard time about tripping over his own feet even though he had been knocked down by a guy who could have been the Hulk during the shootout. Guys would be guys.

———————

Kate loved being with Derek, and she was glad she hadn't skipped out on that first gala that had started them on a whirlwind of dating. In the end, they knew they couldn't resist their wolfish instincts—to love and to hold each other forever more as a mated pair.

To make it official, the whole pack was celebrating their wedding in Hawaii in a couple of weeks.

As for Brenda Connors, she was going to trial soon, and it appeared she might even have to serve jail time! The horror of it. She was out on bail, but she had lost her social connections and was no longer invited to many of the social gatherings. She definitely wasn't a match for a couple of wolves who had found true love.

Next year, Derek and Kate might even have wolf cubs of their own, but for now, they were having a ball being a wolf couple in love.

ACKNOWLEDGMENTS

Thanks so much to my dedicated beta readers, Darla Taylor and Donna Fournier! You ladies make it even more fun…and funny. Thanks also to Deb Werksman, who has stuck it out with me all these years and encouraged me in everything I do, and the cover artists who continue to create beautiful works of art—truly drool-worthy!

ABOUT THE AUTHOR

USA Today bestselling author Terry Spear has written over a hundred paranormal and medieval Highland romances. One of her bestselling titles, *Heart of the Wolf* was named a *Publishers Weekly* Best Book of the Year. She is an award-winning author with 2 Paranormal Excellence Awards for Romantic Literature. A retired officer of the U.S. Army Reserves, Terry also creates award-winning teddy bears that have found homes all over the world, helps out with her grandchildren, and enjoy her two Havanese dogs. She lives in Spring, Texas.

CHAPTER 1

EARLY THAT SUMMER MORNING BEFORE HEADing into work, Kayla Wolff and her quadruplet sister, Roxie, were running as gray wolves on their wooded acreage, not expecting any trouble. Except for a cougar they had to chase off once and a black bear another time, they usually didn't have any wildlife difficulties. They'd had to sic Sheriff Peter Jorgenson on hunters last fall though.

Kayla was excited about getting together for dinner tonight with Nate Grayson, the only wolf she'd dated since moving to Silver Town, Colorado, a wolf-run town. Nate's sister, Nicole, had actually mated their brother Blake.

Kayla loved it here, and she was planning to mate Nate on the Fourth of July in a little over two weeks if he didn't ask her beforehand.

Along with their two brothers, she and Roxie owned and managed the Timberline Ski Lodge nearby. She had been busy serving as the catering manager for a wedding yesterday, so she was glad to get back to working on promotional stuff today.

As wolves, she and Roxie had been playing with each other when they heard the sound of two men speaking on their property. Other wolves in the pack were welcome to run here anytime, but the others usually ran in the pack territory. And their brother Landon had property with his mate, Gabrielle, around her veterinary clinic, so they often ran as wolves there rather than at the lodge.

Kayla didn't recognize the men's voices. She and Roxie drew nearer, circling around and keeping low so the men wouldn't see them, trying to get a whiff of the men's scents before they alerted the sheriff that they had human trespassers. They could be just wolf guests from somewhere else, and Kayla and Roxie certainly didn't want to alienate wolf visitors to the area. Unless they were causing trouble.

The hot summer breeze kept shifting, and they had to keep circling when they normally would avoid humans at all costs. Though Kayla did have the notion of just chasing them off as wolves. That was definitely her wilder wolf side coming to play.

She listened to the men's conversation in the meantime, and finally, a black-haired man with a curly beard and reddish sideburns came into view. He was a stocky figure wearing a T-shirt that stretched tautly over muscled arms and chest, jeans tight on bulky thighs, a black cap shadowing his features, mirrored glasses, and hiking boots. It was early morning and there was no need to wear sunglasses at this time. The woods were shaded and dark and the sun still just dawning. The other man was tall, not as muscled, with short blond hair; he looked about the same age as the bulky guy—mid- to late twenties—and was wearing a blue-jean ball cap, a gray T-shirt, jeans, sneakers, and polarized aviator sunglasses.

"I told you. With your experience, it's a piece of cake. He'll pay us good money to do it," the blond guy said. "His uncle is good for his word."

"You're sure you can trust the others?" The mus- cled guy sounded dubious.

"Hell, yeah. We grew up together. We're all friends. They're eager to do it and to follow your lead since you're experienced at this kind of thing. It's copacetic."

"It better be. You know what happened the last time."

"Yeah, and you didn't know those guys. This time it'll be different."

"I'll talk it over with his nephew first."

The blond guy didn't say anything more, but he looked annoyed, his mouth pursed, as if he expected the bulky guy to go along with the pro- gram based on his words. "Yeah, sounds like a good idea," he finally said, as if he had no choice in the matter.

Roxie was on the move again, trying to get closer. Kayla wanted to woof at her sister to stay with her. She didn't want them to move any closer to the men, afraid that if the two of them did, the men might spy them more easily. Sure, she and Roxie hadn't been able to smell them to see if they were human, but she was all for circling them further. If they were wolves, no problem, unless they were up to mischief. But humans? They could be unpredictable.

"All right, but it better work out." The muscled guy turned around and saw Roxie.

For a moment, everyone froze. Kayla ran at the men to give Roxie time to move, then turned quickly and bolted out of there, hoping her sister was gaining on her and the men were running in the opposite direction and not planning to shoot them if they were armed with guns. She heard movement in the woods behind her and glanced over her shoulder to see Roxie catching up to her, her eyes filled with excitement.

Relieved it was just her sister and there was no sign of the men, Kayla thought she could use less excitement in her life. When she had to serve as a wedding caterer and deal with a bridezilla like she'd had to a couple of weeks ago, that was enough of a "thrill" for her. She and Roxie both managed the brides, but Roxie could get growly with an unreasonable one, so Kayla often just took care of them to avoid problems.

Roxie nipped at her in fun. Kayla nipped back at her, glad everything had turned out fine. Though she was going to lecture her when they returned to their home next to the lodge. She was glad their sister-in-law Nicole hadn't been with them because she was pregnant. She and their brother Blake would run with Roxie and Kayla most mornings, but Nicole had been under the weather with morning sickness of late.

After Kayla and Roxie reached the house and ran in through the wolf door, squeezing in at the same time—their usual routine—they raced up the stairs to their respective bedrooms to shift and dress for work.

Once Kayla had shifted, she called out to her sister, "You shouldn't have gotten so close to the men!"

"You shouldn't have tried to grab their attention so I could get away."

"What if they'd been armed?" Kayla pulled on her panties.

"They weren't. They didn't have anywhere to hide a gun, holster, nothing."

Kayla sighed, glad to learn that. She had really worried about it. She fastened her bra. "All right, but you shouldn't have gotten so close. I was going to circle around them further to catch the breeze headed in a different direction. So did you smell their scents?"

"Human. But since they seemed to be there having a private meeting and then saw a couple of wolves, I figure they won't be hanging around, so no sense in calling Peter to try and locate them and fine them for trespassing."

"Okay." Kayla buttoned up her blouse.

"Hey, you've got to admit that was an interesting aside to our normal morning jaunt through the woods."

"Yeah." Kayla laughed. "It was memorable, all right. But don't tell our brothers. If we do, they'll leave their pregnant wives home to run with us to ensure we stay safe. Even if the guys wanted to stay home with them to make sure they were fine, Nicole and Gabrielle would make them go with us." She finished dressing.

"Absolutely. Mum's the word."

Kayla wondered how long that would last! Within a pack, and with them working so closely with their brothers at the lodge, she suspected the word would get out one way or another.

———————

Eager to take Kayla Wolff for a night out on the town in Green Valley, Colorado, Nate Grayson drove to her and her sister Roxie's house next to the Timberline Ski Lodge. He and Kayla liked to get out of Silver Town on a date on occasion when they both could manage. His private investigator cases had stacked up and she had been busy with marketing strategies for her family-run ski lodge and

restaurant, not to mention handling several catering venues for different celebrations—weddings,
birthdays, anniversaries, retirement, you name it—
that they often couldn't get away.

As soon as she came to the front door of her
home, Kayla was all smiles, wearing a red dress
and high heels, the fragrance of peaches and
cream enveloping her. "Hey, you look lovely," Nate
said, hugging and kissing her, and she hugged and
kissed him right back. He enjoyed having her
scent on him, claiming him as he was claiming her.
Once he'd met her, he'd never been interested in
anyone else.

"You look pretty dapper yourself. I'm glad we
could both get away for this." Kayla looked just as
eager to enjoy the night with him.

He'd dressed up for the occasion too, though
a jacket and tie were required for the restaurant.
It was a warm June night as he walked her to his
car. "Yeah, me too. Even though we know some of
the wolves of the Green Valley wolf pack and they
know us, there aren't as many of them living there
and they don't run the whole town. *Everyone* knows
us in Silver Town."

She laughed. "Are you afraid to be seen out with
me too much?"

He smiled. "Not me." He was more concerned
that *Kayla* wanted more anonymity because she
tended to be shy about things like this. But he was

eager to show she was all his and no other wolf better think she was available.

When they finally arrived at the Great Gatsby restaurant in Green Valley, it was still light out at seven in the evening. The restaurant was all lit up, and it really set the stage for a nice romantic dinner. Nate parked and walked Kayla inside and they were seated at their reserved table right away. A gold and black theme ran throughout the restaurant: gold chandeliers, black tablecloths, black and gold wallpaper, and gold candles on each of the tables. The women on the waitstaff were wearing gold, flapper-era fringe dresses, and the men were dressed in black-and-white striped double-breasted jackets and trousers.

"This is so nice. Thanks for taking me here. I've never been here, and it's really a lovely restaurant, great atmosphere. Everything's so elegant," Kayla said.

"It is. I wanted to make this extra special tonight since we haven't been able to get together lately what with your work and mine. And we're always having meals at your house or mine, so I wanted to do something different. I haven't been here either, and I was waiting to take you here. I'm sure glad to be here with you."

"Oh, me too with you."

One of the waitresses jiggled the gold fringe on her dress at Nate when she came over to take their orders and he smiled, amused. "And what would you like to have for dinner?" she asked Nate first, as if she was coming on to him, but he figured it was part of the Great Gatsby show.

Kayla and Nate ordered T-bone steaks, mashed potatoes, slivered carrots, and glasses of merlot.

"Are you celebrating anything special?" the waitress asked.

Nate said, "Just being in love."

"Aww, now that's special."

Kayla blushed. Nate reached over and took her hand and squeezed. They'd been seeing each other since they'd both moved here a year and a half ago, which was a long time for *lupus garous* to date before they decided on mating. He just felt she hadn't been ready for it yet. But he sure was. Everything about her made him want to be with her day and night.

One of the men served them their glasses of wine and made sure to show Kayla extra special attention. She was blushing furiously, and when the wine steward left their table, she smiled at Nate. "You were looking a little growly."

"I knew it was just an act, but, uh, yeah, I might have not hidden my growly side enough." He smiled. He had to admit he had been feeling a little growly despite his best intention of seeing it as it was.

"That's okay." Kayla clinked her wine glass against his. "If that flapper had wiggled her dress fringe at you one more time, she would have heard *me* growl."

Nate laughed. He just couldn't see Kayla doing that.

Kayla licked the wine off her lips, and he wanted to groan at the sight. He needed to spend more intimate time with her. He wanted to get on one knee, pull her onto his lap, kiss her, and ask her to mate him. But he was determined to stick to his plan to do it at the cabin he'd reserved for her birthday in eight days. He and his sister and parents were planning a surprise birthday bash at the lodge for the quadruplets the night before, though Kayla was actually born after midnight on the following day. They'd celebrate her birthday the next day too, according to Roxie.

Then their meals were finally served.

Kayla cut into her medium-rare steak, took a bite, and practically purred.

He smiled. "Good, huh?" He took another bite of his. Man, the food was the greatest. He couldn't have planned this outing any better.

"Yeah, this is delicious." She reached over and squeezed his hand. "Thanks for bringing me here for such a special night."

"I'm having the best time too."

They enjoyed the music playing in the background, drinking their wine, eating their dinners, and pausing to kiss each other—which felt so right.

"This was truly delightful," Kayla said, finishing up her dinner.

"Being with you, it sure has been." He was so glad they had been able to get away for the evening. He finished eating the last of his steak and paid the bill.

"Did you want to come home with me tonight?" he asked.

She sighed.

He knew that was a no. He sighed. She smiled and they stood up, clasping hands. She kissed him before they left the restaurant, then they headed out.

"I don't want to be with anyone else, you know," she said. "I just have so much on my plate. I'm in charge of a wedding reception coming up and also a fiftieth wedding anniversary party for a couple."

"Yeah. I know." Which was why he wanted to propose to her right after her birthday celebration at the cabin, as long as she'd come with him there. They would have an uninterrupted week of fun. He wanted to mate her and be with her every night, no matter how busy their days were. He wanted to be there with her, for her so she could tell him all about her rough day and he'd help her to chill out, just as he knew she would be there for him during rough times.

"You are the best thing that ever happened to me, Nate. Truly. Don't give up on me."

"There's no chance of that, honey." He kissed

her and then hugged her close. "Being with you has been life-changing."

"For me too. We'll be there soon for sure."

"We will be."

They left the restaurant, ready to head home. He removed his jacket and was putting it in the back seat when he heard gunfire down the street and breaking glass. What the hell?

He grabbed Kayla and got down between the cars for protection, holding her tight.

"Gunfire," she whispered as if whoever was shooting might hear her words and would come for them next if she didn't speak quietly.

"Yeah, at a business a couple of blocks down the street." As a retired Army Ranger, he knew just what gunfire sounded like. And of course with their wolf's hearing, he could place where it was coming from. "Come on, let's go. I want to get you out of here." He didn't hear anyone headed their way that could be trouble. He got her car door, and she climbed in, and he shut the door. Then he hurried to climb into the car, started the engine, and pulled out of the parking lot and onto the street.

"I bet you want to check it out, being a private investigator." Kayla glanced behind her.

"No. I don't want to run into someone who's shooting up a store. And certainly not when I worry about your safety."

They were just getting ready to turn onto the

highway that would take them back to Silver Town when he saw a black pickup truck racing up behind them like it was going to run right over them. Nate didn't have anywhere to pull off, and he wasn't about to tear off at reckless speeds through town to avoid getting rear-ended.

A car was approaching them from the opposite direction, and that's when the jerk behind him tried to pass them.

"What's wrong with him?" Kayla asked, seeing the truck approaching in the sideview mirror. "He's passing."

"Yeah. I don't have anywhere to go, and he's not going to make it before the other car gets here." Nate slowed way down so the truck could safely pass them.

The racing truck pulled around them, but he wasn't going to have enough time to pass them before colliding with the oncoming vehicle. The truck was going, hell or high water. Nate slammed on his brakes. To avoid being rear-ended, he hadn't done that earlier, but now he was trying to give the pickup time to get around them.

As if the driver was experiencing road rage, the truck cut Nate off, nearly hitting his front bumper. Nate swerved to avoid getting hit, and his tire struck the curb so hard it exploded. Instinctively, he threw his arm across Kayla to protect her from hitting the dash, even though she was seat belted in and the seat belt caught her.

"Ohmigod!" she cried out, sounding a little rattled.

"The tire just blew. No one was shooting at us." Which had concerned him at first when he heard the tire blow. He turned off the engine and pulled her into a hug. "Are you okay?" He'd worried more than anything about Kayla getting hurt if the truck bashed into them.

"Yeah, you?" Kayla embraced him hard.

"Yeah. I've got to change the tire. Be back in a minute and we'll get on our way."

"Bastards," Kayla said, getting out of the car at the same time he did.

He unbuttoned his shirt, and she smiled appreciatively as he bared his chest. He smiled and flexed his muscles a little. He shouldn't have, considering the situation they were in, but she chuckled, and it seemed to lighten the mood.

He opened his trunk and pulled out his spare tire and moved it around to the side of the car. Before he could grab the car's jack, she brought it out for him.

"Thanks, but you really didn't have to do that. I don't want you to get dirty." He appreciated her help. He wasn't so macho that he didn't want her assistance, but he didn't want her to get any grease on her pretty dress.

"That's okay. I'm being careful and I'm used to changing a tire when I need to."

As soon as he removed the lug nuts, she held onto them for him. Once he had changed out the tire, she handed him the lug nuts. "I should have gotten their license plate number for reckless—" she said but abruptly stopped speaking when two police cars tore down the road past them, blue lights flashing, heading in the direction of the initial gunfire and shattered glass.

They both turned to look at the police cars.

"Too bad they weren't after the guys speeding down the road," Kayla said.

Which made Nate wonder… "You don't mind if we go the way the police cars went and see what's going on, do you?"

"Always the PI."

"Yeah, sorry. I wouldn't have done it when the gunshots were going off." He sighed. "This is our special date. I really shouldn't have mentioned it." He put the jack back in the car, closed the trunk, and pulled a bottle of hand sanitizer out of his console. He gave it to Kayla first so she could clean her hands. Then he washed his and pulled on his shirt.

Kayla began buttoning it for him. "No, I really want to know what's going on too. Ending a date on an investigative errand works for me."

"Are you sure?" He was dying to learn what was going on, particularly if the truck that had forced them off the road had been involved in a crime—a hit-and-run or something. He wanted to report it to the police. But he didn't want it to take away from their date. Still, when they had first met, Kayla was eager to help him solve a situation of theft at her lodge, so he knew she had an interest in investigations.

She finished buttoning the top buttons on his shirt while he buttoned the lower ones. "Yeah, you know me. I would think about it the rest of the night otherwise, imagining all kinds of different scenarios."

"All right. I feel the same way." He tucked in his shirt, and they returned to the car. Then he drove off in the direction the police cars had gone.